5! Top Pick! "An absolutely must read! From beginning to end, it's an incredible ride."
—*Night Owl Romance*

5 Hearts! "I definitely recommend *Dangerous Highlander*, even to skeptics of paranormal romance — you just may fall in love with the MacLeods."
—*The Romance Reader*

5 Angels! Recommended Read! "*Forbidden Highlander* blew me away."
—*Fallen Angel Reviews*

5 Tombstones! "Another fantastic series that melds the paranormal with the historical life of the Scottish highlander in this arousing and exciting adventure. The men of MacLeod castle are a delicious combination of devoted brother, loyal highlander Lord and demonic God that ooze sex appeal and inspire some very erotic daydreams as they face their faults and accept their fate."
—*Bitten By Books*

4 Stars! "Grant creates a vivid picture of Britain centuries after the Celts and Druids tried to expel the Romans, deftly merging magic and history. The result is a wonderfully dark, delightfully well-written tale. Readers will eagerly await the next Dark Sword book."
—*Romantic Times BOOKreviews*

Don't miss these other spellbinding novels by
DONNA GRANT

DARK KING SERIES
Dark Heat
Darkest Flame
Fire Rising

DARK WARRIOR SERIES
Midnight's Master
Midnight's Lover
Midnight's Seduction
Midnight's Warrior
Midnight's Kiss
Midnight's Captive
Midnight's Temptation
Midnight's Promise
Midnight's Surrender

DARK SWORD SERIES
Dangerous Highlander
Forbidden Highlander
Wicked Highlander
Untamed Highlander
Shadow Highlander
Darkest Highlander

SHIELD SERIES
A Dark Guardian
A Kind of Magic
A Dark Seduction
A Forbidden Temptation
A Warrior's Heart

DRUIDS GLEN SERIES

Highland Mist
Highland Nights
Highland Dawn
Highland Fires
Highland Magic
Dragonfyre

SISTERS OF MAGIC TRILOGY

Shadow Magic
Echoes of Magic
Dangerous Magic

Royal Chronicles Novella Series

Prince of Desire
Prince of Seduction
Prince of Love
Prince of Passion

Wicked Treasures Novella Series

Seized by Passion
Enticed by Ecstasy
Captured by Desire

**And look for more anticipated novels
from Donna Grant**

The Craving (Rogues of Scotland)
Darkest Flame (Dark Kings)
Wild Dream – (Chiasson)
Fire Rising – (Dark Kings)

coming soon!

A DARK GUARDIAN

THE SHIELDS

DONNA GRANT

This is a work of fiction. All of the characters, organizations, and events portrayed in this novel are either products of the author's imagination or are used fictitiously.

A DARK GUARDIAN

© 2011 by DL Grant, LLC
Excerpt from *A Kind of Magic* copyright © 2011 by Donna Grant

Cover design © 2011 by Croco Designs

ISBN 10: 0988208415
ISBN 13: 978-0988208414

www.DonnaGrant.com

Available in ebook and print editions

CHAPTER ONE

Central England, Stone Crest Castle
Summer, 1123

The darkness of night summoned Evil like a warm tavern to a weary traveler. The velvety thickness blanketed any who dared to oppose its will. And the Evil enfolding Stone Crest had one task in mind - the demise of all.

"Faster," Mina whispered urgently into her mare's ear. She bent low over the horse's neck and chanced a look over her shoulder, her hair sticking to her face and neck as the ground raced beneath her.

The dark, menacing road was vacant, but she knew the creature was near. Stalking. Mina's skin tingled with anticipation, and her heart pounded fiercely in her chest as her mare continued to run toward the trees.

A terrible, unearthly scream rent the air. Mina quickly covered her ears. Her mare slowed, then stopped and danced around in fright.

"Nay," Mina hissed while she tried to gain control of her mount. "Run, Sasha, run. Our lives depend upon it."

The mare sensed Mina's anxiety because her long legs

stretched out and the ground flew beneath them once more. Mina gripped the reins and Sasha's mane tightly as her blood rushed wildly with fear and dread. The hair on the back of her neck rose, but she didn't need to look behind her to know the creature followed very close.

Mina focused on reaching the clearing. Her mare was fleet of foot, the swiftest of her family's horses. If anyone could outrun the creature, it was Sasha. At least, Mina had thought so. Now she wasn't so sure.

A small smile formed on her face when she saw the clump of trees that signaled the clearing was just a short distance away. As she was about to reach the trees, the flap of wings overhead reached her.

Something long and sharp passed in front of her face and sliced across her arm. A frantic Sasha reared, and it was all Mina could do to hang on. Then suddenly, the world tilted and Mina jumped clear as her beloved mare collapsed and lay too still on her side.

Mina raised her eyes to the night sky and saw the creature that had come to their small village hovering above her, a sardonic smile on its grotesque face. Its small beady eyes flashed red in the gloom, and she knew her time was at an end.

Long, razor-sharp talons lengthened from its hands. She swallowed her failure like a lump of coal. This wasn't how it was supposed to end.

Fear immobilized her. She couldn't even scream. The creature moved slowly in the air towards her, as if he wanted to torment her prior to killing her. Before the creature's talons carved open her face, she saw a blur of movement out of the corner of her eye. In the next moment, she found herself thrown roughly to the ground and over the side of the hill. The weight of whoever had landed atop her knocked the wind from her lungs in a gush.

As they rolled, she dimly heard the furious screams of the creature.

Just as she thought they might tumble for eternity, they finally came to an abrupt, bone-jarring halt. She was afraid to open her eyes and find that another evil had taken her. After all, it had been the worst kind of wickedness that had plagued her village for a month now.

A deep, soft voice reached her ears through her panic. A man's voice. "Are you all right?"

Slowly, she opened her eyes. Instead of a face, all she saw was the outline of his head. His tone held a hint of concern, but this was a stranger. She had come to mistrust anything that wasn't part of her village.

"Aye," she answered at last.

"I was beginning to think the fall had addled your brain." There was no mistaking the trace of humor in his meaning as he swiftly rose to his feet.

He held out a hand to her. She hated to do it, but she accepted his help. She didn't think she could gain her feet alone after the tumble she had just taken. As he pulled her to her feet, her arm burst into agonizing pain. She could barely move her hand, but she wasn't about to let the stranger know she was hurt and give him an advantage. It was something she had learned early in life. One had to be strong to survive in this land.

"It's not a safe night for a woman to be out alone."

She sensed he wanted to say more but held back. They were mere inches from each other, so she took a step back to offer herself more room. "There are many things which should keep people safely inside at night. Including men."

He bowed his head slightly. "I mean you no harm, lady."

She didn't believe that for an instant. Only a wandering idiot would take a stranger's word.

A bizarre whistle-like noise sounded from atop the hill. The stranger whistled back and then the eerie silence reigned once more. Not even the sound of crickets could be heard.

With her good hand, she dusted off her breeches, and looked around for the dagger she had swiped from the armory. She couldn't believe she had dropped her only weapon.

"Is this what you seek?"

Mina grudgingly turned to the man and saw her dagger in his outstretched hand. She accepted the weapon. "Thank you. For everything." She bit her lip and thought of Sasha. Without another word, she began to race up the hill.

The stranger was at her side in an instant, aiding her when she would have fallen. When they reached the top, she came to a halt as five men on horseback stared at her. They sat atop their steeds like kings, watching her every move. She dismissed them when Sasha's soft cry of pain reached her.

She went to her mare and knelt beside her. She ran her hand lightly over the open gash across Sasha's whither and closed her eyes. It was a mortal wound.

"The mare has lost a lot of blood," the stranger said as he knelt beside Sasha. "I'm afraid she is lost to you."

Tears came quickly to Mina's eyes, and she tried to blink them away. Tears were for the weak. "I'm so sorry, Sasha," she said and leaned down to kiss the mare's head. "I should never have come."

She knew there was no way to save her horse, and to leave her like this was to see her suffer needlessly. With trembling hands, she held the dagger to Sasha's throat, but moments slowly drew on.

A large, warm hand encased hers. "Shall I?" the stranger offered.

Before she could change her mind she nodded. He took the dagger, and she laid her head on Sasha's. It was over in a heartbeat. Sasha never made a sound, but it cut through Mina's soul like a silent scream of anguish.

She gave herself but a moment before she stood and looked around her as the moon broke through the dense clouds. Now she was alone with six men. Six heavily armed strangers.

The stranger rose and faced her. "I am Hugh."

"From where do you come?"

"London," he answered after a bit of a hesitation. He extended his arm to the men on horseback. "My companions are Roderick, Val, Gabriel, Cole and Darrick."

Each man bowed his head as Hugh said his name, and she was quick to note the array of weapons and the large shields. Then, six pairs of eyes were on her.

"I am Lady Mina of Stone Crest."

"Well, Lady Mina, what manner of men would allow you to be out at night unprotected?"

Hugh's question had her thinking of the trap she and some of the villagers had set. "I'm not alone," she said with more conviction than she felt. Her eyes scanned the sky above her, but there was no sign of the creature.

"Where are your men?"

She turned and pointed toward the clump of trees. "In the clearing. I was luring a...an animal into a trap."

When she turned toward the men, the moonlight lit upon Hugh for just an instant, but in that moment she saw his skepticism. "It would have worked," she defended herself. "If Sasha had made it to the clearing."

"I hate to point out the obvious," the man in the middle said. Gabriel was his name. "But your men have yet to come to your aid."

Fear snaked its way through her and nestled

uncomfortably in her stomach. These men could easily kill her. "I have only to call to them."

"Then call, for I would meet the manner of men who would allow a woman to take such a risk," Hugh stated, his voice laden with unspoken anger.

"I would rather see the trap," Gabriel said and nudged his horse forward.

She stood her ground, ready to bolt, as Gabriel and his mount walked past her. She nearly sighed aloud, but recalled that she wasn't alone.

Hugh watched Mina closely. Her hesitation said all he needed to know. The men that should have been with her had deserted her. Had she lied? Was she alone?

The creature she had lured must have frightened them away. Yet, if what she said was indeed true and they had set a trap, then the men wouldn't have deserted her.

"Come," he said and put his hand on her back to guide her toward the clearing.

She walked a little ahead of him, and he tried not to notice that she wore breeches instead of a gown. It had been awhile since he had given in to his urges and bedded a woman, and with one walking just ahead of him with her backside swaying so enticingly from side to side, he found it hard to ignore.

He mentally shook himself and made his eyes look away from her delectable back end. Her hair had come loose from her braid and hung down her back in thick waves. Its exact color was hard to detect in the darkness, but he knew it was pale.

Thankfully, they reached the clearing then. Just as he suspected, no one waited for her. "Where is the trap?" he asked.

"I was to lead the creature into those trees," she said and pointed straight ahead. "Once I passed them, the men would cut a rope that held a spike which would impale the...animal."

Hugh heard the hesitation and wondered when she would tell them exactly what manner of beast had been chasing her. Could it be she really didn't know? Despite his misgivings about the situation, they had been sent to help.

And an order was an order

The creak of leather sounded loudly in the quiet as someone dismounted, and when Hugh looked over he found Gabriel beside him.

"Not a bad plan," Gabriel said thoughtfully as he stared at the trees. "I wonder if it would have worked."

"I guess we'll never know," Mina said softly.

"Scout the area," Hugh told his men. "See if any of Lady Mina's men are still around."

While his men did as ordered he handed Mina his water skin. She drank greedily before returning it to him.

"We aren't here to harm you."

She shrugged her shoulder. "We've learned not to trust anyone. Are you knights?"

"In a manner," he answered. "Do your parents know what you were about tonight?"

"They are dead."

That explained much. "By the beast that was after you?"

She became very still before she briefly nodded her head. "You know what hunts us?"

"I do," he admitted.

"How?" Her voice held doubt and hope.

"I'll explain once you're safe. Do you have any other family?"

"A brother and sister, and they did know what I was doing," she answered before he could ask.

Before Hugh could ask more questions, his men

returned without good news. It was just as he expected, and it left a foul taste in mouth. There was no excuse to leave a defenseless woman alone to face the sort of evil they hunted.

"We will return you home safely." When she hesitated he said, "If you would prefer to face that creature alone and on foot, then we will leave you to it."

He had an idea she was about to do just that when the creature screamed some distance away and silenced any words she might have said. Without waiting for her to agree, he swiftly lifted her onto his horse.

He glanced at his men before he grabbed his horse's reins and mounted behind her. Their expressions said it all.

They had found exactly what they were searching for.

CHAPTER TWO

For a moment, Hugh thought they wouldn't be allowed entrance into the castle despite Mina calling to the guards. Mina's tension was evident by the way she held her back straight. Hugh and his men simply waited, and he knew he wasn't the only one cataloguing the strengths and weaknesses of the castle.

Finally, the chains rattled and the gate slowly opened. There was a soft sound of a sigh. Mina's. He was all too aware of the womanly curves sitting before him, of her long hair tangling about his arms as he gripped the reins in front of her.

There was something different about Mina, something that niggled at the edge of his mind.

He nudged his mount forward, leading his men beneath the large gatehouse. The sound of their horses' hoofs resonated around them as they walked into the cobbled area of the bailey. One glance showed just a smattering of men atop the battlements.

There should have been more guards. Hugh inwardly

cringed. Just how long had the creature been attacking the area? It was just one of many questions he wanted answers to that night.

No one came to greet Mina when they stopped their horses near the stable. He dismounted, but before he turned to Mina, he let his eyes survey the castle and bailey in one sweep.

It was a good-sized holding. From what he could tell from the limited moonlight and few torches, it didn't look as though it needed many repairs. Someone had taken care of it, but with a castle this size, there should be a vast number of people rather than the handful of men seen on the battlements and in the gatehouse. The castle could easily be taken.

"It's not a good idea to stand out in the open too long with it being nighttime," Mina said.

She was right, but Hugh had a feeling the creature wouldn't return to the castle this night. He turned and reached for Mina. His hands came around her trim waist, something he hadn't expected since it was hidden in her manly attire. She kept her eyes downcast as he lowered her to the ground.

To his surprise and annoyance, he found himself wanting to prolong the contact.

It was unlike him, and it disturbed him. He jerked his hands away and took a step back. "Where is everyone?"

She turned and pointed to the stable. "You can put your horses there. There is a lad that will care for them, but you must hurry and get inside."

"We will see to our mounts," he said and leisurely turned to his horse.

Mina knew she should get into the castle, but she got her first good look at the men she had led to Stone Crest and was mesmerized. Hugh's men remained atop their mounts and looked around the bailey as if they were waiting for something, or maybe just sizing up the place.

Had she seen them earlier as she saw them now, she doubted she would have gotten on Hugh's horse. The men were warriors. Not the regular knights who were stationed at the castle, but the warriors one heard about that could - and would - conquer anything that got in their way.

Not only was each man an incredible specimen that would make any woman sigh with pleasure, but they were unlike any knight she had ever seen. They didn't wear the armor she was accustomed to seeing, though they each bore a large shield. Their clothing was simple and unadorned, but it wasn't of the poor class, nor was it of the nobility.

They wore their long cloaks like armor, but beneath them she caught glimpses of their tunics and pants. Leather boots that reached their knees, which were out of place with the short leather shoes that men now wore. All in all, they didn't quite fit in with the day's fashions.

But what she recognized without a doubt were the weapons, and each seemed to favor one above another.

The man farthest from her held a two-headed flail that was larger than anything she had ever seen, with spikes longer than her hand. The next one had a wicked halberd with a downward curved spike on the back. Gabriel gripped a unique bow that made her want to take a closer look at its odd shape.

A double-headed war axe that had to be at least two feet across could be seen strapped to the back of the next knight. The man closest to her, the one with the charming smile, had many daggers peeking out of his clothing. Her eyes went to Hugh's horse and took in the sight of the crossbow slung next to his saddle. It was bigger and thicker than the ones she was used to seeing.

The superior weapons of the men gave her pause, as well as spotting the pommels of swords. These men were certainly warriors of some kind, but of what she had no idea.

"There you are," a surly shout sounded from above them.

Mina took a deep breath and counted to ten. Twice. She had hoped to get inside the castle with her new guests before either her brother or sister saw them. Luck, it seemed, wasn't on her side.

Hugh glanced at Mina before turning his head upward. "Who is that?"

"My brother, Bernard, Baron of Stone Crest."

Hugh knew that circumstances, as they were, could turn many a good man into a coward, but his instincts said this situation had existed before the evil had befallen Stone Crest and the village.

Like it or not, he would have to face the young baron. Better now than later. He felt the reins tug in his hand and turned to find a young lad with bright red hair waiting to take his horse.

"Hello, John," Mina said with a smile. She turned her gaze to Hugh. "He's wonderful with horses, though he cannot speak."

Hugh smiled at the lad and handed him the reins. He leaned down close to the boy. "Watch the roan," he warned of Val's horse. "He's got a nasty bite if you aren't looking."

The lad gave him a bright smile and pointed to his bay. "Oh, this one is as gentle as a lamb. As long as you give him a good rub and extra oats," he said with a wink.

After John had departed with the horses, Hugh straightened and found Mina staring at him oddly. "Is something amiss?"

She shook her head. "Most people avoid talking to

him."

"I'm not most people," he replied. "Now, let us greet your brother."

The hall was quiet and nearly deserted except for the two wolfhounds that slept by the hearth. Mina led Hugh and his men to a table and bade them sit while she found a servant.

Hugh took the seat that faced the stairs in which Bernard would descend, for he had no doubt the young baron would be down shortly, once he was informed of their arrival.

When he should have been watching the stairs, he found himself studying Mina. He smiled when he saw her pull her loose strawberry-blonde hair away from her face to fall in a thick, long braid down her back. Her face was smudged with dirt, but hidden beneath the mud were bright blue-green eyes that took in all around her.

She walked with the grace of a lady and the dignity of a queen, despite her manly attire. It was then he noticed the blood on her arm.

He reached out and grabbed her good arm as she walked past him. "You should have told us you were injured."

"It isn't much. I will tend to it when I reach my chamber."

He ignored her words and called over his shoulder. "Gabriel, your healing skills are required."

Gabriel moved away from the hearth and hurried to the table. He turned Mina's arm this way and that as he examined it. "It's deep. I'm going to need a bowl of water and a towel to wash away the blood."

It only took one look from Hugh to get the servant who had brought the drinks to gather the materials Gabriel requested.

Hugh looked up to find Mina's face ashen. He rose and pushed her into his chair. Gabriel took the seat next to her and pulled out the black packet hidden in his tunic. Hugh never tired of watching Gabriel shift through the unlabeled herbs and grab a pinch of one or a leaf of another.

This time, Gabriel gathered three herbs and began to crush them. Once that was done, he placed two more in a goblet of water. Then, he turned and reached for the towel and wet it. Gabriel's big, war scarred hands were gentle as they washed the blood away to reveal a gash half a hand's length on Mina's forearm.

Hugh noticed the rest of his men had come to watch Gabriel work. He placed his hands on Mina's shoulders to keep her still so Gabriel could tend to the wound properly. Hugh readied himself for her to jump when Gabriel began to pack the mixture of herbs into her wound, but she only twitched slightly.

Every once in awhile, Hugh would hear a sharp intake of breath, but she never cried out. Once Gabriel had wrapped the wound tightly, he grabbed the herbs mixed in the water goblet and handed it to her to drink.

"What is it?" she asked.

"It will help with the pain," Gabriel told her while he rolled up his packet.

She sat the goblet on the table. "Pain lets me know I'm still alive."

Hugh wasn't surprised to find all five of his men raising eyebrows at her words. At one time or another, all of them had said the same thing.

"It will also help to heal the wound," Gabriel added after a brief pause.

With his words, she reached for the goblet and drained it. She placed it on the table once more and rose on shaky legs. "I thank you for tending me. I will see to your drinks now."

"They've already been brought," Hugh told her as he motioned to the table. "Rest," he said and took the chair on her other side.

No sooner had he reached for his goblet of ale than Bernard sauntered into the hall. Hugh felt Mina tense beside him as he rose to his feet.

"Mina," Bernard bellowed and staggered against a table, knocking over a chair.

Out of the corner of his eye, Hugh saw Mina rise and walk toward her brother. Bernard held out a goblet to her and waited. Hugh watched, fascinated, as they stared at each other in silent battle before Mina finally filled the goblet.

"Have you taken to whoring?" Bernard asked after draining half of the drink.

"Nay, brother," Mina replied stiffly. "These men brought me safely home, but then you would know that if you weren't full of ale."

"I see you are still alive," Bernard said as he looked her over, his lip rose in a sneer. "Your plan didn't work."

It wasn't a question. Just for a moment, Hugh saw Mina's eyes flare with anger.

She took a step back and crossed her arms over her chest. "You ordered the men to return."

Bernard laughed. "Of course I did, you silly girl. No one believed your plan would work."

Hugh had had enough. "Her plan might, in fact, have worked had you given it a chance."

The inebriated lord of Stone Crest turned toward him then. "You know nothing of what I speak."

"But indeed I do," Hugh said and walked around the table toward him. "We came upon the creature after it had unhorsed your sister and was about to make a meal of her."

Bernard waved away his explanation. "She always gets away from the beast. Tonight was her night to die."

Hugh hid his surprise, but Mina's gasp was heard loudly through the great hall. Just what type of family had they stumbled upon?

"Why?" Mina asked.

"Why," Bernard yelled as he rounded on her. "It was you who drudged up the demon. It was you it was after when it took our parents. You've been nothing but trouble since the moment you were born."

A shuffle behind Hugh told him his men had reached their limit. When he turned his gaze to Mina, he was surprised to find her hands fisted by her side, as if she thought about attacking her brother.

Hugh decided to take matters into his own hands. He grabbed Bernard by the neck and dragged him outside. Even though the baron kicked and screamed, no one came to stop Hugh. He continued through the bailey until he happened upon the water trough and dunked Bernard's head.

After counting to three, he pulled him free of the water. Curses toward Mina burst from Bernard's mouth, and Hugh dunked him again.

"Do you plan to drown him?" Val asked as he came to stand beside Hugh, his arms crossed over his chest.

"If need be." He allowed Bernard another breath of air before putting him back under the water.

"We need all the men we can find," Roderick stated and kicked his boot against the trough.

Hugh sighed. He knew they were right. He released Bernard, letting him fall to the earth coughing and gasping for air.

"Who are you?" the baron finally asked, his breathing harsh and course.

Hugh reached down for him and almost smiled when Bernard flinched. Once he had the baron on his feet he started for the castle. He didn't answer until they were once again inside the hall.

When Bernard went to grab for a goblet, Hugh caught his hand. "It's the ale that has addled your brains. The world will be much clearer without the blur of it."

For a moment he thought, and hoped, Bernard would fight him, but in the end the baron withdrew his hand. Hugh sighed and returned to his seat.

"My name is Hugh." After he had introduced his men he said, "My men and I are called the Shields. We have come to kill the demon that troubles your village."

Bernard laughed. "We have tried for a month to kill that creature. What makes you so confident?"

"It's what we do," Hugh stated.

The baron's eyes grew round for a moment then he leaned back in his chair. "Who exactly are you?"

"Knights. Of a sort."

Bernard harrumphed and wiped his wet hair out of his face. "You're not like any knights I've seen."

"We *are* knights," Hugh repeated.

The baron's blue eyes narrowed, and he leaned forward. "How did you know about the creature?"

"Word travels quickly these days."

"And there are many of these creatures?"

Darrick grinned. "More than you could possibly imagine."

"Then hasten and be done with it," Bernard said with a wave of his hand as he leaned back in his chair. "I grow weary of its existence. I grow weary of all of this."

When Bernard would have risen and walked away Hugh stopped him. "Why do you blame Mina?"

"It wasn't until she went exploring in the forest and the

old ruins of an ancient Druid temple that the creature appeared," Bernard explained through clenched teeth. "As usual, she was somewhere she had no business being."

Hugh didn't stop Bernard this time as he walked away.

They sat in silence until Darrick said, "I think there's more to this story than we've been told."

"There is always more," Val said cynically.

But he had a right to be cynical, Hugh thought. Val came from the time of the Romans. He was a fierce fighter that mastered any weapon placed in his hand, and he was invaluable to their group.

Talk halted as Mina came towards them. "I will show you to your chambers," she said without looking at them.

They rose to their feet and followed her up the stairs. She stopped at the first chamber. "I apologize, but there are only three chambers available."

"It'll be fine," Darrick said. "We're used to sleeping outside, so this will be a treat."

Hugh watched as she gave Darrick a small smile. Val and Gabriel took the first chamber, and Roderick and Darrick the second. When they came to the third, Cole went in ahead of Hugh.

Hugh waited for Mina to turn towards him. Before he could say anything she said, "I also want to apologize to you and your men for having to witness what happened between me and my brother."

"There is nothing to apologize for."

There was a sound behind him, and when he turned to see who - or what - it was, he only found the darkened hallway. When he turned back, Mina was gone. He shook his head and entered the chamber.

"What do you think?" Cole asked as the others walked into the chamber behind Hugh.

"I was hoping to find out more, but it looks as if we

must wait until morning."

Val leaned against the closed door with his arms crossed over his chest. "I pray the sister is friendlier than the brother."

"I have a feeling she isn't," Cole said and leaned back on the bed. "Still, you won't find me complaining about sleeping in a soft bed."

"That's the truth," Darrick grinned. "And speaking of which, I'm headed to my soft bed."

Hugh waited until the men had left the chamber before he let his mind wander over what had occurred that night. They hadn't expected to come upon their quarry quite so suddenly.

Their orders had been brief and exact. Hunt down and slaughter the creature terrorizing Stone Crest.

"Your mind is going to explode with those deep reflections," Cole said.

Hugh turned to the bed. "Go to sleep."

"Why?" Cole asked and sat up. "And leave you to your dark thoughts?"

"I'm just reviewing what we learned."

"We learned nothing."

Hugh looked at his companion. Cole was an immortal found wandering between realms as a child. His world had been destroyed, and he had been taken in and trained in weapons and fighting by the Fae.

"How old are you, Cole?"

Just a slight narrowing of Cole's blue eyes let on that the question had surprised him. "Three hundred and twenty-one. Why?"

"How long have we been fighting for the Fae?"

"Seems like forever sometimes. What are you getting at?"

Hugh leaned forward and raked his hands down his

face. "With every beast we kill, two more take its place. They are coming faster and deadlier every time."

"Aye, it's the truth," he said and scooted to the foot of the bed. "Do you know something we don't?"

"Nothing." Hugh signed heavily. "I know nothing more than you."

"Ask Aimery."

Hugh chuckled at the thought of asking the commander of the Fae army. "I'd rather not have my thoughts in a jumble, thank you very much."

"Aye, he does manage to do that to all of us."

"I'm glad I'm not alone in that."

A moment of silence ticked by before Cole asked, "How much time do we have?"

Hugh let out a pent up sigh. "Not nearly enough."

CHAPTER THREE

Mina stared down at her bandaged right arm. She had slept like the dead the night before and woke feeling refreshed for the first time in months. Even her arm didn't ache.

It was the truth she'd been relieved when Gabriel had seen to her injury. She knew nothing of treating wounds, and had been afraid she wouldn't tend it correctly and it would become infected. It was a downfall of hers to refuse help from others, but it had also helped her to realize she could do things herself.

Thoughts of the new guests had her contemplating what she'd heard last night. Hugh and his men found and hunted creatures like the one that terrorized Stone Crest. It explained their odd dress and weapons for sure, but she couldn't imagine there to be other creatures. If she were the type of woman to be frightened, that bit of news would have her hiding in her chamber.

She pushed the covers aside and swung her legs over the bed. In her quiet, dull life, her days had never changed until the creature came. She had a feeling these men could rid them of the creature. If she were lucky, she might have an adventure or two before her life went back to the usual monotony as well.

With the morning sun peaking through her window, she combed her hair as best she could with her injured arm, and said a prayer that Bernard and Theresa stayed away from her. It would be a test of pure strength of will if she could keep her temper under control and her mouth closed until Hugh and his men departed Stone Crest.

Dressing was extremely difficult. She threw the gown aside and reached for another, one that she might manage on her own. It was while she was buttoning the gown that Theresa walked into her chamber without knocking.

She bit her tongue and refused to look at her sister as she continued fastening the gown.

Theresa's tongue could flay a person alive. Mina had a sneaking suspicion she'd come to rile her this morning before they went down to the great hall. But Mina wasn't a fool. She could control her temper when need be.

Her sister laughed as she walked around Mina. "Are we dressing to impress our guests, because there is nothing that you could put on that would make you look any better, sister dear. God didn't bless you with anything remotely…pretty. It's a shame that."

Mina didn't even bother to raise her eyes to her sister. Theresa's words used to cut deep, but they had become so constant Mina rarely paid attention to them anymore. She used to gaze upon Theresa's light blonde hair, blue eyes and angelic features with admiration, but despite Theresa's beauty, her attitude made her hideous in Mina's eyes.

"I know what I am," Mina said evenly. "I am simply getting dressed."

"Ah, but you are wearing one of your nicer gowns."

Mina's gaze rose to her sister's this time. In an instant, she knew today would be worse than what Bernard had done last eve. By the time the sun set, Mina knew Theresa would embarrass her enough to keep her locked in her chambers.

If she were afraid.

But Mina had other concerns than what the new guests thought of her. Even if Hugh's dark gaze made her stomach quiver and her heart miss a beat. So what if he were the most handsome man to ever cross her path and that his calming nature made her want to be around him?

She would look from afar. As she'd always done.

After a moment, she said, "I don't want to humiliate you or Bernard by wearing my man's attire."

"Your presence embarrasses," Theresa spat, her red lips pursed tightly. "Do everyone a favor, sister, and remain in your chamber."

Mina didn't let out her breath until the door had closed behind Theresa. Her hand still tingled with the urge to slap Theresa. It was going to take some doing to calm down, and she knew Theresa had planned it all very carefully. Mina had hoped to reach the hall before her sister met their guests, but she had been too slow. Now, there was no reason to go down unless she could control herself around Theresa.

She sank slowly to the bed, her thoughts of adventure flying out the window like her hopes of a happy life. A tapping at her door brought her to her feet. No one begged entrance into her chamber, so it was more curiosity than anything that made her open the door.

To her surprise, Hugh stood before her, his amazing brown eyes meeting hers with a hint of a smile. Last eve she'd been at first in pain and then too angry and embarrassed to notice anything but the dirt on her shoes. But now she was able to see him in the light of day.

He stood tall and proud before her in a tunic of blood

red. It was not decorated but the material looked costly. His dark brown hair fell in soft waves to his shoulder while the sides were pulled away from his face and bound in a single braid at the back of his head. He had a square chin and wide, thin lips. His forehead was high and his nose straight. Dark brows slashed above golden brown orbs that watched at her as a falcon might watch pray.

She should be appalled or even wary. But those weren't the emotions Hugh stirred in her. No, with him, he stirred awareness of his muscular form, cognizance of how he towered over her, and a pulse of...desire she neither knew how to comprehend or react to.

"Good morn," he said softly as if sensing she were off kilter. "How fares your arm?"

Mina glanced at her arm before falling into his golden brown depths once more. What was his allure? What was it about him that drew her – even against her better judgment? Or more precisely, the knowledge she could never have a man like him?

"There isn't much pain," she finally answered.

"Gabriel has the touch when it comes to healing. Did you sleep well?"

She blinked and leaned forward to look down the hall looking for Theresa or someone who might have told him which chamber was hers. "I slept fine. And you?"

"Are you looking for someone?" he asked as he glanced down the corridor in the direction she'd looked.

"How did you find my chamber?"

He shrugged his massive shoulder. "I asked. Is something amiss?"

She shook her head. "I was just on my way to the hall."

"Then allow me."

An arm clad in the deepest red extended toward her. No man had ever offered her his arm, and at first she wasn't sure she should take it. But the crinkling corners of his eyes made her aware he'd issued a silent challenge.

One he somehow knew she couldn't refuse. She accepted his arm and noted the pliability of his tunic beneath her fingers. It wasn't the fine silk a lord might wear. Yet it wasn't the coarse wool of a lowly knight. She had never touched anything so soft.

"There is more to you than you show," she said as they descended the stairs.

He tensed slightly at her words, the sinew in his arms tightening beneath her fingers. "Have you the sight?" he asked softly.

"Nay. I can simply tell that what you show the world and what is inside you is different."

"That can be said of many people. Including yourself."

His words halted her steps as she gazed up at him. "Aye, that is the truth. There is a great evil here. I would see you and your men leave this village today so you don't follow the others to an early grave."

"We cannot."

"There is nothing holding you," she said urgently. "Leave before it's too late."

He gave her a small smile. "Thank you for your warning, my lady, but we knew what was here when we came. I wasn't lying to your brother when I said we've been sent to kill the creature."

"By whom?"

"It doesn't matter."

She stared into his brown eyes and saw the truth of it. "Too many good men and women have died fighting the creature. Most were just about their daily lives when it came upon them."

He smiled gently. "Then we shall have to be sure to kill it quickly."

"I want no more deaths on my conscience."

"This isn't the first creature we have encountered, and I doubt it will be the last. We'll eradicate it."

They resumed walking, and when they reached the hall there was a smile on her lips, thoughts of Theresa and their encounter long forgotten. Until she spotted her sister amidst Hugh's men. Theresa laughed and smiled at the men as they gazed upon her beauty.

Before Mina could turn away, Theresa's eyes lit upon her. "Good morn, sister. You must introduce me to our guest."

Mina swallowed and glared at her sister for a moment before she plastered a smile on her face and said, "Hugh, this is my sister Theresa of Cloister. Theresa, Hugh."

She bit her tongue as Theresa rose gracefully and executed a perfect curtsy while Hugh regally bowed his head.

"I understand we owe you and your men our gratitude for saving our Mina," Theresa said coyly. "She's always getting into some mischief. She never did know when something is better left for a man to do."

Mina couldn't look at Hugh or any of his men in the eye. She should have known Theresa would throw her barbs even with guests around. It was becoming harder and harder to keep her temper in check.

"It was no trouble at all. Actually, Lady Mina was doing well on her own," Hugh replied and turned toward Mina. He held out her chair, waiting for her to sit.

Mina wanted to refuse because it would place her directly across from Theresa, but to decline would show rudeness, and she owed these men much more than that.

"Thank you," she said and took her seat.

"Cloister?" Hugh said to Theresa as he sat. "Are you married, my lady?"

"I was," Theresa said and dabbed at her eye. "He was taken by that foul monster Mina let loose."

Mina wanted to roll her eyes. Instead, her gaze took in Hugh's men. Of the five, she only knew two by name. Gabriel, with his unusual silver eyes had a gift for healing. And she recognized Val because of the wicked looking scar that cut across his face, though instead of detracting from his looks, it only added to them.

As she watched them, she couldn't help but notice that each of them was an attractive man, especially Hugh. The group was a mystery that begged to be deciphered, though she had little doubt anyone, least of all her, would learn more than the Shields were willing to share.

A man, sitting to Theresa's right, laughed at something she said. He was the only one who kept a smile on his face and the only one where the smile actually reached his eyes.

She leaned over to Hugh. "The man talking to my sister. What is his name again?"

Hugh leaned over and said, "That is Darrick. He's the trickster of us. He keeps everyone's spirits up."

So, Gabriel was the healer, Darrick the trickster, Hugh the leader and Val the scarred. Now if she could only recall which one was Roderick and which was Cole.

"Cole has the hair as black as a raven's wing, and Roderick is the only blond among us," Hugh whispered near her ear.

She smothered her laughter, but not before she noticed Theresa narrow her eyes at her. She ignored her sister and turned toward Hugh. "How did you know what I was doing?"

He shrugged. "You were introduced to us in the dead of the night while wounded, and had quite an ordeal to encounter once we returned here. It's only natural you wouldn't have remembered all our names."

"I suppose," she admitted with a smile.

"I'd like for you to show me the Druid ruins."

All talk in the hall halted at Hugh's words. Mina's heart burst with excitement at having a man such as he ask her to accompany him. Maybe she would get that adventure after all.

"I would be happy to show you," Theresa said and gave him a seductive smile. "Mina has chores to do, but I'm free."

Mina curled her hands into fists beneath the table. She shouldn't have been surprised though. It wasn't the first time Theresa had done this to a man that talked to her.

"That is very gracious of you," Hugh said, and Mina's heart sank like a stone to her feet. Once again beauty had won out.

"However," Hugh continued. "It looks like rain, and I know you have no wish to dirty your fine gowns as I explore the ruins."

Mina glanced at Theresa, and for an instant, thought Theresa would shriek with fury as her face mottled with rage. She wasn't used to men turning her down.

Theresa stood and stared at Hugh. She turned to his men and smiled sweetly. "Excuse me, gentlemen, I must see to the duties of the castle."

Once Theresa had departed the hall, Mina let out the breath she'd held. She reached for her goblet of water and found all six men watching her keenly. "Do I have something on me?" she asked as embarrassment engulfed her.

"Nay," Val said.

Their stares began to unnerve her. She turned toward Hugh. "What is it?"

"We are trying to understand how a brother and sister could detest a sibling so."

She sighed and shrugged. "It's always been so. What can you expect from two people who are so beautiful to have someone like me in their family?"

"Do you jest, milady?" Darrick asked, his usual smile gone.

She shook her head and placed a piece of warm bread in her mouth. "There is no need to be kind. I know I wasn't blessed with Theresa and Bernard's good looks. Even my betrothed couldn't stand the look of me and took Theresa instead."

"Are you telling us that Theresa took your betrothed?" Hugh asked, disbelief etched on his handsome face.

Mina nodded. "But don't blame Lord Charles. He had no wish to be bound to one such as me when he could have someone like Theresa."

She jumped as Roderick set his goblet down hard on the table and stood.

"I'll see to the horses," he said before he walked from the castle.

Mina was ashamed of herself. "I didn't mean to speak ill of Lord Charles."

"You didn't," Hugh said. "Roderick was raised differently than most people. He detests seeing someone treated unfairly."

The meal quickly grew unbearable with the men staring at her with a mixture pity and sorrow.

"If you are ready, we can ride to the ruins now."

To her surprise, Hugh held out her chair for her. She wasn't used to having men dote on her as they did with Theresa, and it brought a small smile to her lips.

"Thank you," she said and couldn't believe she sounded so breathless as if she had run to the gatehouse and back. "I'll just go and change."

"There is no threat of rain."

She stopped and gaped at him as he grinned. "I've never known a man who would lie to Theresa. Every man I've ever known has fallen over themselves to gain her attention."

"As I told you last night, my lady, I am not like most men."

"So I've noticed," she murmured and walked from the hall. When she stepped through the door, she found Roderick standing with John holding the horses. John was grinning like a lad who had been given a king's ransom.

When she reached the horse John had selected for her, a gray mare that Theresa usually rode, she found Hugh beside her. Before she could open her mouth, he lifted her onto the horse.

His large hands had touched her gently and left a strange tingling running through her. He almost made her feel like a woman, something she'd never felt before.

Could this be what it was like to be Theresa? To have men so...attentive? She knew they were just being kind, but their compassion meant more to her than they would ever realize.

"Aren't you afraid of meeting the creature during the day?" she asked them.

They exchanged looks before Hugh said, "It only comes out at night."

She narrowed her eyes at them, suddenly suspicious. "How did you know that?"

"Like I told you, we hunt them."

And he *was* a hunter. Just to look at Hugh's chiseled face and rugged features was to know that the man would conquer anything he set his mind to. He was a warrior, a leader.

With a nudge, her mare turned and cantered through the opened gate. She was a little surprised to find the men surround her as they rode. She was used to being alone. Always.

The ride to the ruins was pleasant. Had the circumstances been different, Mina could almost believe she was a beautiful lady being escorted by her faithful knights. Almost. She wasn't foolish enough to actually believe in dreams anymore. She was who she was. Nothing would change that.

The ruins came into view as they crested a hill, and she slowed the mare to a walk. Hugh stayed on her right and Darrick on her left. When she would have continued on, Hugh grabbed her reins.

"Hold a moment," he said and then motioned with his hand.

She watched as Gabriel rode to the ruins and looked around. It was just a few moments later that they heard him whistle.

"Lead on, my lady," Hugh said and released her reins.

She cleared her throat and nudged the mare, but the closer they came to the ruins the harder the mare fought to turn around.

"I don't know what's wrong with her," she said in exasperation. Sasha had never acted like this when they had come.

It wasn't until she allowed the mare to turn away from the ruins that she quieted, but she still trembled. Mina dismounted and rubbed the mare's neck.

"Leave the horse," Hugh said.

"Sasha never acted like this."

"That is because Sasha was used to this place. I doubt this mare has ever been here before."

She raised an eyebrow at him. "Then why aren't your mounts acting up?"

"They are used to the smell of evil," Cole said as he

dismounted and dropped his horse's reins.

She watched Cole walk toward the ruins and found it difficult to swallow. "Evil?" she asked and turned toward Hugh. "There is evil here?"

"Can't you tell?"

She looked over the ruins. "I've come here many times over the years. Only once was I frightened, and that was the day the creature came."

"Show me," he urged her.

She left the mare with their horses and walked toward the ruins. There wasn't much left of them. Just a few rocks standing as tall as the trees, while others had been knocked over and laid on top of each other.

"A child's imagination made these ruins into a castle of her own," Mina said as she reached the first stone.

Hugh watched as she touched the standing stone gently. There was reverence in her touch, but that wasn't what surprised him. It was the fact the evil didn't penetrate her.

To him and his men, the evil was so strong they smelled it not long after leaving the castle. There were more to these ruins than what the surface held.

He followed Mina through the stones that had once been an entrance. They found Cole staring at something on the ground.

"You found it," Mina said.

Cole's eyes jerked to his, and Hugh knew he had indeed found something.

"This is where the earth opened up and the creature came from," Mina said when they reached Cole.

Hugh stared at the burnt patch of earth that was about two strides in width. Around it, in a perfect circle, were flawlessly smooth bright blue stones. Those stones gave him pause. He stared at one of the oval stones.

"Mina, did you put those stones there?"

She shook her head, wisps of blonde hair with a hint of red gathered around her face. "Those stones were scattered throughout the ruins, and I took one back to the castle with me once, but it soon disappeared. I think someone took it."

"You have no idea who?"

"Nay." She looked down at the burnt earth again and wrung her hands. "Are Bernard and Theresa correct? Did I unleash that creature?"

"I don't know," Hugh answered as he stared at the ground.

"Hugh," Roderick called.

"Stay here," Hugh told her as he hurried to Roderick.

Instead of walking around the huge stone, he jumped from stone to stone and landed beside Roderick. "What is it?"

"Trouble," Roderick answered.

Hugh looked up and suddenly found Aimery before him. Whenever the Fae visited, it did mean trouble. "We've only just arrived, Aimery. Give us a few days."

"It's not that," the commander of the Fae army said. "It's something else."

The haggard look on the face of the ever regal Fae alerted Hugh. "What is it?"

"More creatures have been released."

Hugh ran a hand down his face and leaned against a fallen stone. "What's going on, Aimery? We've been tracking these creatures for so long now that I've lost count. Their numbers aren't dwindling like ours. They grow stronger. Just how many more are there to be released?"

"I wish I had an answer."

"We can't leave yet. There is more to this than we've yet to uncover."

"You mustn't leave until this is finished," Aimery said and clasped his hands behind his back. His long, straight flaxen hair never stirred in the breeze, and his swirling blue gaze trapped Hugh's. "Choose two men and send them on the next mission."

Hugh opened his mouth to answer when he saw Aimery's gaze move over his shoulder. Hugh turned and found Mina staring at them.

"Can she see you?" he turned and asked the Fae.

Aimery gave him a droll look. "Of course she can. Invite her over. It's time we meet."

Anytime the Fae said those prophetic words it brought a chill to Hugh's bones. "Leave her out of this."

The intense blue eyes of the Faerie landed on him. "Her Fate is out of my hands."

"Mina," Hugh called without taking his eyes off Aimery. He smelled her fresh, clean scent as she approached.

A long strawberry blonde tendril landed on his arm as she came to stand beside him. She regarded Aimery with intrigue, but a healthy dose of caution.

"Aye?" her soft voice questioned.

He moved his gaze to her face and saw the doubt shine brightly in her blue-green gaze. "You have nothing to be afraid of. Aimery is a friend."

"Who just appeared out of nowhere?"

He would have laughed had the situation not been so serious. Most people, when they saw a Fae, immediately forgot them because their minds wouldn't allow them to believe what they saw. He took a step closer to her, angling himself so that he was almost behind her.

"I've wanted to meet you for a long time, Mina," Aimery spoke, taking a step toward her. "You have shown much courage over the years."

Hugh almost groaned aloud, especially when Mina took a step away from Aimery, which brought her up against his chest. "Mina," he said as he took hold of her arms. "He's a friend. Trust me."

She stared at Aimery for a time before she finally moved toward him, her head moving from side to side as she looked him over. Hugh hated the absence of her warmth and the feel of her feminine curves against him, but he expected nothing less with Aimery around.

After all, no mortal could withstand the lure of the Fae.

Mina watched the stunning blond man before her. Nay, stunning didn't describe him correctly. There was something about him that pulled her to him. He was incredibly handsome, so much so that he was perfect. Everything was perfect, down to the shiny leather of his mid-calf boot.

He wasn't human, of that she instinctively knew. But what he was, she didn't know. "What are you?"

"You know what I am," Aimery said, his unearthly blue eyes intent on her. "What am I?"

The answer came immediately to her lips, but she disregarded it.

"Don't ignore your instincts," he warned.

Her gaze drifted to Hugh who watched her just as carefully. "Fae," she said and looked to Aimery. "You are of the Fae."

Aimery smiled, displaying even, bright white teeth and nodded. "Very good. You learn quickly."

His praise should have boosted her spirit, but the silence of the men around her disturbed her. "What's going on?"

"These men, the Shields," Aimery answered, "have been sent to destroy the creature that terrorizes your village."

"I know."

"They work for the Fae."

Now that did surprise her. "I don't understand. Why don't you kill them yourselves?"

The Fae smiled sadly. "If only we could, but we have our own demons to battle and laws that hinder us." He turned to Hugh. "Choose your men. I'll return later with the destination."

And in a blink he was gone.

Mina turned to Hugh. "You're leaving?" The sudden apprehension of his departure frightened her in ways she couldn't understand. "The creature still lives. You cannot leave yet."

"Only two of my men will be leaving. They have another assignment." He stood and held out his hand for her. "Now come tell me what happened the day the creature came."

She didn't hesitate in placing her hand in his. His hand was warm and strong as it enfolded hers. She told herself it was just because he chose her over Theresa, but it was more than that. If she didn't watch herself, she could find herself becoming besotted with him for the simple fact he paid her attention.

But she had to remember that the real reason he was with her was because she was here the day the creature had come. That's what really held his interest.

"What were you doing?" he asked when they were once again standing beside the burnt earth.

She pointed to the stone over his shoulder. "I was sitting there."

"Doing what?" Cole asked.

"I come here for solitude," she said after a moment. She hadn't wanted to admit she came to escape the castle.

Hugh stepped closer to her. "Then what?"

"The sky became black as if night had fallen in the middle of the day." She lifted her face to the sky. "I looked up at the clouds, and then the earth began to shake. It knocked me off the stone, and lightning began so fiercely that I feared I would be struck."

She stopped and wrapped her arms around herself as she gazed at the burnt earth. "When the lightning stopped, I heard the most awful, bone-chilling scream. When I looked up, it was to see the creature flying towards Stone Crest."

"And that is all that happened?" Hugh asked.

She nodded. "After that, I ran toward Sasha and raced to the castle. Since then we've been plagued by the creature every night."

"How many has it killed?" Val asked.

"So many I have lost count. The castle and village used to be full of people, but they soon ran for their lives. The ones who stayed have been picked off, one by one, every night."

"I find it odd that in a month it hasn't destroyed everything," Gabriel said as he put his foot on one of the fallen stones.

She looked from Gabriel to Hugh. "What?"

"The creature's mission is to kill off everyone in your village," Hugh explained. "Whoever is controlling it is keeping it from killing too many at once."

Gabriel turned and looked at the castle in the distance. "The question is why. The creature could have killed everyone in a week's time."

"By the saints," she whispered and slumped onto a stone.

"Then it's time we put a stop to it," Hugh said and gently touched her hand.

Hope blossomed in her heart. She raised her gaze to him. "Do you have a plan?"

"I always have a plan."

CHAPTER FOUR

Hugh looked over his men once they were inside his chamber. They hadn't been separated since their first assignment, and he wasn't happy about this. But he also didn't have a choice. Mankind depended upon them, whether they realized it or not.

"Any of you wish to volunteer?" he asked.

All five of them stared at him and waited. It was just as he expected. None of them wanted to go, but they all knew someone had to. It would be up to him to make the decision.

The role as leader of the Shields had come upon him without him even wanting it. The decisions he made would affect them all for the rest of their lives, however long that might be. Truthfully, he didn't want to send any of them. He should be the one that went, but as soon as the thought entered his mind, it was replaced with the thought of Mina.

He gazed at his men again and took a deep breath. "Roderick, you and Val will take Aimery's new orders," he said. And as he anticipated, neither man disobeyed him.

"Aye," they replied.

His chamber suddenly seemed too small. He longed to stretch his legs and walk around without carrying weapons hidden in his clothes, or wondering when the next foul creature that Hell spat out would attack.

"Did Aimery say where we're headed?" Val asked.

Before Hugh could answer, Aimery appeared next to him. "You will be going to the future," the Fae said.

None of them thought much about that. Hugh himself had been brought forward from 1036. Traveling through the realms of time was something that occurred often in their line of work.

Roderick rose from his seat by the hearth. "Where exactly?"

"To a place called Texas."

That got everyone's attention.

"I've never heard of this place," Hugh said. "In what realm is it in?"

"This one," Aimery said. "Just nine hundred years from now."

Val whistled softly as he placed the dagger he had been sharpening back in his boot. "Then I suppose Roderick and I better prepare. When do we leave?"

"Immediately," Aimery said. "Ride to the woods. I'll meet you there."

And with that he was gone.

It didn't take Roderick and Val long to gather their few belongings. Hugh and the rest of his men walked to the bailey to see their friends off.

After brief good-byes and Godspeeds, Val and Roderick rode their horses through the open gate toward the forest. Hugh didn't know if he would ever see them again, but he sure hoped he would. These men had become friends. Family even.

They had lost men before, and they would again, but he refused to believe he would lose either of them. Val had seen much while fighting for the Romans, and Roderick was immortal. They would survive.

He turned to follow Cole, Gabriel and Darrick into the castle when he spotted Mina atop the steps. He stopped when he came to her.

"I won't ever see them again, will I?" she asked.

"I honestly don't know."

She looked past him. "I wish them well."

He waited until she had entered the castle before he followed. They had wasted most of the morning instead of preparing for the creature. The sooner they killed this one, the sooner he could meet up with Val and Roderick.

His men and Mina waited in the hall for him. "Tell me about your trap," he urged Mina as he sat down.

"It didn't work," Bernard stated as he walked to the table. "That was proven last night."

"What was proven, was that you told the men to return here," Darrick said. "You left your sister to die."

Bernard's pasty face flushed with anger. "It's she the creature wants."

"How do you know that?" Hugh asked. "Did the creature tell you?"

"Don't be ridiculous," Bernard hissed and reached for a goblet a serving girl handed him.

Hugh's gaze flickered to Mina to see her eyes downcast. He couldn't tell if she was angry or embarrassed. He didn't understand why Bernard and Theresa held Mina in such contempt. Mina's explanation of her brother and sister's good looks didn't make sense since Mina herself was pretty.

"Then how do you know?" he asked Bernard again.

"It only makes sense." Bernard drank deeply and slammed the empty goblet on the table. "It was she who let it loose. That creature will trouble us until he has her."

"We don't know who let the creature loose."

Bernard laughed. "Do you think I would believe the word of a traveler? A Shield," he said with contempt lacing his voice. "I am lord here."

"Frankly, I don't care what you believe," Gabriel stood and began to unsheathe his sword.

"Gabriel," Hugh said softly in warning. It would do them no good to kill the lord of the castle, regardless of whether Bernard was a pompous pain in the arse or not.

To his relief, Gabriel resumed his seat though he kept his gaze on the baron. Hugh knew there would be trouble unless they could convince Bernard to help.

"Don't you want to see your village free of the terror that hangs over you?" he asked the young baron.

"Of course," Bernard answered without raising his gaze from his goblet.

Hugh rose to his feet and walked toward Bernard. "Then aid us instead of hindering us."

"But Theresa said I shouldn't allow you to help," he said and looked at Hugh, his bloodshot eyes staring coldly.

Hugh looked into the blue eyes of Mina's brother. "You are lord here as you said, not Lady Theresa. What does your instinct tell you?"

For several tense moments, Bernard stared hard at the table. Then finally, he raised his eyes to Hugh's. "It tells me not to stand in your way."

Hugh let out a breath and found himself smiling at his little victory. "Then let us plan."

For the next few hours, they huddled around the table plotting the evil creature's demise. When their plans had been finalized, Hugh leaned back to find Theresa standing in front of him and directly behind Mina.

"You all have been very busy," Theresa said and let her

eyes roam over the men until they reached Bernard. "I would see you privately, brother."

"Not just now," Bernard said and poured himself more ale. "We're busy. Find me later."

Hugh looked at Mina in time to see her flinch, and then his eyes found Theresa's fingers digging into Mina's shoulders. But Theresa seemed oblivious to her actions as her gaze shot daggers at Bernard.

In the silence, Bernard looked up. "You're still here, Theresa? Run along. This isn't a place for a lady."

"Mina is here," Theresa said.

Bernard rose and opened the map of the castle on the table. "Yes, well, Mina isn't exactly a lady."

Mina bit her lip and tasted the metallic tang of blood as Theresa's fingernails dug agonizingly into her neck. Just as she was about to cry out, Theresa loosened her hold and flounced from the hall.

With her eyes closed against the pain, Mina thought over Bernard's words. So, she wasn't exactly a lady. His words shouldn't upset her, but they did. More than usual.

Mina opened her eyes to find Hugh staring at her. His dark gaze was always on her. In the end, she knew it was pity that brought his attention to her.

"Are you all right?" he asked.

She gave him what she hoped was a bright smile. "Never better."

To her surprise, the corners of his mouth tilted upwards. "You aren't a very good liar."

"I know." It never occurred to her to lie again, it just wasn't in her nature.

"Did I miss something?" Bernard asked as he looked up from the map.

"Not at all," Mina hurried to say. She leaned up at the same time as Hugh, and their heads bumped together. She grabbed her head. "I'm sorry."

He rubbed his head and eyed her warily. "I beg your pardon. Ladies first."

She laughed as she once more leaned forward, but the laughter died on her lips when she saw Bernard staring at her oddly.

"Strange," Bernard said.

"What is?"

"Have your eyes always been that unusual blue color?"

Would her family never cease to embarrass her? "Aye."

"I never noticed," he said softly.

She wanted to ask him just what he had thought the color of her eyes were all these years, but Cole had pointed to something on the map that took Bernard's attention.

It was just as well. He would probably say something harsh to hurt her again.

Hugh watched brother and sister and noted the differences. Bernard and Theresa's eyes were blue, whereas Mina's were bluish-green. Bernard and Theresa had blonde hair, and Mina had strawberry-blonde.

Could it be that Theresa and Bernard treated Mina differently because she had a different father or mother? He suspected that was the case and Mina just didn't know it.

~ ~ ~

Mina smoothed down the tight fitting bodice of her pale green gown and ran her hand along the wide, floral patterned trailing sleeves. She wrapped the braided belt around her waist and hips and tied it so that it hung down her front, the tassels at the ends brushing against the floral pattern on the hem of the gown.

She looked into the mirror and was rather pleased with what she saw. The gown had belonged to Theresa. She hadn't liked the pattern, but Mina loved it and had hurriedly accepted the gown before Theresa changed her mind.

As quickly as she could with her still injured arm, she braided her hair in two separate braids that hung over each shoulder and fell across her breasts. She then wrapped thin strips of leather around each braid from base to tip for added effect.

It was the first time in years that she actually felt somewhat pretty. Even her bandaged arm couldn't be seen. Before she lost her nerve, she left her chamber for the hall below.

She took a deep breath and walked to the dais. Not even Theresa, sitting between Bernard and Cole, could upset her. It was the first time in years she felt like a lady, and she planned to act like one, just as her mother had shown her.

When Mina approached the table, the men rose. The only chair available was at the end, but she didn't mind. It put her well away from Theresa and Bernard.

"Here, my lady," Darrick said as he scooted out of his chair. "Take my seat."

Mina raised her eyes and saw Hugh staring at her. She offered him a small smile. Once she had taken her seat, and Hugh and Darrick resumed theirs, the food was quickly brought out.

"You look lovely," Darrick said when she passed him a platter.

Not one to hear compliments, Mina found herself uncomfortable. "Thank you."

"You do look beautiful," Hugh murmured next to her ear. "That dress becomes you."

Her heart fluttered at his praise. She turned her eyes to him and her mouth went dry. "Th...thank you," she stuttered.

His warm brown eyes crinkled at the corners as he smiled. "I'm only speaking the truth, my lady."

Mina knew she ought to look away, but men like Hugh didn't come to Stone Crest. He was all muscle, good looks and warrior. A perfect combination, to her way of thinking.

He turned away to listen to something Bernard said, and she took that time to let her eyes roam over his body.

His hair was still damp at the ends. She found that she wanted to reach up and tuck the hair behind his ears as he pushed it out of his face. His large, rough hands bespoke many battles, proving he was a man to fear.

Tonight, he wore a tunic of dark brown that complemented his eyes and hair nicely, though she imagined there wasn't anything that would look bad on him.

He spoke, his deep treble soothing her. Never had a man affected her like the mere presence of Hugh. What was it about it him that drew her?

She held her breath when he placed his hand on the table next to hers. The need to reach over and touch him was so strong, that for a moment Mina found herself doing just that. She stopped herself in time.

"Something wrong?" Darrick asked.

She jerked her head around. "Nay. Where are your families?" she asked quickly to change the subject.

One side of his mouth lifted in a smile. "With what we do, it is better if we don't have families."

"So, none of you is married?"

"Nay, my lady."

She nodded and turned back to her trencher. She had been ravenous when she'd come into the hall, now all she could think about was the man sitting beside her and the pull he had on her.

Mina made herself take a bite, making sure to keep her

eyes anywhere but on Hugh. It wasn't easy. Especially when his leg or arm would brush up against her, but she was nothing if not determined. If she could survive years with Theresa and Bernard, then she could survive a few hours next to Hugh.

"We begin tonight."

She was so engrossed in turning her attention away from Hugh that she almost didn't hear his words.

"What do you begin?" she asked before she could stop herself.

He turned toward her. "The hunt for the creature."

Whatever hunger she had conjured up immediately disappeared. She hadn't expected them to start tonight. Didn't they need to practice or something?

She kept her thoughts to herself, and listened as Hugh and his men explained what would happen. It was obvious they expected her to go to her chamber once the meal was finished. She, of course, had other plans.

~ ~ ~

Hugh watched as Mina walked from the hall. When he turned back to his men, it was to find Darrick watching him.

"She's up to something, isn't she?" Darrick asked as they walked from the hall to the armory.

Hugh briefly thought about feigning ignorance, but he realized it would be folly. "I suppose."

The laugh that followed his words did little to comfort Hugh. He didn't even glance at Darrick, but that didn't stop his friend from speaking his mind.

"I noticed how you found it hard to concentrate tonight at the meal."

Hugh stopped and let the others go on ahead of him.

He waited until they were out of earshot before he said to Darrick, "It's because I haven't been around a lady in some time."

Darrick smiled and shrugged. "That's a pretty good reason, but I didn't see you having that problem with Lady Theresa."

Hugh ran his hand through his hair. "What is it you want?"

The smile left Darrick's face. "I don't know. I saw how Lady Mina watched you. You intrigue her."

"Do you worry I'll harm the maid?"

"Never," Darrick said with conviction. "But I also have never seen you act like this around a woman before. At least not since..."

Hugh knew Darrick wouldn't finish the sentence. There wasn't a need. He knew exactly who Darrick referred to. "We have a mission to complete. Let's concentrate on that right now."

Darrick seemed relieved that he didn't chastise him for bringing up a painful part of his past. In truth, Hugh was more than pleased to drop the subject.

~ ~ ~

After she had changed into her man's attire, Mina walked to the table where Hugh and his men gathered their weapons in the armory.

"Just what are you doing?" Bernard asked as he strode up to her.

She didn't look to her brother because her gaze was locked with Hugh's. Hugh's golden brown gaze watched her with intelligence and cunning. The question was, what would Hugh do?

"I'm gathering my weapons."

Bernard sputtered at her side. "The hell you are. I've been a fool before, but not this time. You'll stay in the castle where you will be protected."

She didn't answer him. There was only one man who could make her stay. Hugh.

"Hugh," Bernard said. "Tell her to stay put."

The men quieted and stilled, waiting to hear what Hugh would say. Mina found herself holding her breath. Would he give her the right to fight the creature who had taken her parents and terrorized her village? Or would he treat her like a pampered lady and keep her locked safely inside while others risked their lives?

His eyes looked deep into her soul, and where she thought she might see coldness, she saw heat. Blatant desire flared in his eyes, and it caused her blood to quicken. Everyone faded away until it was only she and Hugh in the armory.

Only their breaths.

Only their heartbeats.

She silently begged him to understand her need to go. If anyone could understand, surely it was Hugh. And though she would never admit it to another, she wanted to go just to be near him. He made her feel alive, as if she were valued. And all the danger in the world was worth that.

"We need every person that can help," Hugh finally answered.

His voice was like velvet as it scraped over her skin, soft and deep. It became difficult to breathe as she fought not to reach out and cover his hand with hers.

"I am lord here, and I demand that you return to your chamber," Bernard said as he grabbed her arm.

She hid her wince as his fingers bit into her arm, and looked up at Bernard. He was dressed in his armor, armor that hadn't been worn in a long time. "Why? Last night you wished me dead. What has changed between then and now?"

"I don't know." His brow furrowed deeply as his eyes clouded. "I truly don't know. It's as if I've never really seen you before."

She stared at her brother, his blond hair reaching to just below his ears. He had seemed so young yesterday, now it was as if he had grown into a man suddenly. Gone was the pampered boy she had known. Before her was the lord their father had been.

"There isn't much to see," she said and started to walk past him when he stopped her.

"The years are blurred, Mina, but I do know that I said and did many hateful things. I don't know why I said them, but I would ask your forgiveness."

Was this another ploy to hurt her? Regardless, he was her brother. She had to take a chance that he was sincere. She reached up and smoothed a lock of hair from his eye. "I forgive you."

He smiled and threw his arms around her for a hug. She froze, for neither of her siblings had touched her thus in many years. Slowly, her arms rose until she returned his embrace.

Tears stung her eyes as she realized how much she had missed belonging. Theresa had always made her feel like an outsider, but her parents and Bernard had been family. Bernard had been changing for a few months, but it wasn't until their parents died that things became so bad for her.

"I couldn't bear it if something happened to you," Bernard whispered and squeezed her tighter.

"It's time," said a voice she was coming to know quite well.

She turned from Bernard to find Hugh standing next to

them. She reached for a wicked looking dagger that had a curved blade when a large, calloused hand descended on hers.

"Bernard is right. You really should stay in the castle. You have no fighting skills, and you might be more of a hindrance than a help."

Hugh's words wounded her, though he was correct. "I understand. If it's better for me to stay, then I will. I will do whatever it takes to kill this creature."

He didn't move. His hand was warm but gentle over hers. The contact of his skin against hers was exhilarating. She looked down at his brown hand atop hers as a thought took root. "Can a lady not be armed even if she is to stay inside?"

His dark gaze probed hers. "Arm yourself, but do not lie to me."

"Can I help it if I refuse to sit idly by and watch my people, brother, or friends fall, whilst I am safe inside?" she asked, her anger simmering just beneath the surface at feeling so helpless. "I want to feel like I'm needed, like I can help somehow. I'm being blamed for this creature's release. Can't you understand why I need to be out there?"

He nodded and released her hand with a sigh. "Stay close," he warned.

She swallowed the lump of fear that formed in her throat. What had she just committed herself to? She wasn't a warrior, just as Hugh pointed out. She didn't even know the first thing about fighting, and the practice she had done alone in her chamber with her dagger didn't count.

But she refused to be a hindrance. She had her duty to perform, and she would carry it out, even if it meant her life.

She walked outside to the bailey to find the remaining villagers barricading themselves inside. A look to the heavens and the clouds painted various shades of pink confirmed that dusk had arrived.

No sooner had she noticed the sky than the scream that put terror in even the bravest of souls reverberated around them. Shrieks from villagers became so loud that the small group of hunters could no longer hear the creature.

Mina watched as Bernard and his knights ran to their places on the battlements. When she turned back, Hugh was gone. He had told her to stay close, but she hadn't been paying attention.

Her eyes scanned the skies for any signs of the creature. She gripped her dagger and started to run toward safety when Cole stepped in front of her. His war axe rose above his head, but it was his gaze that caught her attention. He looked above her.

She slowly leaned her head back and saw the creature hovering over her.

CHAPTER FIVE

Hugh couldn't believe his eyes. The creature hovered above Mina and watched her fervently. Hugh took stock of the creature as he got his first good look at it. It was like nothing the Shields had encountered before.

Its body was that of a man with skin as thick and course as a dragon's, but its hands and feet were that of some animal with elongated talons. The wings were wide and thin as they held it stable in the air over Mina.

Though he had seen many demons, this creature's skull had an odd look. The head and face were small, but the jaw extended forward enormously. A huge, wide mouth that showed rows of sharp teeth, beady red eyes, a flat nose, pointed ears and two horns rounded out the head.

It took Hugh only a moment to realize Mina wasn't going to run. He rushed from his hiding place and grabbed her. As he tossed her to the ground, he reached for his crossbow. He fired his first shot, and the creature deftly moved aside as the arrow flew harmlessly by.

"Take your places," Hugh bellowed to his men.

The creature turned its horned head away from him. It had spotted a villager running toward safety, and had quickly swooped down and captured the man in its claws.

"Nay," Mina cried and gained her feet, but Hugh seized her before she could run to the creature.

He held her between the ground and his body as they watched the creature rip the villager to shreds. She buried her face in Hugh's neck, and he simply held her as he watched the beast. When the creature was finished, it turned back toward them and smiled cruelly.

The creature flew toward them and knocked Hugh to the ground as he pushed Mina behind him. He quickly rolled and reached for his crossbow only to have the creature's claws rake across his back.

Determined not to bellow his rage for the pain that ran through him, Hugh gritted his teeth. A thick, warm substance rolled down his back and into his tunic. Despite the burning on his back, he willed his body to move and came up on his hands and knees. He got no farther when he found himself suddenly holding onto air instead of earth.

He didn't need to look behind him to know that the creature had picked him up, but he'd be damned if he would go down without a fight. Hugh grinned as he retrieved the dagger from inside his boot.

It was as if the creature knew what he had planned, because when Hugh glanced up he was headed straight for the castle doors. He put up his hands to block the brunt of the force, but in the process, lost his grip on the dagger. Once he hit the castle doors, the creature loosened its hold, and Hugh crumpled on the steps. He was viciously thrown onto his back, and then the creature leaned close to his face.

"Leave, Demon Seeker, or you'll be next to die," the

creature hissed before flying off.

Hugh stared transfixed as the creature burst through a cottage and killed all within. Never before had any of the creatures they had hunted and killed ever spoken to him.

"Hugh!"

He looked to his right and found Darrick and Cole atop the battlements pointing to the creature. In spite of the pain, he jumped to his feet and raced across the bailey for his crossbow. He grabbed it and aimed it at the creature.

His first shot hit the creature's wing but did nothing other than anger it. It threw down its current victim and screamed its wrath at Hugh.

As quickly as he could, Hugh began to reload the crossbow. This time, however, the bolt wouldn't load into the chamber. He glanced up and found the creature coming at him again. No matter how hard he shoved and pushed, the bolt wouldn't fit into the crossbow, and his time was running out.

Mina had hidden behind a hay wagon while Hugh had fought the creature, but now he needed help. His men were too far away to aid him. Without thinking of the consequences, she grabbed her dagger and ran toward Hugh.

Even when he dropped to the ground and rolled from the creature's clutches, she didn't stop her assault. This was her opportunity to end the terror for good.

She raised the dagger over her head and launched herself at the creature. The dagger embedded deeply into the beast's chest. The smile she wore at her victory was soon replaced by fear when the creature simply pulled the dagger from its body. He tossed the blade aside and took hold of her as he rose to hover above the bailey.

"So you wish to die," the creature said, the jubilation evident in his snake-like voice. "I had planned to save you for last, but now is as good a time as any."

The fact that the creature spoke brought ice to her veins, but it was nothing compared to the lump of dread residing in her stomach at hearing she was to die.

Just as the beast was about to carry out its threat, it shrieked and released her. Her own scream followed the creature's as she plummeted toward the ground. Instead of landing on the hard earth, she found herself cradled in Hugh's arms.

"Thank you," she managed to get out past the panic coating her throat.

One side of his mouth lifted in a grin. "Anytime."

She could have stayed in his embrace forever. Within his strong arms and against his muscular chest, she knew she was safe. From everything but losing her heart.

He set her on her feet and pushed her toward the castle. "Get inside. It has outwitted us this night."

She looked up and saw several arrows in the creature's back. As she began to follow Hugh toward the castle, she saw the creature turn toward the stables. Her eyes instantly found John, who was coaxing a frightened horse back inside the stable. She called out to John, jumping up and down and waving her arms, but he never saw her.

"Hugh," she yelled, but he couldn't hear her over the shrieks and cries of the villagers.

She looked around anxiously and found a spear someone had abandoned. With her only thought to save John, she picked up the weapon and raced toward the stable.

Hugh stood by the doors and hurried people inside the castle. If they could get everyone inside, then they would be safe for the night.

"Mina!"

Hugh's gaze jerked to where the yell had come from

and spotted Bernard trying to get through the doors, but Gabriel held him back. Hugh followed Bernard's gaze, and found Mina once again racing toward the creature, this time to save the stable hand.

Hugh unsheathed his sword and took off after her. His long strides quickly caught up with her, and he threw himself at her while hurling his sword at the beast. He wrapped his arms around Mina and rolled so that he would take the brunt of the fall as his sword plunged into the creature's chest. With his eyes still on the creature, he rolled over until she was beneath him.

During all of this, John had managed to get the horse inside the stable without knowing he was in peril. Hugh would have laughed except the creature still hadn't died. It pulled Hugh's sword from its body and immediately healed itself before dropping the sword and flying toward the forest.

Hugh breathed in deeply and looked down at Mina cradled against his body. "Do you have a death wish, lady?"

"Nay," she said softly, her eyes large, and her voice whisper soft.

"You wouldn't know it by your actions tonight."

Her tongue peeked out to lick her lips, and it was then that he realized he was on top of a beautiful woman, and her soft, warm frame was against his. His body, already ignited from the battle, flared painfully to life. His gaze lowered to her mouth. And that was all it took.

He found it impossible not to lean down and taste it. His head was lowering to hers, his mind already wondering what she would taste like.

"I couldn't let John die."

Hugh paused. He tried to ignore the blood pounding loudly in his ears as his body called for release. "You should have called me."

"I did."

Her eyes, even in the darkness, were like beacons. He was trapped in her gaze, ensnared by an allure that was all her own. Just one taste. That's all he needed. He dipped his head and whispered, "Mina."

"You saved her," Bernard shouted as he raced up.

Hugh squeezed his eyes closed and jumped to his feet when Bernard's voice penetrated the haze of his desire. He should be grateful to Bernard for saving him from making a fool of himself, yet his body cursed the baron for interrupting as his cock throbbed with need.

He held out his hand to help Mina up, but Bernard pulled her to her feet himself. "Thank God for Hugh," Bernard said. "I just knew you were going to die, Mina."

Hugh could feel her eyes on him. He didn't have the courage to return her gaze, afraid that he would find revulsion, or worse pity, in her blue-green depths.

"We must get inside before the creature returns." Hugh turned toward the castle to find Gabriel and Cole watching him closely.

He ignored them and hurried into the castle. He needed some time alone. Now. The monster within him begged to be released, and if he didn't get away from Mina it would burst from him.

Thankfully, Mina and Theresa set about making the villagers comfortable. He and his men, along with Bernard, made their way to his chamber.

"It has never come this early before," Bernard said.

Hugh noticed Bernard's hand shake as he reached for a goblet. He had wondered when the illness would come, and he had been surprised it had taken this long. Suddenly, he caught a whiff of the ale. The odor was barely noticeable, but to anyone that was on the lookout for any type of evil, they would recognize that the ale was drugged.

He tried not to move too much because of the pain in his back as he closed his chamber door. Blood had run down his back into his trousers and boots. He longed to change, but knew there was too much yet to do.

"Bernard, we should get you to your chamber."

"I'm fine," the young baron said. "I will stay and help with the planning."

Hugh said no more on the subject. "What time does it usually come?"

"Well after dusk when there is no light in the sky other than the moon."

That *was* odd. "I wonder what brought it out early this night?"

A loud crash jerked him out of his thoughts. He looked at his feet to see Bernard on the floor. Hugh kneeled beside him and found him covered in sweat.

"I need ale," Bernard whispered.

"That's the last thing you need, my friend. You've been drugged for a while now."

"Drugged?" Bernard repeated thickly. "By whom?"

"I say whoever let the creature out," Cole said.

Hugh nodded his agreement. "We need to get you to your chamber so you can get the drug out of your system. It's going to be a rough night."

"I'll make it," Bernard vowed as they dragged him to his feet.

With Bernard guiding them to his chamber, they got him inside. While Cole and Darrick got him in the bed, Gabriel fixed a strange blend of herbs mixed with water, and Hugh gingerly put his back to the door. No one would be allowed inside tonight.

"Drink," Gabriel commanded Bernard. "It will help with the shaking."

Bernard obeyed without question. Hugh was impressed.

If he could shake the addiction to the drugged ale, he would be a fine lord for his people. He had been led astray somewhere, but where exactly? And by whom?

~ ~ ~

Mina wiped the sweat from her forehead. The villagers' wounds had been seen to, and they had all found places in the hall to sleep. There were so many bodies lining the hall that she could barely see the floor.

But they were safe. For now.

She sighed and scanned the room for her brother or Hugh and his men. They were all conspicuously absent. She hurried from the hall and went first to Hugh's chamber. It was empty. There was only one other place they could be.

With her hand in a fist, she knocked on her brother's door. "Bernard?"

It opened so quickly she almost fell forward. "Hugh," she said when she saw who was before her. "I knew I would find you here."

"Now isn't the time," he said and tried to shut the door.

A moan from inside the chamber reached her before Hugh was able to shut the door. She quickly squeezed through the door and past Hugh's big body. Her gaze found Bernard on the bed moaning and thrashing around.

She raced to him. "Bernard?" she said as she put her hand to his head. She jerked her hand away. "He's burning up."

"I know," Hugh said as he came to stand on the opposite side of the bed.

Anger flared within her. "No one told me he was injured."

"He isn't," Gabriel said as he brought water to Bernard's lips.

She watched as her brother drank greedily and fell back as though exhausted. Her eyes rose to Hugh. "What is going on?"

He walked around the bed and held out his hand to her. "Come, and I will explain."

She took his hand and allowed him to lead her to the two chairs before the hearth. He sat her in one and took the other. For long moments, he stared into the ashes of the hearth.

"Just tell me," she begged him.

He closed his eyes for an instant, but when he opened them they flashed eerily in the light of the chamber. "Your brother is fighting off an addiction he has toward the ale he's been drinking. The drugged ale."

The breath went right out of her as if she had been punched in the stomach. "Drugged? By who?"

"Didn't you think it odd when he said he didn't realize the color of your eyes?"

She shook her head, not wanting to hear the words.

"Last eve, I dunked him in the water trough to shake off the effects. Apparently, he went to bed without any ale and only had a little this day. It was enough to show him what was going on around him."

"Who would drug him?"

"Whoever called forth the creature."

Her eyes snapped to his face. There wasn't gentleness in his handsome face now, but truth. "I shouldn't believe you. I don't know you, yet I find myself taking your words as certainty."

"Bernard asked that no one be allowed in his chamber until he could get through the worst of this."

"For the first time in my life my brother saw me, spoke to me. Don't make me leave," she pleaded.

Hugh should refuse her, but he found he didn't have

the heart. Besides, he was fast losing what energy he had with his loss of blood.

Despite all of that, he didn't think he could stand the look in her eyes if he told her no. She gazed upon him as if he were a savior, and God help him, he needed that from her. He opened his mouth to answer, but remembered that Bernard had made him promise no one would be allowed in.

Surely though, Mina wouldn't have drugged the ale. Or would she?

Hugh's instincts, which he relied on so heavily, were failing him now. For a moment, he forgot everything but the swell of Mina's breasts through the tunic that molded to her wonderful curves.

"Please," she begged and touched his arm.

His body silently roared its need to have her touch more of him. It was always so after a battle.

Answer her and get away. Quickly. Before you do something stupid like kiss her full, ripe lips or cup her breasts.

By the saints, he couldn't remember a time when a woman had captivated him so. An answer. He had to give her an answer.

But what was the question?

CHAPTER SIX

Mina wasn't used to dealing with men of any sort, that was Theresa's expertise, but she wasn't going to give up easily. When Hugh didn't respond, she pushed away from her chair and fell to her knees before him.

"You saw for yourself how he treated me last night, and the difference today. I will not leave him when he needs family."

His eyes shifted slightly as if weighing her words.

"It's not as if I'm asking to be alone with him. Just allow me to stay near in case he needs me."

"It's not going to be a pretty sight," he warned, his eyes flickering to her mouth briefly. "Bernard might say things he doesn't mean, and some that he does."

She swallowed hard and met his steady gaze. "I've listened to many things my brother and sister have said. What comes out of his mouth this night will not affect me."

"I hope I won't regret this," he said slowly. "You can stay."

She smiled and grabbed his hands. Without thinking, she brought them to her lips and kissed them. "Thank you. Thank you."

After a moment of silence, she looked at the hands within her grasp. They were balled into tightly clenched fists. The triumph she had felt at being able to stay vanished in a wink. How could she have forgotten so easily how repulsive she was?

"I'm sorry," she said and began to turn away when he grabbed her shoulders.

He wouldn't allow her to look at him, but he brought her ear close to his lips. "Roderick did not lie this morn. Do not listen to the foul words your sister spouts. You are neither homely nor ugly."

"I--" she began, but he put a calloused finger over her lips halting any words she might have said. For a moment, she forgot everything but the heat of his body and his finger touching her mouth.

"You have been told for so long that they think you are homely that you believe it. I have nothing to gain from telling you otherwise."

She closed her eyes against his words. He couldn't know what they did to her. She almost cried out when he took his finger away, but he only moved it to her chin so he could turn her face to his.

"Open your eyes, Mina," he ordered, his voice husky.

She opened them to find his face mere inches from hers. She saw the golden flecks in his brown eyes and watched them darken. Her body responded with a shudder of...she couldn't put a name to it, but whatever it was, it affected her deeply.

"Know the truth I speak. Your beauty outshines that of Theresa. She has told you those lies for her benefit. Listen to them no more."

Her gaze left his eyes and drifted to his firm mouth. His words were spoken softly but with conviction as if he believed every syllable.

As suddenly as his hands had touched her, they left. She gasped at the loss and raised her head. He had leaned back in his chair. She spotted the muscle in his jaw ticking and what she could have sworn was a flash of pain.

"Go to your brother," he said.

She didn't know what she had done, but she wanted to take it back. She yearned to hear his words again, to feel his touch, his heat.

"Now."

She jerked and would have fallen when her feet became twisted had he not caught her. Her eyes closed when his hands touched her again.

He groaned and set her away from him. "Go, Mina. You know not what you tangle with."

She gripped the arms of the chair to keep from falling against him. What was wrong with her that his simple touch could affect her so? Had she been so hungry for kind words that they addled her wits when she heard them?

Not that she minded hearing them from someone as gorgeous as he, but she had never been one to fool herself. She squared her shoulders as she stood, took a deep breath and went to Bernard.

Hugh gripped the chair arms until he heard the wood crack. By God, he had almost taken her right then. Her inviting pink lips had been but a breath away, and the tantalizing shadow of her cleavage had beckoned him.

She had wanted him. Her body had opened for him with just words and a touch on her lips. He shifted to relieve the throbbing between his legs, but it only grew. There was only one thing that would ease the ache.

Mina.

He hadn't lied to her. She was more beautiful than even Rufina, the Fae Queen, who was the most striking creature he had ever laid eyes upon.

At first, he had thought Mina used a ploy, but she honestly thought herself ugly. And he could understand why. After hearing, day after day, how repulsive someone thinks you are, one could start to believe it.

Theresa wasn't homely either. But it was the hatred festering within her that made her beauty fade. Aye, Mina outshone Theresa in every way.

He shut his eyes and pictured Mina with her eyes closed and lips parted on a sigh. All he would have to do was lean down and taste her, but he had made a point to stay away from the people he helped.

It made for a lonely life, but it was even worse when he had to leave them to hunt the next monster. Besides, in all the years he'd led the Shields he had never returned to the same place twice, and likely never would.

He would just stay as far away from her as possible. For the sake if his sanity, he had to. With that resolved, he rose to his feet and turned to face his men and Mina.

She stood at the foot of Bernard's bed watching her brother closely. Her hands were clasped in front of her, and every time he moaned, she flinched.

Aye, he already regretted allowing her to stay. He tried to lean against the wall, but his back was apparently worse than he had thought. He couldn't see to it because he couldn't leave the chamber, and he wanted Gabriel to concentrate on Bernard.

~ ~ ~

It was in the hour of midnight, but Hugh couldn't sleep, not with Mina in the chamber with him and his back throbbing with pain. Gabriel hadn't left Bernard's side, and even now as Bernard dozed, he sat by the baron's bed.

Mina had taken the chair on the other side of the bed,

and had fallen asleep with her arms cradling her head on the bed. Cole and Darrick sat on either side of the door to make sure no one entered.

The night hadn't gone as badly as Hugh had thought it might, but then again it wasn't over. As soon as that thought flitted through his mind, Bernard sat up in bed bellowing and punching anything he could hit.

Hugh moved as fast as he could from his place beside the hearth, but he didn't reach Mina in time to block the blow that Bernard aimed at her.

She fell back onto the floor with a loud thud. Hugh glanced to make sure his men contained Bernard as he reached Mina. He gently picked her up into his arms and carried her away from the bed. He sat her in the chair she had occupied several hours before when they had talked. Her hand covered the right side of her face.

"Let me see," he said and eased her hand away. He breathed a sigh of relieve to see it wasn't as bad as he had feared. "It's a busted lip. You might bruise a little on your cheek, but I'll have Gabriel fix something for you."

He called to Gabriel who threw him a wet cloth. "I'll be gentle," Hugh said as he reached up to wipe the blood away.

"It's strange to find someone with such strength be so gentle."

He shrugged. "I do what I must."

"How is she?" Gabriel asked as he walked up.

"A cut lip and maybe some bruising on her face," Hugh told him and moved so Gabriel could look at her injury.

Hugh found himself wanting to yank Gabriel's hands away from Mina as soon as he touched her. That emotion hadn't been experienced since he had lost his family, and frankly, he'd prefer that it go away as quickly as it had come.

But it didn't. And the longer Gabriel touched her, the worse it became. When he next looked, he found Gabriel watching him oddly.

"Hugh?"

"What is it?" he asked, afraid that Mina was hurt worse than he had thought.

Gabriel stood and moved away from Mina. "She's fine."

He narrowed his eyes as Gabriel turned and walked back to Bernard.

"Stay here," he told Mina as he followed Gabriel. He stopped Gabriel before he reached the bed. "What is it?"

Gabriel stared at him fixedly with his silver eyes. "You."

"Me? What are you talking about?"

"You growled when I touched her."

Hugh blinked and took a step back. "I wouldn't."

"You did," Gabriel said. "Not that I blame you. She's stunning, but I wasn't laying claim to her."

"I know," he said and looked away. "I apologize, my friend."

Gabriel shook his head. "No need. Take what comfort you can, for it never lasts. Now tell me why you didn't inform me of your back?"

"You were busy."

"I'm never that busy. It can become infected. Let me see to it now."

Hugh sat in a chair as Gabriel helped him remove his tunic. Hugh settled his elbows on his knees as Gabriel set out wiping the blood away. Hugh looked up and found Mina watching him.

He wanted...he didn't know what he wanted anymore. In truth, there was nothing for him to do but continue. He couldn't return to his time. Everyone thought him dead.

His hands fisted as Gabriel rubbed a foul stinking

mixture onto his back.

"No stitches?"

Gabriel grunted. "The funny thing is, the creature could have killed you, but it didn't. The talons opened the skin, but not far enough to stitch."

That puzzled Hugh. "It's almost as if we are sport to it."

"Could be," Gabriel answered. "Let the mixture dry for a moment before you put on another tunic."

Hugh moved to the wall so he could watch Bernard but stay out of Gabriel's way. Despite the urge to check on Mina, he was determined to stay right where he was.

His body might be away from her, but his gaze constantly found its way back to her. It was galling that he didn't have enough control over himself to keep his mind focused.

They all jumped at the sound of the creature's scream as it circled the castle. He reached down and gripped the hilt of his sword. One could never be too safe.

"I am beginning to think we should leave this place," Mina said as she rose from her chair, her gaze on the window.

"That thing won't stop with just your village," Cole said. "It has its own mission."

"Cole," Hugh said to stop him, but it was too late.

Mina took a step toward the door where Cole stood. "What mission?"

"They are out to kill every person they encounter," Cole answered.

Hugh found Mina's gaze turned to him. "Is it true?"

He nodded solemnly.

"But you know of a way to stop it."

He sighed, hating these questions. "With every creature we hunt it's different. We have never encountered the same creature twice."

"In other words, you have no idea how to kill this one."

Damn, she was perceptive. "That's correct."

She paced the chamber while he watched Gabriel mix more herbs for Bernard. Hugh wanted to tell her they could kill it tomorrow, but only a fool would make a promise such as that.

"Hugh," Gabriel called. "Help me lift Bernard so I can get this mixture down him."

Hugh pushed off the wall and walked to the bed to lift Bernard. Sweat covered Bernard's body, and he shook so badly the goblet kept knocking against his teeth. Hugh began to wonder if the baron would survive the addiction.

In the next instant, the goblet went crashing to the floor as Bernard shoved Gabriel aside. "Ale," Bernard called. "I need ale. Now!"

"By the gods he has strength," Gabriel said as he immediately began to mix more herbs. "We must get the water down him."

"Mina, grab his legs," Hugh called out as he grabbed one of Bernard's arms.

Cole quickly captured Bernard's other arm before he was able to hit Gabriel, while Darrick helped Mina hold Bernard's legs. Even with all four of them practically on top of Bernard, he still fought the water Gabriel tried to give him.

"What is in the water?" Mina asked.

"It will aid him past the addiction," Gabriel explained. "The sooner we get it down him the sooner he'll get past it."

"Ale," Bernard murmured.

Mina bit her lip as Hugh physically opened Bernard's mouth and Gabriel poured the water down his throat. For a moment, she thought Bernard might choke, but they got him to swallow somehow.

"I'm not strong enough," Bernard said as he opened his eyes and looked at Mina.

She smiled and climbed off his legs. "You were strong enough to begin this, and you will be strong enough to finish it."

"You don't understand, Mina. So many lies," he said and trembled.

She pulled the covers around him thinking he was finally calm.

"Nay," he said and swiftly took hold of her arms. He looked over her head to Hugh. "Get her out of here. She needs to be safe. She will die if she stays!"

"She'll be safe," Hugh's deep voice said behind her.

"You don't understand," Bernard said, the frustration evident by the lines in his young face. "None of you understand. She can't stay here any longer."

Before she could say anything, Bernard fell back onto the bed seemingly asleep. She rose on shaky legs and turned to face Hugh.

"I don't know what he means. This is where I was born and raised. I cannot leave."

"Mayhap he just wants to see you safely away from the creature," Darrick said.

She looked at her brother on the bed, so vulnerable and young. It would not be too long before he would take a wife. Where would she be then? His new wife wouldn't allow her to stay, and she wasn't naïve enough to believe she would ever find a husband. But the convent was not for her.

With her future clouded in unanswered questions, she took Bernard's hand and resumed her seat by his bed. She would not leave him this night. Not even the creature that still circled the castle could move her.

CHAPTER SEVEN

Hugh watched Mina slowly wake. She hadn't moved from Bernard's side all night. She had stayed to help get the healing water down his throat and soothe him in the long hours of the night.

But it had taken its toll on her. Dark circles marred her beautiful face, making her blue-green eyes larger than usual. Hugh moved on silent feet to her side as she worked the kinks from her neck.

He and his men had concluded there was more to Bernard's ranting than he'd let on, and they would get to that as soon as Mina was in her own chamber.

"Come," he said and took her arm.

She tried to pull away from him. "I won't leave my brother."

Hugh opened his mouth to speak, but Bernard's voice, low and raspy came from the bed. "I will be fine, Mina. I couldn't have done it without you, but you need your rest. There is a creature to kill," he finished before his head lolled to the side.

She stood there and stared at her brother before turning her gaze to Hugh. "I suppose he doesn't need me anymore."

"He will always need you," Hugh whispered. "I'll walk you to your chamber."

The sun was just breaking over the horizon as they walked along the deserted hallway. The sounds of people waking from the hall below reached them.

They reached her chamber and he followed her inside where she immediately went to her bed and laid down. She was asleep before he took two steps toward her. After he removed her shoes, he covered her with a blanket and quickly walked from the chamber before he climbed into bed with her and buried his rod deep within her tight sheath.

He lengthened his strides and hurried back to Bernard. Upon entering, he found Gabriel and Darrick helping the baron sit up in bed.

"How do you feel?" Hugh asked as he walked toward Bernard.

The baron laughed dryly. "Like I've been dragged behind a wagon being led by six wild horses."

Hugh chuckled and straddled the chair, leaning his chin on the back. "You're past the worst of it, thanks to your sister."

"I saw her lip." Bernard looked down at his hands. "Did I do that?"

"By accident."

Bernard sighed loudly and raised his eyes to Hugh. "I meant what I said last night. You must get her away from the castle. Now. Before it's too late."

"Why?" Gabriel asked.

Bernard hesitated for a moment and looked down at his hands again. "She will be safer away from here."

"Everyone would," Hugh said. "But that creature will only move on to another village if we don't destroy it. You and Mina have already begun to mend your relationship. Everything will work out."

"You don't understand," Bernard said and slammed his hand against his thigh.

Hugh decided it was time to stop playing around. "Then tell me. There is someone in the castle that let loose that creature, and I'll wager that same someone has been drugging your ale. Do you know who it is?"

Several tense moments slipped by.

"Nay," Bernard said with a shake of his head. "I sorely wish I did though. So much has gone amiss."

Hugh didn't like this, not one bit. It was one thing to battle an evil he knew, but another to fight one blind. His gut knew Bernard lied, but there would be no getting the truth out unless the baron wanted to admit it. It was Bernard's tone when he spoke of getting Mina away from the castle that intrigued Hugh. Why Mina and not Theresa?

The questions were mounting, and it did little to soothe him.

"Darrick, keep an eye on Mina," Hugh said, as he studied Bernard. "Don't let her see you, but make sure she stays safe."

"What are you thinking?" Bernard asked.

"I just want to be sure no one else in your family is harmed. Cole, keep watch on Theresa."

"Don't bother," Bernard said. "That woman could skin the creature herself if she put her mind to it."

Hugh looked at Cole and Darrick pointedly and waited for them to leave the chamber. He turned to Gabriel and Bernard then. "We must keep a vigilant eye out to keep everyone safe. If something looks out of the ordinary, tell us immediately, Bernard."

The baron snorted. "That is going to be difficult since I really don't know what is ordinary anymore."

He had a point. Hugh scratched his chin as he thought over their options. "I think it would be better if everyone still thinks you're a drunk. Don't change your attitude toward anything, especially Mina."

"Aye, I can do that. What about Mina?"

"We'll tell her ahead of time. We don't want her acting any differently either," he said.

"I don't know," Bernard hedged. "I'm not sure I could do it."

"We'll help you."

Gabriel rubbed his hands together and grinned. "I see a plan forming."

Hugh smiled at his friend. "If everything goes right, not only will we kill that creature, we'll free this castle and the village from the evil that holds it."

"Then, by God, I hope your plan works," Bernard said.

~ ~ ~

Mina opened her eyes and moaned. Her body ached from the position she had kept it in most of the night, but it was worth it to see Bernard over that awful addiction.

With a smile on her face for the first time in months, she rose from the bed. A bath would be just the thing to ease away these aches, she thought. She opened her chamber door and headed toward the bathing chamber.

Her step was light, as if a great weight had been lifted from her shoulders. She had her brother, and he treated her like a sister for the first time since she could remember. Things were looking up, especially with the arrival of Hugh and his men. Just thinking about Hugh brought a flush to her body and a strange sensation between her legs.

She walked into the bathing chamber and came to a sudden halt. Inside the large wooden tub sat Hugh. He was facing her, his arms stretched out and holding onto the sides, while his head rested back against the tub with his eyes closed.

If she were a proper lady she would turn and leave, but her legs wouldn't obey her. Her eyes feasted on the expanse of muscular chest that glistened with water in the sunlight that streamed in from the window above him.

Dark hair littered his torso, and there was no denying the taunt muscles bulging in his arms, shoulders and chest. His hair clung to his head and water fell in ripples down the hard planes of his face as though he had just surfaced.

Breathing became difficult as she let her eyes wander over his splendor. She had seen many men without their tunics as they toiled in the bailey, but none compared to the warrior before her now. The sinew in his arms and chest came from years of wielding a sword.

And if his arms looked that good, what would the rest of him look like?

Her face flamed at her thoughts, but the simple truth was she would do almost anything to know. She bit her lip and let her eyes roam lower, wishing she could see through the water.

The water rippled from movement, and her gaze jerked to his face to find his eyes open.

And staring at her.

Her heart hammered wildly inside her chest, but it was the heat from his dark brown gaze that held her immobile. Her lips parted, and the breath rushed from her lungs when he stood.

Never was there a man that walked in this realm or another that could compare to the magnificence before her. He exuded power as if it were a second skin. She drank in her fill of him, following the water as it ran down his chiseled abdomen through a trail of dark hair that disappeared in the water just below his waist as he stood.

A small moan escaped her lips when he took a step toward her and she caught a glimpse of his manhood as the water moved. When his hands gripped the side of the wooden tub, she knew he was about to leave the water and come to her. His gaze caught and held hers, as if he were giving her time to flee. But she wouldn't take flight.

She wanted this.

Wanted him.

"There you are," Darrick said as he came around the corner.

She didn't turn towards Darrick, for her eyes were riveted on the dark warrior before her.

"Ah, sorry," Darrick said hurriedly.

She heard his footsteps as he left the chamber. She closed her eyes wishing they hadn't been interrupted. What would Hugh have done once he left the tub?

"Forgive me," she said and hurried from the chamber before she embarrassed herself more.

Hugh gripped the tub painfully as he watched Mina run from the chamber. He had been thinking of her creamy skin and full lips when he'd opened his eyes to find her standing in the doorway. He hadn't known how long she had been there and hadn't cared.

His blood had surged to his cock as he watched her gaze roam over him, but it wasn't until he stood that he saw the desire flare in her eyes. He forgot where he was, what he was, and that she was a lady. All that mattered was having her in his arms while he molded her body against his.

He had been about to leave the water to do just that when Darrick walked into the chamber. Although he wanted to bash Darrick's face in, Hugh probably owed him a debt of thanks for saving him.

"Aimery, you gutter pig. If you set this up I will have my revenge," Hugh muttered to the empty chamber. It was just like the Fae to meddle in affairs such as these if they thought it would ease him somewhat.

But what Aimery didn't realize, is that having Mina would only make it so much worse. She was like Heaven, just out of reach.

Hugh took a deep breath, stepped from the tub and began to dry himself off. He had to kill the creature and leave this place before it was too late.

Though it might be too late for him anyway.

~ ~ ~

Mina shut her chamber door and leaned against it, her breathing harsh and labored. Even without closing her eyes, she could picture the perfection of Hugh.

Her body trembled with a need he had risen within her with his heated brown eyes. Her breasts had grown heavy from wondering if he would touch her. He was a temptation she had never encountered before, and the yearning to have him overwhelmed everything around her.

She didn't even care about the creature anymore. She just wanted...Hugh. Marriage wasn't even a necessity. All she craved was to feel his strong arms wrapped around her, making her forget the world and the evil that surrounded her.

But it was something that wasn't meant to be. If he would have anyone, it would be Theresa. Everyone wanted Theresa. For the first time in years, she hated her sister. She pushed away from the door and walked to the mirror she rarely gazed into, but she couldn't look at herself. Nothing had changed since the last time she dared to peek, and it never would.

She was still as ugly as she always was.

The mirror forgotten, she turned and stripped off her gown to wipe herself down with the water from the bowl in her chamber. Once she had changed into one of her daily gowns, she plaited her hair and made her way down to the hall.

To her surprise, Bernard sat breaking his fast with Cole and Gabriel. But where was Hugh?

"Mina."

The deep sound of her name on Hugh's lips brought a chill to her skin. She slowly turned to find Hugh standing behind her.

"I need to speak with you," he said softly as he glanced around her.

She nodded and led him away from the entrance down the hallway. "What is it?" she asked and prayed it wasn't about seeing him at his bath.

"I need to ask you to do something. We need you to act as if nothing has changed between the two of you."

She knew he wouldn't ask unless it was important, and despite the fact she hated to lie, she would do it if it meant they would catch whoever released the creature. "All right. May I ask why?"

"Because I have a thought that whoever was drugging Bernard also let loose the creature. If that person thinks nothing has changed, there is a chance we can catch them."

She was impressed. "That's a good plan."

"I wanted you to know that Bernard is going to pretend to be drunk. He won't actually drink the ale, but to everyone else they'll think he is."

"And you really think this person is in the castle?"

"They have to be in order to get the ale drugged."

She thought about that for a moment. "If it is one of the servants, it would have to be several because all of them bring him his ale."

"We'll find who it is," he vowed.

And she believed him. He was the type of man that carried through with his word.

He escorted her into the hall and placed her at the dais. Bernard didn't even look at her, and she made sure not to look over at him. His life was at stake, and she would suffer through however many days, weeks, months or years it would take to find out who would do such a thing to her brother.

She ate in silence trying to ignore Hugh, who sat beside her. When she looked up and found Theresa walking toward her she groaned inwardly, hoping against hope that her sister would leave her alone this morn.

But there were men in the castle, and that meant that they were Theresa's.

"You are in my seat," Theresa said as she came to a halt in front of her.

Mina, for just a moment, wanted to tell her there were many other seats in which to choose from, but decided against making a scene. Hugh had asked that she act as she normally would.

She grabbed her bowl and goblet and moved to another table with her back to them. She might have to hear Hugh and Theresa, but by God, she didn't have to look at them smiling and laughing. The food didn't taste as good, and her good mood vanished upon hearing Hugh's laughter though.

"Do you mind if I sit here?"

She looked up and spotted Darrick. "You wish to sit with me?"

"Unless there is a ghost next to you, aye," he said with a bright smile.

"Please," she said and pointed to the chair.

Theresa laughed again. Mina closed her eyes and wished she could close her ears to it as well.

"It's all a ploy," Darrick said before he took a bite of the porridge.

"Excuse me?" Maybe she hadn't heard him right.

"Hugh and your sister. He is doing it because it's what she expects."

"I don't care what he does," she lied. She glanced at Darrick to see if he bought the lie. His wink told her he didn't.

"She isn't his type of woman."

As much as she hated to admit it, she wanted to hear more about Hugh. "Men have a certain type?"

"Indeed, we do." Darrick said it with a wide smile and raised eyebrows.

"And what is your type?" she had to ask. His teasing brought a smile to her lips.

"Any woman who would want me."

She chuckled.

"It's the truth," he said. "I'm not as fair as Roderick, I don't command a room full of people like Hugh, and I don't make the ladies swoon like Cole does. Though with Gabriel, the ladies swoon because he frightens them so."

She began to laugh in earnest. "Stop," she begged. "You're making my cheeks hurt."

When she stopped laughing, she looked up to find him staring oddly at her. "When is the last time you laughed?"

She thought for a moment. "I'm not sure. Why?"

"Look around the hall."

She did and found everyone watching her. "Why are they staring at me?"

"Because when you laugh, you outshine the sun."

She grinned, thinking he teased her again, but when her gaze returned to him she found he was utterly serious.

"Thank you," she whispered, unsure of what to say.

He suddenly rose and held out his hand for her. "They are waiting for us."

"Who?" she asked as she took his hand, but found her answer when he led her toward the solar.

Hugh, Gabriel, Cole, and Bernard watched as she walked with Darrick toward them. And true to what Hugh had warned, Bernard did look and act as if he had drunk all night. He swayed as he stood beside Hugh and garbled his words when he spoke to Gabriel.

"Why must she be here?" Bernard bellowed his slurred words so that the entire castle could hear him.

Even though she had been cautioned that her brother would do this, it still hurt. More than she liked to admit. She flinched at his words and walked past him into the solar. Her gaze fell on a seat beneath the window and she hastened toward it.

No sooner had she taken her seat and the door closed behind the men than Bernard rushed towards her. He fell to his knees and took her hands.

"Mina, you know I didn't mean it, don't you?" he asked and ran a hand down the side of her face. "Hugh said he would speak with you."

She smiled and touched Bernard's hand. He was sober. Relief washed through her. "Aye, Hugh spoke with me. I acted as I always do."

Bernard's head fell to her knees. "I won't ever be able to thank you enough for what you did last night."

"There is no need. I did what any sister would do."

He snorted and rose to his feet. "Really? And where was our dear sister? Theresa was in her chamber with whatever knight she could entice into her bed."

She waited until Bernard took the seat beside her before she allowed her eyes to drift to the one person in the solar who could make her tremble.

Hugh clenched his teeth together as Mina's gaze turned to him. He had secretly watched her all morn as she dined with Darrick and laughed at his jokes. When her laughter had quieted the entire hall, he'd seen why. She was beautiful, and when she laughed, a light inside her shone even brighter.

He understood why Theresa became enraged and left the hall. No one could compare to the loveliness of Mina, and despite what Mina thought, everyone else knew she was stunning.

Now, as Mina sat watching him so innocently, all he could think of was getting her to his chamber and ripping off her gown so he could feel her delectably soft skin next to his, to see her head thrown back as her body convulsed around him.

Why did it have to happen now? Hadn't he suffered enough? Couldn't he do his assignment without having her close, but just out of reach? Was he being punished for something he had done before the Fae came to him?

He shook those thoughts away, and took a deep breath before he began speaking. "We were unprepared last night. We cannot be again. We must be equipped to fight the creature before the sun begins its descent."

"I'll make sure everyone is inside the castle," Bernard said. "Odd that the creature didn't try to smash through the castle doors."

"That is odd," Hugh said. "It's strong enough to bring the castle crumbling around us. There must be a reason it stayed away."

"It doesn't matter as long as everyone is safely inside," Bernard stated.

"It does matter," Gabriel said, "if it isn't coming for the castle because the one that controls it is inside."

Hugh propped his foot on a chair and leaned on the bent knee. "True, Gabriel. And if that's the case then we must lure it."

"Lure it?" Bernard repeated. "How?"

"Bait," Darrick said and rubbed his hands together. "Do I get the honors, Hugh?"

Hugh laughed. "Not this time. It's my turn."

CHAPTER EIGHT

"Nay!"

Hugh's gaze jerked to Mina. She had risen to her feet, her eyes wide. "What?"

"You...you'll be needed to kill the creature. You need someone who can move fast enough to keep out of its clutches."

He knew what she would say before she said it.

"You need me."

"Nay," Bernard and Darrick said in unison.

Gabriel stepped forward. "She doesn't have the training."

Hugh stared at her, hating that she might just be right. He had seen her agility. She might not have the training, but she was quick, and lighter than he or any of his men. "I don't wish to put you in danger. In fact, I wanted you in the castle this night."

"You won't be able to keep me inside unless you lock me in the dungeon."

"Don't," Bernard said as he walked toward him. "Hugh, don't. Let her have a weapon if she must, but I cannot allow her to stand defenseless while that creature chases her."

Hugh moved his eyes from Mina to Bernard at the same time that Mina walked to them.

"I have faced it twice," Mina told her brother. "It had the chance to kill me last night but didn't. It told me I was to be last."

"What?" Hugh said as he grabbed her shoulders and turned her toward him. "It spoke to you? Is that all it said?"

She nodded.

"By the gods," Gabriel said and raked a hand through his auburn hair.

"Aimery," Hugh called. He needed answers, and he was going to make sure he got them. Now. "Aimery!"

"You called?"

Hugh spun around to find the Fae commander standing beside Gabriel. "Did you know?" Hugh demanded. "Did you intentionally keep it from me?"

"Nay."

Hugh waited. "Just nay? No explanation?"

"Who is this, and where did he come from?" Bernard asked, bewilderment scrunching his face. "I'm beginning to think I'm seeing things because that man just appeared here."

"He's Fae," Hugh answered.

Bernard laughed. "Fae don't exist."

"Really?" Aimery asked. "Who do you think used to rule this world? Who do you think keeps it in balance with the other realms?"

The baron's face went ashen, and he promptly sat down. Hugh turned to Aimery. "Enough of the games. I need to know what we are dealing with."

"I learned about the creature speaking the moment you did, and not an instant sooner."

Hugh sighed and closed his eyes. "Tell me I didn't send

Val and Roderick to their deaths facing something like this alone?"

"Val and Roderick will be fine. Worry about this creature," the Fae warned.

And before Hugh could say another word, Aimery vanished. "Damn." He paced the solar for a moment. "Mina, you'll be the bait, but only because I'm short two men and need every weapon I can get. Bernard, are you good with a bow and arrow?"

The baron nodded slowly, his eyes still focused on the spot where Aimery had stood.

"Then you and Gabriel will be on the battlements. Cole, you and Darrick will be stationed on either side of the bailey with swords and crossbows."

"Where will you be?" Mina asked.

He turned to her. "Close to you."

"We could use some spears and battle axes," Cole said.

"The armory will have everything you need," Bernard said and rose to his feet.

Hugh dragged his gaze from Mina. "Arm every knight and man you can. We'll station them in the bailey, on the towers, and at the battlements."

"There aren't many knights anymore," Bernard said. "Most left a month ago. We might have six left."

Gabriel shook his head. "Might?"

"I haven't exactly noticed much lately," Bernard said in self-defense.

Hugh waited as they filed after Bernard to the armory. When he and Mina were left alone he fisted his hands and said, "I beg your forgiveness if I frightened you this morn in the bathing chamber."

She bit her lip and twisted her hands as she glanced away. "It's I who should beg your forgiveness," she quickly interrupted him. "I should not have stayed."

They stared at each other as the silence grew in the small solar. There was so much Hugh wanted to say, but he couldn't find the words. And it was better that way. He needed to keep himself apart.

She walked past him, and he wanted to reach out and touch her strawberry blonde hair. He forced himself not to move, not to even breathe. But his hunger grew anyway. He would have to be careful and stay clear of Mina for she was a siren that called to him.

~ ~ ~

Mina left the solar on shaky legs. There must be something wrong with her to make her act so strangely around Hugh. He must think her addled.

She strolled through the hall and smiled to a few of the tenants. But it was the others, the ones who had ignored her as Theresa and Bernard had that offered her a smile.

At first, her smiles were hesitant, but by the time she reached the armory she knew her smile spread across her entire face. She raced to Bernard and said, "The villagers and servants smiled at me."

Her brother smiled kindly. "They always have, Mina, you just never looked up to see it. Theresa and I did that to you," he said, his forehead creasing with angst.

"Nay," she said. "No more bad thoughts. You are back as you should be, and with Hugh and The Shields here, the creature will be destroyed. Fate has smiled upon us."

He laughed and touched her cheek. "You just might be right."

"I am. The Fae wouldn't have sent the Shields if they couldn't kill the creature."

"She has much faith in you," Bernard said, staring over her shoulder.

She slowly turned to find Hugh watching her. "Because he is a man of his word," she said. "He'll do what he has promised, and we, in turn, will do everything to help him."

With her stomach feeling as though it was about to take flight, she spun around and acted as though she was examining the weapons, when in truth she listened for Hugh. He never commented on her statement, and after a few moments, she realized he had better things to do.

Even though there wasn't a weapon she truly knew how to use, it made her feel safer if she could have one. She'd lost the dagger she had used on the creature, and she mourned its loss. It had fit her hand nicely, as if it had been made for a woman or a lad.

"I thought you might want this back," Hugh said as he handed her the dagger.

She gasped and reached for the weapon. "I thought I'd lost it."

"John found it and brought it to me this morn."

She smiled and cradled the dagger in her hands. "Thank you."

"It was made for a woman to use. Keep it with you always."

With a nod, she tucked it against her leg to hide in the folds of her skirt and hurried from the armory. By the time she reached her chamber, she knew she was going to get the adventure she craved. And it would start tonight.

Life was turning around. At least she thought so until she spotted the small blue stone sitting in the middle of her bed.

She glanced around the chamber to see if anyone was there. Her excitement vanished like the early morning mist to be replaced with gnawing fear and apprehension. With feet dragging, she walked to the bed and stared down at the extraordinary rock.

It was just like the others in the Druid ruins, only smaller, no bigger than the size of a child's palm. She knew without touching it that it would be warm and as smooth as her mirror. It had disappeared out of her chamber over a month ago, the night she brought it home from the Druid ruins and placed it on her bed to change for supper.

And now it had returned. Mysteriously.

She backed away and fumbled for the door latch. Once it opened she continued to back out of her chamber and closed the door. She leaned her head against the wood and sighed. There was only one thing to do. Tell Hugh. But would he believe her?

It was a chance she had to take.

She pushed away from the door and hurried toward the armory, but the men were no longer there. When she retraced her steps and was about to enter the hall, she found Theresa blocking the doorway.

"Where have you been?" Theresa asked in a low voice.

Mina wasn't fooled. Theresa may be acting as though she really didn't want to know, but in fact, if given the chance, Theresa would rip the hair from Mina's head to find out.

She decided honesty would be best. "I am looking for Hugh."

Theresa lifted her hand and examined her nails. "You know he is only paying attention to you because he pities you."

"I know." And the truth of it stung deeper than any barb Theresa had thrown in years.

"He has asked that you not embarrass him again. He is too noble to tell you himself, so he sent me."

Mina fought to keep from showing Theresa just how hurt she was. So, he had been mortified that she had walked in on his bath. Why hadn't he told her himself?

Because you daft fool, he didn't wish to hurt you.

"Thank you for letting me know," Mina said and tried to walk past Theresa, but her sister didn't move.

"I'm warning you now. Hugh is mine."

Mina met Theresa's gaze. "I have no need of him."

Theresa laughed, her eyes shooting flames of hatred. "I've seen the way you watch him. Given half a chance you would throw yourself at him."

Had she been that obvious? The shame of it washed over her. Hugh hadn't been about to leave the tub to kiss her; he had been reaching for his towel to cover himself. How could she have been so stupid? She blinked rapidly to fight the tears that threatened to spill down her face.

"Ah, I see I was right," her sister said with a laugh. "Your emotions are easy to read. Maybe if you weren't so apparent, you might find a man interested in you. They like to be led along, you know."

"Nay, I wouldn't know. Move so I can leave," she demanded. For the briefest of moments, she saw Theresa's eyes flare in surprise.

"I'll let you pass when I am done with you."

"Then be done."

Theresa laughed and took a step down to come even with her. "Remember, Mina. I can have any man I want. I took your betrothed, didn't I? I am loved here, and you are pitied. Do not try to make yourself better than you are. Everyone knows their place."

With that Theresa spun on her heel and stalked off. Mina slumped against the wall. Her sister's words had cut deep. When would she learn?

She forgot about finding Hugh and telling him of the stone. All she wanted was some time alone to let the tears fall unheard.

After sneaking out of the castle unseen, she walked to

the postern door in the bailey. She slid the bolt free and glanced around to make sure no one was watching her before she slipped away.

CHAPTER NINE

Hugh looked around the bailey for Mina as they readied it for the trap, but he hadn't seen her since she left the armory that morning. She hadn't come to the hall for lunch either, but Bernard told him that wasn't unusual. But when Darrick lost her, Hugh couldn't dispel the knot of worry that had formed.

"How could you lose her?" he asked.

Darrick shrugged. "I don't know. I saw her talking to Theresa, and then she was gone."

"Where did she and Theresa talk?"

"Mina was coming up from the armory as if she were looking for us."

"Did you check the armory?"

Darrick raised an eyebrow in agitation. "Of course. She wasn't there. I've checked everywhere."

"Even her chamber?"

"I knocked, but she didn't answer."

Hugh relaxed. "She's there, she just didn't want to see anyone."

He called to Gabriel and told him where he and Darrick were headed. Hugh took the stairs three at a time, and didn't slow until he reached her chamber. He knocked, and as he expected she didn't answer.

"Mina," he called out and reached for the latch. "It's Hugh."

He threw the door open and found the chamber empty except for the blue stone on her bed.

"By the saints," Darrick said as he came to stand beside the bed.

Hugh didn't want to believe what the stone signified, but it was difficult not to. It was as if he had been blindsided. Again.

He didn't want to believe Mina had something to do with the stone and the creature, but it was hard to think otherwise, especially with what was sitting on her bed.

"She did tell us she took a stone," Darrick said as he walked to the bed and looked at the stone.

"And she said it was stolen," Hugh pointed out.

The evidence was damning, and for the first time since he had answered the Fae's call, he hated what he did. "We must find her," he said and walked from her chamber.

Darrick quickly caught up with him. "Don't condemn her until you've spoken with her."

"In all the time we've done this, when have your instincts ever been wrong?"

Darrick lowered his eyes. "Never, but there is always a first time for everything."

"Then pray that this is the time."

"Hugh!"

He turned from the stairway and saw Gabriel run into the hall.

"Come quick," Gabriel called.

Mina would have to wait.

~ ~ ~

Mina lifted her face to the warm sun. The Druid ruins had always soothed her, and today was no different. She sighed and ran her hand over the ancient, cool stones.

"I wish the Druid's were still here," she whispered.

"But they are."

She whirled around and found the Fae, Aimery, behind her. It hurt to look at him he was so beautifully perfect and regal. "I don't think I'll become accustomed to you appearing out of thin air," she said and righted herself on the stone.

He smiled, and his extraordinary blue eyes twinkled. "You will."

"Does that mean you'll be around for awhile?"

He laughed and sat next to her. "All you have to do is call, and I will answer."

"I'll have to remember that." His presence lightened her mood. "Were you serious about the Druids?"

"I'm always serious where the Druids are concerned."

"Then why did they leave here?"

He looked over the ruins. "They were driven away. Humans are fickle creatures, and are easily swayed to believe there is evil when, in fact, there is none."

"And blind to the evil in front of them," she finished.

"Exactly."

"It's comforting to know the Druids weren't completely driven away. I would have liked to meet one some day."

They sat in silence for a moment until he turned her head towards him. "Tell me what troubles you?"

She looked away from his eyes that probed too deep and tried to smile. "You have better things to do than worry about the affairs of a mere human."

"Actually, the Fae and Humans are connected in ways that cannot be explained. We need you as much as you need us."

"Then why is it that humans don't believe you are real?"

"That is the way we wish it. Long ago, when we roamed this realm, there were humans who wanted power, namely our power. They didn't comprehend that it isn't something we can give."

"And your immortality? Is that also true?"

"Ah," he said and raised both eyebrows. "That is something they coveted more than our power."

"Is it something you can give?" She didn't know what propelled her to ask.

He tilted his head to the side, his long flaxen hair glistening in the sunlight. "What do you think?"

"I think, like your power, it is something that is distinctly yours."

He smiled and winked. "It's becoming late. You missed lunch."

"I'm not ready to return." She turned away from him, not wanting him to see the turmoil within her.

"Theresa and Hugh will still be at the castle. This little reprieve is just that. You cannot run away from it forever."

She covered her face with her hands. "Just for once, I wanted a man to reject her. I know that is awful of me, and I shouldn't wish for something that petty, but it's the truth." She lowered her hands and glanced at him out of the corner of her eye.

Aimery took a deep breath. "One thing I learned about humans is that most are vengeful and vindictive, but those emotions usually come because someone has something they want." He turned to look at her. "You have something your sister wants."

She laughed. "For a moment there, I believed the things you said, but you are showing you are as daft as I."

"I am far from daft. Can't you think of something you

have that your sister might covet?"

"Everything I've ever wanted or had, is hers," she said not being able to keep the sadness from her voice. "Even our brother preferred her to me."

"I want you to remember something," he said as he rose. "Not everything is as it seems. Look beyond what you see with your eyes."

"What?"

He smiled then. "You're smart, Mina, you'll understand my words soon."

And with that he was gone.

"Soon?" she said and looked around her. "Can't I understand them now?"

But there wasn't an answer.

~ ~ ~

Hugh followed Gabriel as he ran down the hallway. He turned the corner and found Cole standing beside a door with his sword drawn.

"What happened?" he asked Cole.

"I'm not sure."

He walked past Cole into the chamber and came to a halt. Theresa was on the floor, her sleeve ripped and a gash on her forehead. He knelt beside her and gently rolled her onto her back. She moaned softly.

"Lady Theresa," he called, but she didn't wake.

He picked her up and carried her to the bed where Gabriel had already gotten out his herbal bag and shifted through the medicines within.

"Tell me what happened?" Hugh told Cole.

"I waited down the hallway, out of sight, just like you told me," Cole said. "I heard her scream, and I came running to her door. I called out, but she kept screaming."

"Did you hear anyone else?"

Cole shook his head. "I tried to open the door, but found it barred. It didn't budge when I put my shoulder to it."

"So how did you open it?"

"That's the strange part," Cole said, his blue eyes clouded with worry. "I heard something shatter, and then silence. After a moment, the door opened on its own."

"Magic," Hugh said. "Did you sense anyone or anything?"

"Just Theresa."

"The wound is light," Gabriel said as he dabbed at her forehead.

"Good," Hugh said and raked his hand down his face.

"Where are Mina and Bernard?" Cole asked.

Hugh had hoped Mina's presence, or the lack of it, wouldn't be noticed. "Bernard is in the bailey. Mina is missing." All eyes turned to him. "Darrick and I found a blue stone in her chamber."

"I have a hard time believing it was her," Darrick said.

"We'll know when we find her," Hugh said. "Cole, keep watch on Theresa."

Hugh left the chamber and walked to the bailey. It was time he found Mina.

CHAPTER TEN

Mina couldn't stay at the ruins once Aimery left. His words kept repeating in her mind, and the answers were as elusive as the Druids. With her peace shattered, there was no reason for her to stay.

She began the walk back to the castle, but she was in no hurry to return. It wasn't until she noticed the sun lowering in the sky that she knew more time had passed than she had realized.

The gate was closed, so she had to get back inside through the postern door. Only when she tried to open it, she found it locked.

Panic welled up inside her. She didn't want anyone to know that she had been gone, but now, that she was locked out, she would have to alert the entire castle in order to be let back in. Then, she would have to answer questions as to where she had been and why she had left.

She laid her head on the cool stone of the castle wall in despair.

"So. We find you at last," said a deep voice.

Her heart stopped at the voice she was coming to know, laced with such coldness it could have frozen her on the spot. She gradually raised her head to find Hugh and Bernard staring down at her from the castle wall.

"Where have you been?" Bernard shouted down at her.

She licked her now dry lips and pulled her eyes away from Hugh. "At the ruins."

"Unlock it," Hugh said over his shoulder.

In a matter of moments, she heard the bolt slide free and the door opened. She found Darrick holding the door for her, but he wouldn't meet her eyes.

Exactly what was going on? What was wrong with her going for a walk? She wasn't a prisoner.

She stepped into the bailey, and found it deserted except for a few chickens wandering around. The closing of the postern door behind her was like a door closing out the sun. She squared her shoulders and walked toward the castle when Bernard called out to her. There was nowhere for her to run that he couldn't find her. It was better to face him now.

"You have some explaining to do," he said as he came to stand in front of her.

She didn't have to look behind her to know Hugh and Darrick were at her back. "I'm sorry for leaving without a word to you. I needed some time to myself."

"It was always odd that whenever something bothered you, you would run to those ruins."

It was the catch in his voice that let her know something was wrong, dreadfully so. "What has happened? You've never cared before that I went."

Bernard hung his head. "Theresa was attacked."

Mina began to smile until she realized how serious he was. Her smile vanished as she took a small step toward her brother. "How badly is she injured? Did anyone see who attacked her?"

"Nay," Hugh said and came to stand beside Bernard.

"Cole heard her scream from her chamber, but he wasn't able to get inside to see who attacked her."

She looked from Hugh's cold dark eyes to Bernard's resigned expression as realization dawned on her. "You think I did it."

"Everyone has been accounted for but you," Bernard said.

"Ah," she said and looked around the bailey. "So, if I wasn't here then it must be me who, not only got inside her chamber, but blocked Cole from entering. All the while attacking my sister."

"Mina--" Bernard started, but she didn't wish to hear what he had to say.

She knew all she had to do was ask Aimery to verify where she was, but she was too angry at being falsely accused by the one man who had shown her the most kindness in years. That's what she deserved for giving her trust to Hugh, a man she didn't know.

"Theresa already spoke to me. There is no need for you to go to these extremes. I'll not bother you again," she said to Hugh and brushed past Bernard.

She didn't get two steps before Hugh's iron grip clamped down on her arm. He held her tightly without hurting her as he spun her around, his jaw clenched tightly.

"Explain yourself," he demanded.

She laughed while blinking the tears away. "I've been put through more than most people endure in a lifetime. I don't have to repeat what was said to me, especially in front of others."

"Then I'll walk you to your chamber, and you can tell me there."

She jerked her arm out of his grasp. "I think not. I was wrong about you. You're not the man I thought you were."

Hugh watched her walk away, her gait long and fast.

There had been anger and hurt in her gaze when he had accused her. He had expected her to plead her innocence, but the fact that she had said nothing gave him pause.

"What if I'm wrong?" he asked Darrick.

Darrick's eyes followed Mina as well. "You've never been wrong before."

"I cannot believe that it's her," Bernard said. "I hope this is the first time you are mistaken, Hugh."

Hugh didn't want to admit it, but he was hoping for the same thing. "Darrick."

"I'm going," Darrick replied as he trailed after Mina.

Hugh turned to survey the bailey. Almost everything was in order. The handful of knights who were still at Stone Crest lined the battlements. A few would be placed about the bailey behind anything that would keep them hidden from the creature.

"Who is going to watch over Theresa and Mina when the creature comes?"

Hugh glanced at Bernard. "I have a feeling Mina will still take her place as bait for the creature. As for Theresa, we'll put a servant inside her chamber, and a couple more outside."

"Then I'll go see that the servants are in place," Bernard said and then stopped. "If it is Mina, what will happen to her?"

"Let us concentrate on killing the creature first." Hugh waited until Bernard was inside the castle before he dropped the mask he'd worn since finding Mina outside the castle walls.

He looked to the sky and saw there was still time for him to take a quick walk. Gabriel joined him as he stared at the postern door.

"What are you thinking?" his friend asked.

Hugh didn't answer but walked to the door. He slid the

bolt free and opened the door. "Lock this behind me. I'll be back shortly."

"What are you looking for?"

"Innocence."

He walked through the door before Gabriel could question him further. He followed the path that led from the door, and found himself at the back of the castle.

The door wasn't seen because of the trees surrounding it. He hurried down the path and quickened his pace to the ruins. When he reached them, the sun still shone enough light for him to see by. He didn't know what he searched for, but he would look just the same.

The ruins showed him little more than he had seen the first time. The circle of blue stones stayed as they were, but he was able to find where Mina had sat. As far as he could see, she had come into the ruins and immediately sat on the fallen stone.

He sat on the great rock as she would have, and looked about. The view she saw would've been of the few remaining stones amid the rubble and the rolling hills. The castle was to the right. He turned and looked over his shoulder to find the forest.

Most people would prefer to gaze at the forest in hopes of seeing a bird or small animal, but Mina stared at the stones. He had a hard time figuring out exactly who she was, mostly because she was so different from anyone he had ever encountered.

Even in his own time, he could easily foresee how a friend or foe would act or react to a situation. What made Mina so different?

The lengthening shadows told him he didn't have long before the creature arrived. He jumped to his feet and began the trek back to the castle.

When he reached the postern door, he banged his fist

on it and whistled. The bolt immediately slid free, and the door opened.

"Just in time," Gabriel said and pointed to the sky.

Hugh followed his gaze, and saw the darkness coming. When he looked back down, it was to find Mina talking to John. She wore the same dark brown pants she'd worn the night he had rescued her, but her tunic was the lightest shade of brown, and contrasted with her strawberry blonde hair nicely.

The dagger was sheathed at her waist, and she held a spear in her left hand. She kept motioning for John to go into the stables, but he only shook his head.

"What's wrong?" Hugh asked as he walked to them.

She didn't look at him as she said, "John wants to help kill the creature, but I told him I needed him to watch the horses."

Hugh looked at the lad holding a sword he could barely lift. He began to reach for the sword, then thought better of it. "Lady Mina is right. We do need your help. We need those horses, without them we cannot battle the creature. I need you to take this sword and guard those horses."

John's eyes lit up, and he nodded his head and turned to go to the stables, the sword dragging behind him.

Hugh waited for Mina to thank him, but she walked away. He easily caught up with her. "I'm only doing what the Fae have commanded."

"How pleasant for you," she said and stopped beside the castle wall directly in front of the doors.

"You have not cried your innocence."

"You wouldn't hear me if I did. You've already condemned me."

He moved to stand in front of her so she would have to look at him. "Then prove me wrong."

Her blue-green eyes stared back at him. "I've told you it

wasn't me. That should be enough."

"I need more."

"Do what you must. It matters not."

And what scared him the most was that he knew she meant it.

There was no use arguing with her. It would have to wait until after they killed the creature. No sooner had that thought crossed his mind than the sun descend into the horizon and the spine tingling scream of the creature echoed around them.

"You know what to do?" he asked Mina.

"I stand here and wait for it to attack me."

"If you change your mind-"

"I won't," she interrupted before he could finish.

He nodded and walked to his position, which was just to her right behind some water barrels.

They didn't have long to wait to hear the loud flapping of the creature's bat-like wings. From his hiding spot, he could see the dark shape of the creature as it flew toward the castle gatehouse. It rose high into the air and let out another scream.

Hugh glanced at Mina and saw her watching the creature. "I won't let it touch you," he whispered.

"I'll hold you to that promise."

He smiled despite himself and adjusted his grip on the crossbow. The creature had flown down until it hovered above the bailey. In the growing darkness, Hugh could see its red eyes searching.

To his surprise, it landed in the middle of the bailey and folded its wings. It took a step, its long talons scraping the ground. It cocked its head to the side and peered at Mina.

"I told you, it's not your time. I've been asked to keep you for last," the creature hissed.

Mina shrugged. "If you want to kill tonight it'll have to

be me."

The creature smacked its jaws together. "I wouldn't want to disappoint you," it said and jumped at her.

"Now," Hugh bellowed as the creature lunged. He fired his crossbow, and then dove at Mina.

He landed on top of her. "Are you all right?" She nodded, but he could feel her shaking. "Stay here."

After putting another arrow into his crossbow, he charged the creature who stood fighting off the attack in the bailey. He put another arrow into the creature, but nothing phased it. It continued to fight while yanking arrows out of its body.

Hugh got close enough to shoot an arrow at its heart. The beast laughed as it pulled the arrow out and healed itself. He was unable to move in time as the creature backhanded him. Hugh landed hard enough to knock the breath from his lungs.

"Mina," someone shouted.

Hugh raised his head to see the creature advancing on her. She tried to run to the left, but it jumped in her way. Wherever she went, it stopped her. Hugh got to his feet and unsheathed his sword.

He began to run towards Mina when the beast extended its right arm, its talons glistening in the moonlight. "Nay," he bellowed.

Out of the corner of his eye, he saw Darrick running toward Mina. Darrick jumped in front of her as the creature swung its arm downward. Hugh watched, horrified, as Darrick slumped to the ground. The beast raised its face to the moon and shrieked loudly before it flew to rest atop one of the castle towers.

When Hugh reached Darrick, Mina was already cradling his head in her lap.

"Darrick," she said as the tears coursed down her face.

"Do something," she screamed at Hugh.

Hugh looked down to see Darrick's chest slashed open. "Gabriel!"

"I'm here," Gabriel said and moved Hugh aside to kneel.

Hugh stood back and watched as Gabriel looked their friend over before he dropped his head.

"You must do something," Mina said.

Gabriel lifted his gaze to her. "I can heal almost anything, but I cannot bring someone back from the dead."

Hugh took a step toward Mina, but Bernard reached her first and pulled her into his arms. Mina cried the tears Hugh, Gabriel, and Cole never would.

"Not Darrick," Cole whispered as he reached them.

"Come," Hugh told him, as he and Gabriel reached for Darrick's body. "We must get him away from the creature before it returns to dine. We'll tend to him once the dawn has come."

"Put him in the blacksmith's cottage," Bernard said.

Once they placed Darrick in the cottage and covered him, they walked back into the bailey where the creature awaited them. Hugh looked around.

"Where is Mina?" he asked Bernard.

"I think she went into the castle."

But Hugh knew she wouldn't do that. "I don't think so. She must be somewhere in the bailey."

"We don't have time to find her," Cole said as he drew his sword. "The creature will descend upon us any moment."

Hugh watched the beast closely as it flew lower to land on the battlement. Its head turned slightly, and its eyes watched something outside the castle walls.

"Dear God," Hugh murmured under his breath. "Mina is outside."

CHAPTER ELEVEN

"Outside?" Bernard repeated, his tone disbelieving. "Why, in all that is holy, is Mina not inside these walls?"

No one moved as they watched the creature spread its wings and fly from the castle.

"It's headed toward the forest," Cole shouted.

Hugh never heard Cole, for he was already running toward the postern door. He threw it open and raced down the path, heedless of his own safety as he broke through the trees. The field from the castle to the forest seemed to stretch forever as he watched the creature reach the trees.

He heard footfalls behind him, and knew that at least one of his men was with him. He didn't chance a look back. He couldn't. He had to keep his eyes on the creature, which was easier said than done once it moved down into the trees.

Hugh's legs stretched longer as he neared the forest, but once he broke into the dense growth, he stopped. With his chest pumping from the exertion, he listened for any sound of the creature or Mina.

"Where is it?" Gabriel whispered as he ran up beside Hugh.

"I don't know."

Cole came to stand on the other side of Hugh. He leaned close and spoke softly, "Shouldn't we have heard her screaming by now?"

Hugh grimaced at Cole's choice of words. "You would think."

"Where is Mina?" Bernard bellowed as he crashed into the forest and ran to them.

They all turned and hushed him.

"We're trying to hear," Hugh told him.

For several more moments they stood wordlessly, listening to the eerie silence.

"This is spooky," Bernard whispered into the gloom. "I've never heard the forest this quiet."

Hugh nodded. "It's the creature that frightens the animals."

"Well, that's not the only thing it frightens."

Hugh's respect for the baron grew. There were few men who would admit their fear, and fewer still who would face it.

"Split up. If you hear something, whistle," Hugh said and moved forward through the trees."

Behind him he heard Cole whisper to Bernard, "Come with me."

With all of his senses tuned toward finding Mina before the creature did, Hugh noiselessly slid his sword from its scabbard. He adjusted his grip on the pommel as he readied himself to react to the slightest threat.

He had gone several paces without hearing anything, and was about to think Mina had gone elsewhere, when the distinctive sound of footfalls running reached him.

He looked to his left and saw a shadow. From where he stood, he couldn't tell if it was Mina or someone else, but he was going to find out.

~ ~ ~

Mina ran, her hair coming free of the braid and sticking to her face, hampering her vision. She stopped next to a tree and gulped in much needed air as she wiped the sweat soaked strands of her hair away from her face.

She couldn't see the creature, but she could feel it. It was close, much closer than she wanted.

But leaving the castle had been the right thing to do. She wanted to give the men time to regroup. Their plan had failed. Again.

She had thought she would be able to reach the old cottage deep in the forest before the creature reached her, but she had become turned around in her hasty flight from the castle. It had been a very long time since she'd ventured from the main road in the forest at night.

And now her mistake would cost her her life.

Her breathing was nearly back to normal when her ears pricked. Behind her and to her right, she heard a creak of a tree limb. The creature. He was toying with her, but why? He had said she was to be killed last, though it had been willing to kill her tonight.

Or had it?

It had come for her in the bailey, but its talons weren't fully extended, and they didn't extend until Darrick had stepped in front of her.

She shook her head to clear those thoughts, and glanced around the forest. The moon filtered through the dense clouds and allowed her a brief view of the trees, and she was able to finally find her way. The cabin was to the left.

After she had taken a deep breath to stiffen her courage, she took off running again, but this time, she refused to look behind her. She would stay focused on where she was headed. At least that was her original goal, until she heard the flap of wings over her head.

Fear devoured her. She didn't want to die. Not yet.

And then she saw it. The cottage. She pushed her fright aside, and stretched her legs as far as they could go. She could make it, she had to. But just as she reached the cabin door, something hit her from behind.

She fell against the door, and it flew open beneath her weight. With the added heft of whatever was behind her, she hit the floor with a thud. Outside the cottage, she heard the beast scream in displeasure.

"Get moving," Hugh whispered in her ear.

She didn't stop to ask him what he was doing there, just did as he commanded. While he went about trying to bar the door, she pushed the limbs aside that had crashed through the roof, and began pulling up the floorboards.

"What are you doing?"

"There's a tunnel below the cottage," she answered as she yanked up a board.

Hugh was immediately by her side helping. Outside, the creature continued to howl and bang against the old cottage, and then it landed on the roof. With Hugh's help, they got through the floor quickly and pulled open the tunnel door.

He helped her down and ran to the cottage door.

"What are you doing?" she yelled.

"I've got to tell my men I have you." With that, he opened the door and let out a loud whistle that she was sure everyone in the countryside could hear even over the creature's screams.

She climbed down the ladder that would put them in the tunnel, and waited for Hugh. She didn't have to wait long. He climbed down far enough to close the door, then he put his feet on the outside of the ladder and slid down.

"Where does this lead?"

She looked down the black tunnel before her. "It was used to escape the Normans. There is a fork up ahead. One tunnel will return us to the castle, and the other takes us deeper into the forest near the old monastery."

"Do you know which way is to the castle?"

She opened her mouth to answer when the door above them creaked. He shoved her ahead of him.

"Run."

She stumbled along the tunnel as she tried to get her legs moving. She didn't know how long she ran until she tripped over a root and fell to the ground. There wasn't time to warn Hugh of the root, and he too fell.

"Are you hurt?" he asked as he rolled off of her and sat up.

"Just exhausted," she said and slowly sat back on her knees. "I don't hear it anymore."

"Hopefully we confused it."

She sighed. "I guess we should continue. I hate not being able to see."

"There were probably some torches at the entrance, but we didn't have time to look."

Suddenly his hand touched her face, then moved to her arm. "Let me help you up."

She allowed him to aid her, mostly because she was too weary to do it herself, but there was also a part of her that wanted his touch.

"I'll take the lead now," he said. "Keep a hold on me."

She wasn't about to balk at having free rein to touch him. With his hand as a guide, he moved hers until it rested against his waist. The strange fabric of his tunic beneath her hand heated.

He moved forward, and she gripped his tunic. For what felt like endless hours, they stayed like that as he moved them deeper into the tunnel.

"How long is this tunnel?"

"I don't remember. I haven't been here in years. There is only one fork, and you'll know when you come upon it."

"So, it's something like this?"

She peered around him and saw the dark outline of the tunnels as they branched off. "That's it."

"Which way to the castle?"

"Left."

They trudged onward. Many times she wanted to ask him to stop, but she held her tongue. She was weary and hungry, but she refused to appear weak in front of him. She must have dozed as they walked because she ran into his back when he stopped.

"What's wrong?" she asked.

"The tunnel is blocked."

She moved to his side, wide awake now. "What? How can that be?" But it was solid earth before her hand.

"The ground must have caved in." He was silent for a moment. "We must turn back and head to the monastery."

She couldn't go another step though. "Hugh, I know you wish to return to your men, but I need to rest."

"Forgive me," he said. "I'm not used to having a lady around."

She heard the grin in his voice as she slumped to the ground. "It's I who should apologize. Not only did I leave the castle, but I'm holding you up." She saw his outline moving around her. "What are you doing?"

"I found a piece of wood. I wanted to see if there was more, and there is. I think I'll be able to build us a fire so we can see."

For the first time that evening, she smiled. "That would be wonderful."

And as amazing as it sounded, it wasn't long before he

had done just that. She looked across their small fire to the man that had saved her for a second time. As she looked, he watched the smoke from the growing fire.

"What are you doing?"

"Making sure there is a vent somewhere so we don't inhale the smoke. See how the smoke drifts away, then up? There must be a small hole nearby where the smoke can escape to."

She sighed and realized she was very lucky to have him with her.

"Tell me why you ran from the castle?" he asked while feeding more limbs to the growing blaze.

"I wanted to give you and the men time to get inside the castle before the creature killed anyone else."

"You were safer inside the castle walls. We all were."

"I thought for sure I could have reached the cottage before it caught me. And I would have, if I hadn't become lost."

"Brave, but foolish." His eyes burned golden in the firelight. "Don't do it again."

"I won't," she promised. She looked down during the silence that followed her response.

"I don't understand you."

Her head jerked up at his words. "There isn't much to understand of me. There isn't another more complex man on this earth than you."

He chuckled. "I guess you could say that. I have a reason to be as I am."

"And you're saying I don't?"

"Nay. Tell me about your parents."

She leaned her head back against the tunnel wall, and let him change the subject. "Everyone loved them. The villagers would do anything for them. While they lived, Stone Crest prospered."

"Did you spend a lot of time with them?"

"Not really. They had so much to do with the castle and villagers. My mother never turned anyone away in need, and Theresa commanded a lot of her attention."

"And your father?"

She smiled to herself. "I used to sit in the field and watch him riding. He was a great horseman. He fostered many young men at the castle, and he was a magnificent leader. Bernard was with him almost constantly."

"So when did they spend time with you?"

"Whenever they could."

"Give me an example," he prodded.

She looked away from his gaze. "I didn't need them like Theresa and Bernard did, and they knew that. I spent most of my time with my mother's old nurse, Gertie." Hearing the words out of her own mouth brought back all the painful feelings she had tried to bury. She blinked rapidly, but moisture collected in her eyes anyway.

Hugh shifted to move next to her. She refused to look at him, but it wasn't hard to see the tears in the firelight. He reached up and wiped a lone tear from her cheek.

She raised her gaze to him. "Is there something wrong with me that would make my own parents shun me?"

"Nay," he said and wrapped his arm around her shoulder.

She turned toward him, and he let her cry against his shoulder. He wondered how long she had held the emotion inside.

"Whether you believe it or not," he said against her hair, "there will come a time when your life will sort itself out."

She leaned her wet cheek against his shirt. "I think for most people it does turn out that way. I know I'm not the only person to have my parents treat me like they did."

"No one can say why parents act the way they do."

"It wasn't as if they were cruel to me," she explained. "They always gave me a smile, and a pat on the head."

"You just didn't feel part of the family."

She nodded. "I always thought it was because of how I look."

"I've already told you, Theresa lied about that."

She raised her face and placed her finger on his lips. "And I've already told you, I know what I look like. I think my parents were too kind to tell me the truth, so Theresa did."

Hugh barely heard anything she said once she placed her finger against his lips. She was in his arms, snuggled against his chest with her face tilted toward him. All he needed to do was lower his head.

"You have no idea how alluring you are, do you?"

She smiled and wiped the tears away. "I've never known a kinder man than you."

"I'm not kind. I speak the truth," he said and found his arm tightening around her.

The fullness of her breasts could be felt against his chest, and the heat of her body mingled with his, giving him a heady sense. He began to shake slightly with a need he had not experienced in decades.

Pull away. She could be part of the evil.

The incessant words his conscience continued to repeat were soon lost as he looked at her plump lips and wondered what they would feel like kissing him.

He gazed into her blue-green eyes and was immediately lost. It didn't matter if she controlled the creature or if she attacked Theresa. All that mattered was that his body craved her like a starving man. He knew to push her away now would be to deny what he needed most.

"Mina," he said and lowered his head.

CHAPTER TWELVE

Hugh watched Mina's pink lips part as his head drew nearer. He closed his eyes when his mouth finally met her soft, full mouth. He began to pull back, knowing he had crossed a line that shouldn't have been crossed, when her fingers dug into his chest and her head moved toward him.

It was all the encouragement he needed.

He cradled her head in his arm while his other hand reached up and around her neck. He slid his tongue along her lips, and heard her moan softly. With his thumb, he gently pulled her chin down until her mouth opened for him.

It was his intention to go slow and not scare her, but when her tongue peeked out and hesitantly touched his lips, it sent him over the edge.

He pulled her tight against his chest as his mouth slanted over hers. His tongue delved into her hot mouth and found such sweetness that he thought he might die.

Mina wrapped her arms around his neck and held on tight, afraid he would let go. His kiss was hot, demanding and sensual. He plunged his tongue into her mouth and mated with hers. Her body began to heat as his kiss brought a new sensation to her that quickly spread everywhere. When his large hand moved from her neck to her arm then down her side to her leg, she didn't stop him.

With his every touch, the fire within her intensified until she knew nothing but him and the heat he wrought from her. She let her head drop back against his arm, and his lips moved from her mouth to her neck, leaving a trail of kisses in his wake. She held her breath, eagerly waiting to see what he would do next.

Her eyes closed, letting her body feel all of him. His hand moved slowly up from her knee. His fingers touched her thigh, her stomach, and then skimmed over her breast. She moaned and moved against him as her nipples peaked and hardened.

His hand moved back and cupped her breast as if testing the weight of it. His adept fingers began to knead her breast and tweak her nipple through her tunic. She squeezed her legs together, and felt a sensation at the junction of her thighs that brought another moan.

She threaded her fingers through his dark brown hair, and was surprised to find it thick and silky. With a small movement of her head, his mouth slanted over hers again and robbed her of both thought and will.

She had a single purpose now...him.

And despite what might happen afterwards, she would not turn back. Not even when his hand cupped her most private part. She jerked at his touch, but then heat infused her. His hand moved in a small circle as he pressed against her, and it wasn't long before her hips rose to meet his hand. A thrill raced through her at his deep, primal moan.

He pulled his head back and ended their kiss. She started to reach for him again, but one look into his dark eyes and she knew something troubled him.

"What is it?" she asked, unable to take her hands from around his neck.

"We shouldn't do this. You are a gentle born lady."

She smiled and ran a finger across his jaw. "We both know I will not receive any marriage offers. My betrothed chose Theresa, if you recall."

"I remember," he said and pursed his lips.

"I am not looking for marriage, if that is your concern." She lowered her gaze to his chest since she knew she couldn't continue looking into his eyes and not reach up for another kiss. "I have never felt like this before, and I don't want it to stop."

Nothing but the crackle of the fire reached her ears. Then, he turned her face to his and smiled.

"If it is a woman you wish to feel like, then I will oblige you, but I'll not take you."

She opened her mouth, but he held up his hand.

"Not here, Mina. Not on the dirt floor of a tunnel. You deserve better than this."

Who was she to argue with that?

She returned his smile and leaned up to kiss him. His arms wrapped around her and brought her fully onto his lap. She breathed in his scent of mystery, man and power. His lips moved over hers with skill as he pushed his tongue into her mouth and teased and cajoled until she was panting with a need and yearning that confused her as much as it excited her.

It seemed that he knew exactly what she needed when she needed it, because his hand moved to settle between her legs. She instantly rocked her hips against his hand, and let out a groan when strange sensations quickened through her and moisture pooled between her thighs.

She gasped when his expert fingers deftly unlaced her trousers and slid inside to touch her bare skin. But that gasp quickly turned into a moan when his fingers touched her sex. He moved his fingers to dip inside her, then spread her own arousal over her throbbing clitoris that begged for more of him.

"My God, Mina," he whispered against her forehead.

She barely heard him as his fingers moved against her. With her eyes closed and head thrown back, she let herself fall into the pleasure that was taking control of her.

Hugh didn't know if he could keep from plunging into her. She was hot, moist and ready for him. All he had to do was move her until she straddled him, but like he told her, she deserved better. So, he would suffer through this torture and give her the gratification she deserved.

His fingers parted her nether lips, and he slipped a finger inside of her tight, wet sheath. She gasped and moved her hips against him. She was made for loving. She had much passion inside of her that had just waited for the right man to unleash.

Her fingers dug into his upper arms as she lost herself to the throbbing that grew by the moment. Soon she would orgasm. That thought made him so hard he had to shift to relieve some of the pressure. He was in a bad way, worse than he had ever been.

He looked down and found her staring at him. With one hand cradling her against him, and the other pleasuring her, he couldn't move.

"Remove your tunic," he said, his voice sounding strained even to him.

She complied without question, and the sight of her bare breasts made his cock jump painfully. Her breasts were full, and her nipples hard, just waiting to feel his mouth. He pulled her toward him, took a taunt pink nipple into his mouth and suckled, while his fingers increased the tempo inside her, and his thumb teased her swollen clitoris.

He moved to the other breasts and felt her legs tighten. She screamed his name as the climax took her, and she convulsed around him. He held her until the last spasm of pleasure faded. Then, he withdrew his hand and wrapped both arms around her. Neither spoke. He didn't want words to spoil what had happened.

He leaned his head back against the tunnel wall while she laid hers on his chest. It wasn't long before her breathing evened and sleep took her.

~ ~ ~

Mina awoke to a heartbeat in her ear and a warm, very male body next to hers. Hugh. She smiled and thought back to what he had given her. He might not have taken her virginity, but he had taken away any innocence she might have had. And that suited her just fine.

"Did you sleep well?" he asked.

She raised her head and grinned. "Actually, I did. Did you sleep at all?"

"A little."

His warm hands moved over her back, and she remembered she no longer wore her tunic. She shivered when she thought about what his mouth had done to her breasts.

"Are you cold?"

She shook her head. "Remembering."

He moved one of his arms and brought her tunic to her. She pushed from his warm chest and slipped on her tunic. When she turned back to him, his eyes were on her breasts. He looked as if he were about to speak.

"If you are going to apologize for last night. Don't. I don't regret it."

He raised a dark brow. "That's good, because I wasn't about to apologize."

"Really?"

"Really. Now are you ready to make our way to the monastery?"

She jumped to her feet and laced her pants. "I am now."

The fire was almost out, and Hugh quickly fed it to make it grow. "Find me the biggest limb you can."

She set about doing as he asked. She found some, but they weren't long enough to be a torch. Just as she was about to give up, she found a limb hidden behind a root.

"Here," she said and handed it to him.

He examined it. "Perfect." He quickly made it into a torch, and once it was lit, kicked dirt onto the fire. "Let's go."

She followed him as they retraced their steps from the night before. This time it was much easier since they had the torch. Since they were able to move faster, they also reached the fork in the tunnel quicker.

"The tunnel to the castle is much longer than the tunnel to the monastery."

"I hope you're right," he said over his shoulder.

They walked in amicable silence. She watched the way his long, muscular legs strode with determination and grace. His eyes were constantly looking around for some sign of danger, and when they did reach the end of the tunnel at the monastery door, he pushed her behind him.

"Hold the torch high so I can see," he said.

She held up the torch, and watched as he reached for the handle on the door, his arm muscles bunched as they readied. He took a deep breath and pulled. It didn't budge. He tried a second time with no results. With a mumbled curse, he looked around and found nothing barring the door.

"It must be bolted from the inside," he said.

"That doesn't help us since the monastery is

abandoned."

He cursed in a language she had never heard before. There was so much she wanted to know about him, but so little time to find out everything.

"Go over there," he pointed behind her.

She couldn't imagine what he was going to do, but she walked to where he pointed. Once she was there, he ran to the door and hit it with his shoulder. Dust rained on him in a thick coating.

"I think that's solid oak," she pointed out.

He ignored her, and put his shoulder into the door again. This time there was a creak. The third time there was a definite fragment in the wood.

She saw the material torn from the arm of his shirt. His shoulder was red and would most likely bruise. "We could always return to the cottage."

"How do you know its dawn and that the creature isn't waiting for us?"

She hadn't thought of that. "It's better than watching you hurt yourself."

He flashed her a bright smile before he ran at the door again. This time the door splintered and flew open. She moved toward him and the broken door. Stale air assaulted her as she walked from the tunnel into a room.

"The smell of damp earth was better than this," she mumbled as she covered her nose with her hand.

"Do you always complain so?" he teased.

"Pretty much, though the only person who usually hears it is myself."

He chuckled and took the torch from her. There was a sound ahead of them, and he quickly drew his sword in preparation.

"If something happens to me, run to the cottage entrance," he whispered.

CHAPTER THIRTEEN

Mina gripped the dagger at her waist and slowly followed Hugh into the monastery. They were in what looked like an old library of sorts. The bookcases were bare, and many of them broken and turned over.

They walked by a set of bookcases that had partially fallen, the shelves were dust laden and many held spider webs. The silence was deafening, yet both of them knew something, or someone, was in the chamber with them. She tried to step where Hugh stepped so whoever was in the chamber wouldn't realize she was with him.

Her heart began to pound with a mixture of fear and excitement at what they would find. She had little doubt that Hugh could take care of whatever it was. He was, after all, a weapon the Fae used to kill the creatures that terrorized villages.

He stopped and held up the torch above his head. For several heartbeats, he stayed just as he was, silently waiting as if he were a stone statue. She wanted to ask him what he paused for, but held her tongue instead.

To her surprise, he leaned toward a set of bookcases and peered into the darkness. There was a loud hiss, and a cat shot out from between the shelves. Mina gasped, and stepped out of Hugh's way as he jumped back.

He turned and looked at her, and she couldn't stop the giggle that escaped. As her laughter grew, she saw a smile begin to spread on his face, and it wasn't long before they were both laughing.

Once her heart had slowed its beating, and she had wiped the tears of laughter from her eyes, she looked at him. "Is it safe now?" she asked while trying to stop another bout of laughter.

"I think so."

It was his lopsided grin and his playful shrug that made her catch her breath as she realized just how much she'd come to trust him.

"Are you ready to move on?"

She gazed at him as the sunlight filtered through a window above them to shed its light on him. Flecks of dust could be seen dancing in the air, and all she wanted to do was touch him to see if he was really with her and not a figment of her imagination.

"Mina?"

His face had grown serious as worry etched his brow. She inhaled and put a smile on her face. "Aye, I'm ready."

They moved through the wreckage of the library, and had to step over many broken pieces of furniture. She had never been inside before today, and it upset her that someone would have destroyed a house of God. "Someone must have done this once the monks departed."

"How long has the monastery been abandoned?"

She thought for a moment. "Before I was born. Longer I believe."

"It could have been raided and everything stolen."

"I cannot imagine anyone doing that to a church or monastery."

He shrugged his massive shoulders. "If you aren't

Christian it doesn't matter to you. Other people worship different gods."

"Well, I don't revere their gods, but I wouldn't dream of destroying a place where they worshipped."

He stopped and turned to look at her. Through the light of the torch, she saw him studying her. "What is it?"

"Nothing," he answered after a moment and continued.

They came to a door that opened to stairs. They climbed them with Hugh holding the torch in one hand and his sword in the other. Though they didn't encounter anything or anyone, he never lowered his sword.

They passed many doorways as they climbed the stairs, but he persisted onward. When they finally reached the top, he pushed open the door and sunlight flooded the chamber.

He lowered his sword and stepped into the chamber. She followed and looked around as she walked to a window and gazed out at the countryside. They were at the top of the monastery, and the view was spectacular.

"I was hoping it was daylight," Hugh said, as he came to stand beside her. "How far is it to the castle?"

She looked at the sun. "It's not even mid-morning. We could make it there by noon if we start now."

"Then let's go."

She pushed away from the window and followed as he walked down the stairs until he came to a doorway to their right. They followed the hallway until it led them outside.

"How did you know where to go?" she asked.

"All monasteries are pretty much the same."

He didn't say more, and she didn't persist. They walked out of the gates that had once barred any woman from within. She turned to give the monastery one final look. She had forgotten the many strange, evil looking creatures that had been carved into the structure.

"They are meant to ward off evil," Hugh said.

She shivered. "They would certainly keep me away."

"That's the point as well."

She turned and began the long trek back to the castle. Along the way, she and Hugh walked side by side, rarely saying anything, but it was a comfortable silence.

When they reached the castle, guards yelled down from the gatehouse, and quickly opened the gate. They walked beneath the gatehouse, through the bailey and into the castle without being stopped by anyone. She tried to keep the smile from her face as they stepped into the great hall, but no matter what she did, nothing could make her lose her happy mood.

"How could you?" Theresa screeched and dove at her from the stairs.

Mina raised her arms to shield her face from Theresa's claws. Her injured arm took the brunt of the attack, and even though it rarely bothered her, it now throbbed so badly it almost brought her to her knees.

"Enough," Bernard bellowed, and pulled Theresa off her. "I told you I would take care of this," he told Theresa.

Mina held her arm and swallowed down the nausea that had suddenly assaulted her. "What is going on?"

"You always play the innocent," Theresa spat as she struggled in Bernard's arms. "But you won't get away with it this time. I told them it was you who attacked me."

Mina would have rolled her eyes if she didn't think it would make her pass out. "I don't know why you are lying, but you know it wasn't me."

Instead of the retort she expected from her sister, Theresa merely gave her a small smile that sent chills over Mina's body. Just what had Theresa done?

No one spoke, and it was then that she noticed how crowded the great hall was. She turned to Bernard, but he wouldn't meet her eyes. When she turned her gaze to Hugh, her blood froze in her veins.

Gone was the man who had held her so tenderly and shown her what it was to be a woman, and in his place was the warrior that did the Fae's bidding.

"Ah, I see," she said around the growing lump in her throat. "Guilty just because Theresa said I was. What about my side of the story?"

Bernard pushed Theresa away from him. He turned to Mina and grasped her shoulders as he said, "I think you should go to your chamber."

"If I'm to be a prisoner, then shouldn't I be in the dungeon?"

"Don't be silly," Bernard hissed.

"Oh, I think that would be wise," Theresa said. "She is controlling that creature after all."

Mina waited for Bernard to say something, anything, but he didn't. She raised her chin and squared her shoulders. "So be it," she said and turned toward the dungeons.

Footsteps sounded behind her. It wasn't long before a hand clamped on her shoulder and spun her around. Hugh stared at her, a muscle working in his jaw. "This isn't necessary."

"Bernard is in charge of this castle, not you, and he obviously wants me in the dungeon." She looked over his shoulder and nodded. "See," she said, as a guard walked toward her.

The hall began to spin around her, and she would be damned before she collapsed in front of everyone. With one hand supporting her along the wall, she walked down the steps that would take her to the cold, dank dungeon.

The musty, stale odor made her stomach churn painfully. She barely waited until the guard had left the dungeon before she lost the contents of her stomach. She hadn't eaten since noon yesterday, but her body didn't seem to care. She longed for water, but she knew she wouldn't receive anything for quite awhile.

She leaned against the damp stone and slowly lowered herself to the floor. She couldn't move her right arm or hand. It throbbed and burned so badly that it brought tears to her eyes. She had no idea what Theresa had done to her, but whatever it was, it was something awful.

Off to her left came a squeak. She glanced over and saw a small brown mouse. "You won't get anything from me, I'm afraid. They'll forget about me soon enough. They always do."

That thought brought Hugh to her mind. Why had he turned on her? Had she done something wrong between the monastery and the castle? Shouldn't a person be asked and questioned about a crime before everyone judged them?

The sound of crying and heavy footsteps reached her from above in the great hall. Though she was far below, the stairs were directly in front of her and brought the sound to her clearly. It sounded like a funeral, and then she remembered.

Darrick.

He had given his life for her. Out of all of them, he had never turned on her. She buried her face in her hand and cried for his loss of life, for not being there to see him put to rest, and because she didn't know how much longer she could go on with her life.

She wiped away her tears, and memories of the night before assaulted her. She took a deep breath and made a fist with her right hand. The pain shot through her like a lance and brought the blessed darkness she craved.

~ ~ ~

Hugh stood with Cole and Gabriel as they buried Darrick. He'd been surprised to see the entire castle attend, but there was one person he knew should have been there.

Mina.

He inhaled deeply and glanced around at the lush foliage that would guard Darrick's resting place. Cole had wanted to have the traditional funeral where they burned their warriors, and had they not been staying at Stone Crest, Hugh would have done just that.

A shadow out of the corner of his eye caught his attention. He turned and found Aimery and several of his Fae warriors. It warmed Hugh's heart to know that the Fae really did care about them. He wasn't surprised the villagers didn't see the Fae, for Aimery had only allowed Hugh a glimpse.

Once the priest finished blessing the ground, and Darrick had been placed in the earth, Hugh turned toward the castle. Bernard nodded and pivoted before reaching out and grabbing a hold of Theresa to lead her back to the castle.

"Did you see Aimery?" Cole asked.

Hugh nodded as he watched the baron and his sister.

"I knew the Fae would be here," Gabriel said and crossed his arms over his chest.

"What is it, Hugh?" Cole asked.

"I'm not sure."

Cole flexed his hands. "It must be something for them to catch your attention like they did."

Hugh shrugged. "It's just a nagging in the back of my mind."

"Like you forgot something?" Gabriel asked.

"Nay," Hugh shook his head. "Like I'm not seeing something."

Gabriel snorted. "What's there to see other than a

spiteful, vengeful woman and her drunken brother?"

"Not to mention a lady that is not only beautiful, but seems as innocent as a new babe," Cole finished. "Are you sure it's Mina controlling the creature?"

"My instincts have never failed me before," Hugh said and strode to the castle.

~ ~ ~

"What the Hell?" Hugh said once had descended into the dungeon. He rushed toward the door that held Mina when he spotted her.

He hadn't been able to stay away, needing her to realize what was going on, and how detrimental it could all be. But he hadn't been prepared to see her passed out on the damp stones.

"Guard!" he yelled.

The guard came running toward him. "My lord?"

"Find Gabriel and the baron and get them down here immediately," he said as he took the keys from the guard's waist.

While he went in search of Gabriel and Bernard, Hugh unlocked the door and went to Mina. He touched her forehead and found her skin warm.

He didn't think it was her wound on her arm since Gabriel had healed it, but something kept telling him to check anyway. He pulled up the sleeve of her tunic, and saw the skin red and blotchy. The talon marks that had begun to heal and fade were raised and turning green.

The sound of boots running down the steps drew his attention. He turned and spotted Gabriel. "Hurry!"

Gabriel immediately came to his knees beside Mina. "By all that is holy," he breathed. "Who did this to her?"

Hugh raised his eyes to Bernard. "She was fine until we

walked into the castle."

"Will she be all right?" Bernard asked, his brow creased in concern. "I didn't want her down here."

"Then you should have told her," Hugh snapped. "I've never seen anything like this wound. Gabriel, can you heal her?"

Gabriel felt her head and shook his head. "I honestly don't know. There's magic involved."

"Let's get her out of here," Hugh said and picked her up in his arms.

"Theresa won't like this," Bernard whispered.

"Frankly, I don't give a sheep's arse what Theresa likes." But it gave Hugh pause. What if he was wrong about Mina and she was innocent? "Is there another way to reach Mina's chamber without going through the great hall?"

Bernard's face lit up. "Aye. Follow me."

They managed to reach Mina's chamber through a back stairway without being seen by anyone. Hugh walked in first and went to her bed. It wasn't until after he lay her down that he realized the stone was once again gone.

"Bernard, look for the blue stone while I aid Gabriel."

The baron nodded and went straight to searching the chamber.

Hugh watched Mina's face become paler. "Hurry, Gabriel," he urged.

"I don't know if this will work," Gabriel said as he added what looked like bits of grass into the goblet of herbs and water. "Raise her head. She must drink all of this."

Every time they put the goblet to her lips she would turn her head away, no matter how many ways they tried to get the liquid down her, she wouldn't open her mouth.

"She acts as though she wants to die," Gabriel murmured.

"The Hell she does," Hugh thundered, and turned her

face to him. "Mina. Open your mouth. You will drink. You won't let Theresa win. Prove her wrong. Prove me wrong." He waited a moment then whispered, "Please."

This time when Gabriel brought the goblet to her lips she allowed the liquid to pass. Once that was done, Hugh laid her back down as Gabriel reached for her arm.

"Hold her," he told Hugh.

Hugh leaned over her and put a hand on either of her shoulders. He watched as Gabriel took out his dagger. "What are you doing?"

Gabriel's silver gaze widened a fraction in surprise. "You've never questioned me before."

"Go ahead," Hugh said and looked away.

"Just what happened last night?"

"No questions, Gabriel. Do your work."

But he didn't stop watching his friend as Gabriel set about reopening Mina's wounds. As soon as the skin was open, a foul odor penetrated the chamber.

"The red jar," Gabriel called out anxiously.

Hugh reached over and handed it to Gabriel who hastily wiped the yellowish mixture on Mina's open wounds. Mina cried out and tried to jerk her arm away. Hugh held her down while Gabriel finished putting the mixture on and wrapping her arm.

When he finished, Hugh released Mina. "Will it work?"

Gabriel ran a hand through his tousled hair. "I hope so. Whoever, or whatever, did that to her meant for her to die."

"The only people to touch her were Theresa and Hugh," Bernard said.

"She was with me all night in the tunnel beneath the monastery. If it was something there, I would also have it."

"True," Gabriel said. "Just in case, let me see your back."

Hugh raised his shirt. "Anything?"

"Nothing," Gabriel said. "The marks look better than I had hoped. I think you'll come away without much of a scar."

"It's strange the creature didn't kill you," Bernard said.

"I know," Hugh agreed. "It's had plenty of opportunities."

"And it has had ample opportunity to kill Mina as well," Gabriel pointed out.

"Mina told us that it spoke to her and said she was to be last. That whoever was controlling it wanted her to witness everyone's death."

"Well," Bernard said and slumped into a chair as though he had been punched. "That either means she's innocent, or a liar and controlling it as well as poisoning me and attacking Theresa."

"She has good reason to want revenge against both of you," Gabriel said.

Bernard hung his head. "Unfortunately, that is too true."

"So, Hugh, what do we do?"

Hugh looked at the sleeping woman, the same woman who had come alive in his arms last night, the woman who made his blood pound and desire fill him. "I don't know. Everything points to her as the culprit."

"But?" Gabriel prompted.

"She could be being set up. Who hates her the most?"

Bernard began to laugh. "That is an easy one. Theresa. But I can honestly say Theresa knows nothing of magic or these blue stones."

"Are you sure? Would you stake your life on it?" Gabriel asked.

Bernard paused.

Hugh blew out a long breath. "Did you find the blue

stone?"

"Nay."

"I didn't think you would. Why would Mina place the stone out so that any of us could see it, and then hide it again?"

"She could have forgotten to replace it." Gabriel shrugged.

"Possibly," Hugh conceded.

"And the evil surrounding the Druid ruins didn't bother her."

"Look," Bernard said as he gained his feet. "Dusk is coming. I don't wish to see any more of my people die. Do you know of a way to kill the creature?"

Hugh walked to the door. "Gabriel, don't leave Mina. Bernard, get your people inside their homes. I'll find your answer."

CHAPTER FOURTEEN

Mina didn't wish to open her eyes. She wanted to return to the darkness where the pain in her heart and her arm didn't reach her.

"Mina. You must wake now."

She turned away from the insistent voice, silently begging him to leave her be.

"It's important. Please, Mina."

Since the nice, but relentless, voice had dragged her out of her darkness and wouldn't leave her alone, she had no choice but to open her eyes. She blinked and looked around as her gaze focused. She was in her chamber, though she couldn't remember getting there.

"Hugh carried you."

She turned her head and found her brother and Gabriel staring down at her. "Go away," she croaked out.

"Mina, where is the blue stone?" Bernard asked. "Where did you hide it?"

"I don't have it." She tried to lift her right arm to rub her eyes, and cried out from the pain.

"Shh," Gabriel said, as he gently took her arm and laid it carefully beside her. "Don't move it for a while."

"What happened?"

Gabriel's silver eyes lowered for a moment before he met her gaze. "Dark magic."

"What does that have to do with my arm?"

"Whoever used it intended for you to die. Had Hugh not gone to the dungeon when he did, I wouldn't have been able to save you."

She didn't want to owe Hugh a debt of thanks. "I would have liked to say good-bye to Darrick. He saved me. I miss his teasing and laughter."

Gabriel nodded. "Aye, he will be greatly missed. He gave his life for you because he believed in what we do. And because he liked you."

That brought a small smile to her lips. "Thank you."

"About your arm, I have heard of Dark Magic being used in such a way, but I have never encountered it. I don't know if my herbs will assist at all."

"I wish you would have let me die."

"Mina," Bernard chastised her.

"How would you feel if people thought you were an evil person setting a creature to kill everyone? How would you feel if no one would believe a word you said?"

Gabriel placed a hand on Bernard to halt the words he was about to say. "She needs to rest. Give her some time."

When Bernard left her chamber, she turned to Gabriel. "Thank you."

"Thank me later," he said and brought a goblet to her. "Drink this."

~ ~ ~

Hugh walked the battlements in agitation, the sun sinking lower in the horizon every moment. He had been calling to Aimery for some time now, but the Fae wouldn't answer him. He slammed his fist onto his thigh, and walked into the tower only to find Aimery.

"I wondered when you would come inside," the Fae said.

Hugh clenched his jaw. "It would have been nice had you let me know you were in here."

"Now what would be the fun of that?" When Hugh didn't smile at his joke, the Fae straightened from the wall. "What is it?"

"Was Mina at the Druid ruins as she claimed, or was it she who attacked Theresa?"

"What does your instinct tell you?"

Hugh paced the small tower. "It tells me that it's Mina who controls the creature."

"But, you don't want to consider that. Is it so hard to believe her?"

Hugh spun around and looked into the glowing blue eyes of Aimery. "Aye, it is hard to believe. After everything I've done and witnessed, all I have is my instinct to rely on."

"That does put you in a bit of a fix," Aimery said nonchalantly.

"Why won't you just tell me what I want to know?"

"Because I have been ordered not to."

Hugh laughed dryly, not surprised at all by Aimery's answer. "And who ordered that?"

"Me," said a female voice behind Hugh.

Hugh spun around and froze. Only once had Hugh seen the exquisite Fae Queen, Rufina. He had been stunned speechless by her splendor, and even now he couldn't string two words together. She had the same glowing blue eyes of Aimery, a trait of a Fae, as well as the long flaxen hair, but it was the simple perfection of everything about her that made her so beautiful it hurt to look at her.

"It's no wonder you don't allow mortals to see you," Hugh grumbled, and turned away from her so he could think again.

She laughed, the sound twinkling like little bells. "You always were a flatterer."

He rolled his eyes and glanced at Aimery. "Is she always like this?"

Aimery shook his head. "She's in a good mood, my friend. If I were you, I would take advantage of that."

Hugh sighed and gathered his thoughts before he faced Rufina. "Can you tell me if Mina is speaking true or not?"

"Let me ask you something," Rufina said and threw her long, loose hair over her shoulder. "Do you care for this mortal?"

"If I didn't care about them I wouldn't risk my life to kill the creatures terrorizing them."

She smiled, her full, red lips turning up seductively. "I know what happened between you and Mina in the tunnel. You wanted her, Hugh. It's been many years since you've found a woman who stirs you as Mina does."

"Enough," he said and ran his hand down his face. "I hate that you cannot answer a simple question."

"You didn't answer mine either," she pointed out.

"That doesn't give you the right to pry into my private life."

She raised a perfectly arched flaxen brow. "You are a warrior for the Fae. You and your men are the only things that keep this world living. I pry into your lives to make sure everything is as it should be."

"Just tell me if Mina is lying," he said, his voice resigned.

"Nay. That you will have to determine on your own."

He had just about had enough. He turned to Aimery. "Then tell me why my arrows or sword do not kill the creature."

"What?" Aimery and Rufina asked in unison.

Hugh barked out a laugh and raised his eyes to the ceiling. "I thought you were all knowing."

"Don't press your luck," Aimery warned as he pushed off from the wall. "Why didn't you tell me earlier about the creature?"

Hugh shrugged. "Like I said, I thought you knew."

Long, slender fingers with each nail the same length and shape, wrapped around his wrist. "Do you have any idea how many people roam the realms?" Rufina asked. "Do you even know how many realms there are?"

"Nay."

"If we opened our minds to everyone out there we would go insane. It isn't unless we focus that we know what is going on at any given time."

He narrowed his eyes as he saw the concern pulling at Rufina's face. He slid a glance to Aimery and saw him pacing. "The fact this creature cannot be killed is something you haven't encountered before?"

Rufina shook her head and walked to the tower door. "We knew that the creatures were becoming stronger and lasting longer with each of their deaths, but I had hoped this day was farther off."

This wasn't what he needed to hear right now. "What day are you speaking of?"

She turned her shimmering blue eyes to him. "I think it's time we told you what you've been fighting for."

~ ~ ~

Hugh walked into Mina's chamber and found Gabriel alone. "How is she?"

"She woke briefly, but I gave her another draught to

keep away the pain while she heals. She'll sleep the rest of tonight."

"Good. Did she say how she was attacked?"

"She doesn't remember anything."

Hugh nodded. "Where's Cole?"

"Following Theresa."

Just then the door to Mina's chamber flew open, and Theresa stood there with her eyes wide. "I was just in the dungeon. Why isn't Mina there? Have you allowed her to escape?"

Hugh took a step toward Theresa as both Cole and Bernard walked up behind her. "We haven't allowed her to escape."

Theresa's eyes moved beyond him to Gabriel and the bed. Her already wide eyes nearly bulged with indignation. "How dare you!" she screamed and ran toward the bed.

Hugh caught her in time, and held her as she clawed and kicked him.

"She tried to kill me," Theresa shrieked. "She wants me dead, and she'll stop at nothing until she succeeds."

"She was attacked herself," Hugh said.

Theresa continued to fight and shriek, and it took both Cole and Bernard helping Hugh to subdue her.

Hugh took her face in his hands. "Enough!"

"I don't understand why you can't see it," she said as the tears spilled from her eyes.

Hugh straightened and sighed. "Bernard, I think it might be best if you took your sister to her chamber. Did you get everyone inside their homes?"

"Aye," Bernard answered as he drug Theresa to the door.

Once Bernard and Theresa left, Hugh turned to his men. "We need to talk. I had a visit from Aimery and Rufina today."

"The queen?" Cole asked, stunned. "I only met her once, when I agreed to become a Shield."

"Me as well," Gabriel added.

Hugh found himself staring at Mina as he recalled his conversation with the Fae. "They have no idea how to kill the creature."

"Well that isn't good," Cole said and sat in the chair beside Mina's bed.

Gabriel rubbed his chin. "They didn't give you any hints?"

"Nay. In fact, they were both very worried. It seems that they knew this day would come, but they hadn't expected it this soon."

Cole blew air out of his mouth. "What does that mean for us?"

"It means it is up to us to kill this creature."

"If it can be killed," Gabriel said.

Cole studied Hugh for a moment. "There is more."

Hugh nodded. "It's the beginning of the end of this realm."

CHAPTER FIFTEEN

"The beginning of the end?" Cole repeated. "What is Rufina referring to?"

"It seems," Hugh said, "that the creatures are becoming immune to anything we have to kill them. The first sign was how they leaped from this time to nine hundred years from now."

"So, even if we manage to kill this one, the creatures will continue to evolve," Gabriel said.

"Exactly. Whoever is releasing them is growing in power, and giving that power to the creatures."

Cole snorted. "And the Fae can't help us?"

"Nay."

"Can't, or won't?" Gabriel asked.

Hugh drew in a deep breath. "They aren't sure what needs to be done. The realm of Earth has always been open to them because they once roamed here, but the other realms are as closed to them as the Fae world is to us."

"There has to be some way to stop these creatures, and the people controlling them," Cole stated.

"There is. We just have to find it."

Gabriel sighed. "Aimery told us long ago that it was

someone from another realm using people from Earth to bring forth the creatures."

Hugh stared at Gabriel for a moment as he recalled that conversation with Aimery. "And I bet if we find that blue stone Mina had we could begin to solve this puzzle."

"Mina said she didn't have the stone," Gabriel said.

"It has to be in this castle somewhere, especially if she brought it here and it disappeared."

He turned to Cole to find him staring at the bed. He followed Cole's gaze to find Mina watching at him. Hugh didn't like the way her beautiful eyes regarded him as if he were an enemy instead of her friend.

But then again, what did he expect since he also believed she was guilty. Or was she? Hugh no longer knew.

"You're supposed to be sleeping," he said.

"How can I with Theresa yelling?"

He walked to the bed and reached for her hand, but she flinched away from him. The pain that caused bothered him more than he cared to admit or show. "Tell me where you put the stone when you first brought it to the castle?"

She laughed dryly. "Why? You won't believe anything I say. I've told you I don't have the stone, that I don't know who put it in my chamber after it had been stolen."

"If you truly are innocent, then you won't let what is between us stand in the way of seeing you proved right."

She tried to sit up and cried out when she put weight on her injured arm. Hugh reached to help her, but she jerked away from him so hard that she tumbled off the bed. He stared helpless as Gabriel rushed to her side and helped her back onto the bed.

"Mina?" Hugh said and peered closely at her.

She turned her blue-green eyes to him. Where they had been filled with laughter and arousal only hours before, they were lifeless now. There were many things he was ashamed of, and things he wished he could take back, but what he wanted most of all was the light back in her eyes.

"All my life I've had to deal with the tongue lashings from Theresa, and having been ignored by my parents," she said. "Then you came. You give me back my brother, and made me see things I had missed before."

She paused and looked down at her hands. "Then you gave me the one thing I have always wanted." She lifted her gaze to him. "You paid attention to me. You gave me hope. Then promptly took it away. I see no reason to help you when I cannot count on your assistance."

He took a step back as the impact of her words hit him. "I didn't take away your hope."

"Forgive me," she said and gave a wry laugh. "I foolishly thought that if anyone would have seen my guiltlessness it would be you. I foolishly thought that after our night in the tunnel, you had seen my innocence. I hadn't realized you could use people like you do."

His throat tightened as if a noose were around him. "I want to believe you are innocent, but you won't give me proof that you are."

Her eyes flared with anger. "You want proof? The day Theresa was attacked I was in the ruins speaking with Aimery."

It was like a punch in the gut. Hugh recalled asking Aimery, and Aimery being vague. How could he have been so stupid as to not see the truth before now? "Why didn't you tell me before?"

She turned away from him and slid down under the covers. "It is too much to want someone to believe me?"

~ ~ ~

Mina flexed her hand and bit her lip from grimacing.

"Don't rush it," Gabriel said. "Let's take a look at it, shall we?"

She held out her arm as he sat on the bed and unwrapped the bandage. The skin around the wounds was tinged with green, but it was now pink.

"They're healing nicely."

"Aye," she said and gazed at the three slashes that went the length of her forearm. She raised her eyes when she felt Gabriel staring at her.

"Things could be worse than having scars," he said.

"You mean like having people think you are controlling a creature that is killing them?"

He sighed as he rubbed more cream on her wounds. "I don't know what happened between you and Hugh, but I can tell you in all the years we have been hunting these evil, vile monsters, he has never been wrong about who is controlling them."

"I've already heard that bit of news."

"There is a first time for everything though." He smiled, and began to put on a new bandage.

She returned his smile. "Hugh doesn't believe me about Aimery does he?"

Gabriel shrugged. "I haven't spoken to him about it since he left this morning."

She glanced to her window and saw the sun lowering. "I can't believe I slept all day. Did the creature come last night?"

"Aye," Gabriel murmured. "Despite the villagers being inside their homes, the beast was still able to get to them."

"How many did it kill?"

"Nearly a dozen, and destroyed several cottages as well as some cattle and sheep."

She leaned her head back and sighed. "It doesn't matter what we do, it always manages to kill."

"You won't be leaving this chamber tonight," Gabriel warned.

"I know. I can't hold the dagger, and I'm too weak to run. What is the plan?"

Again Gabriel shrugged.

She chuckled. "So, Hugh asked that you not tell me."

"Something like that."

The door to her chamber opened, and Hugh filled the space. "Gabriel, I need to speak with Mina alone."

Without a backward glance at her, Gabriel left the chamber. She wanted to call him back, but she knew he wouldn't return. Instead, she took a deep breath and looked to Hugh.

"Why didn't you tell me of Aimery before?" he asked for the second time.

Mina wanted to ignore him, but she couldn't ignore someone like Hugh. He dominated the room and her gaze. She hated that she couldn't look away from his handsome face. "I already told you. I wanted you to believe me because I asked you to."

"I don't do things that way. I have to have proof."

"Then ask Aimery. He'll tell you."

The silence followed that made her apprehension grow.

"I have," Hugh said after a moment.

She swallowed nervously. "And what did he say?"

"He won't deny or agree to being with you."

She began to laugh. "This is just wonderful. I finally tell you the one thing that can prove where I was, and Aimery won't confirm it. So, where does that leave us?"

"I don't know," Hugh said and sighed heavily.

She looked at him and saw the lines of worry around his eyes. "Whether you believe it or not, I would tell you where I put the blue stone if I had it."

"But you don't have it?" he asked.

"Nay."

He looked away and up at the ceiling as though contemplating a great strategy. "I lost track of how many years I've led these men after these creatures. I've killed so many of the evil things that I lost count." He lowered his head and walked to the bed.

"I don't even know how old I am anymore. I have relied on my instincts as the only known source as we traveled through different times. Without trusting those instincts, I am lost."

She lowered her eyes, not able to hold his questioning gaze. "Exactly where were you born?"

"South England, not far from London in the year 1011."

She digested his words and the surprise that followed them. Then she raised her gaze to him. "If I were another person I would say you are daft. But I believe you. Why can't you believe me?"

"Because the facts point to you."

She sighed. "How can I prove my innocence?"

"Help me find the blue stone and the person controlling the creature."

"What if I'm that person? Aren't you afraid I'll attack you?"

He snorted and crossed his arms over his chest. "You could try, but believe me when I say you won't be able to."

She didn't know how to answer him.

"Mina, we saw the stone on your bed while you were at the ruins. Where is it?"

"I already told you I don't have it. It was stolen from my chamber. I walked in here that day to find it on my bed. I immediately went in search of you when I encountered Theresa and she said..."

"What?" he prompted after she fell silent.

Mina recalled Theresa's words with accuracy, and then she remembered the feel of Hugh's hands on her, of how he brought her such pleasure without taking any for himself.

"Her usual insults," she lied. "And I went to the ruins for solace. When I returned to my chamber it was gone."

"The mystery deepens," he said softly. "Will you help us find the stone?"

She watched him for a moment. Despite her heated words, she still longed to feel his lips and hands on her body. He'd hurt her, but she would forgive him in a heartbeat if he but asked.

He was asking her to spend time with him, and even though he still thought her the one controlling the creature, he was giving her a chance to prove him wrong.

"I'll help you."

~ ~ ~

Hugh searched Mina's chamber again with her directing him from the bed. He found hiding spots that he knew no one had discovered earlier, yet there wasn't a blue stone to be found in her chamber.

He straightened from looking through her chest. "The stone isn't here."

She gave him a look that said 'I told you so', but she didn't utter the words.

"The castle is a very big place with lots of hiding places. It could be anywhere."

"The best time to search is at night when everyone is asleep," she said as she swung her legs over the bed.

In two strides, he was beside her. "What do you think you're doing?"

"You don't know this castle like I do. If you want to

find this stone, then you're going to need me."

He clenched his jaw, and was saved from having to answer by a knock on her door.

"Enter," she called while still staring at him.

Gabriel and Cole walked into the chamber.

"What do you think you're doing getting out of bed?" Gabriel asked as he rushed to her and pushed her back onto the bed.

"I'm fine," she argued.

Hugh shook his head. "I don't think you realize how close to death you were."

"Oh, I know exactly how close I was, and I was content to be there. You should have left me."

He was stunned by her words. "It's not your time to die."

"And who are you to decide that? Only God has that authority."

"Actually," Cole started, but Hugh quickly interrupted him.

"Where is Theresa?"

"She's locked herself in her chamber saying that she can't trust anyone anymore, and she refuses to come out until that creature is dead."

"We'll have to find a way to get her out to search her chamber," Mina said.

"That will have to be for last," Hugh said. "There are many other chambers to search first. If we are lucky we'll find it before there is a need to search hers."

"Whoa," Cole said. "What is going on here? Why are we discussing searching chambers?"

Gabriel cocked his head to the side. "I'm thinking it's the blue stone."

Mina gave him a bright smile. "Correct. I'm going to prove I don't have the stone by finding it myself."

"With me by your side," Hugh stated. His protectiveness toward her was growing, and all he could do now was pray that she was innocent, and his plan to get her involved in the search to keep an eye on her worked. His heart couldn't take another betrayal.

"Great. Where do we begin?" Cole asked.

The men looked at Mina as she tried to stand. Hugh reached her before her knees gave out. "You aren't ready yet."

"I can show you places to search," she pleaded. "You need me. We have a pact."

Hugh clenched his jaw tightly. He and his men could move easily throughout the castle, but they needed Mina to guide them, which would be doubly hard since she was still weak.

The ear-splitting scream of the creature ricocheted around the chamber.

"I don't think we have time to think of that right now," Cole said as he looked down the hall. "The castle is already filled with the villagers."

Hugh turned and looked at Mina. "We're going to need parchment and a quill, Cole."

"On my way," said the black-haired warrior.

"And tell no one where you are headed," Mina called after him.

Hugh looked up at the window. "There will be no hunting the creature tonight. We need to plan for tomorrow and tonight."

CHAPTER SIXTEEN

Mina shuddered and drew the blanket around her waist. The weakness from almost dying had taken its toll on her, but she was determined to fight it. She wanted to be there to prove to the Shields she was innocent.

Hugh, Cole and Gabriel sat around her bed as she described the castle in detail and Cole drew. They examined the completed drawing a few hours later after Gabriel had returned with food. They munched on cold meat and bread with the platter of food balanced on her legs.

Though she knew each of them held reservations about believing her, it was nice to have them listening to her as well as willing to take her help.

"Where is Bernard?" she asked.

"He had some castle business to see to," Hugh answered.

Then an idea struck her. "Are you going to bring him in on your search?"

"Of course."

She touched Hugh's arm to get his attention. "You know I love my brother?"

"Aye. What are you getting at?"

"It's because I want to prove my innocence that I have a suggestion."

Hugh leaned back in his chair and crossed his arms over his bulging chest. "I'm listening."

"Search what you can tonight, but only go by yourselves. If you don't find it tonight, we'll search more tomorrow. But, the point is, if you find it, it was by my help. If you don't, you only have me to blame."

"With Mina being the only one knowing we're searching, it would make sense that she would be the only one to keep moving it," Gabriel said. "Good logic."

She smiled at Gabriel, but she waited for Hugh's reply. She wrung her hands and bit her tongue to keep from asking him to answer her now instead of making her wait.

Finally, he leaned forward and said, "It does make sense. I agree. We keep it between us."

"But with us gone, she could easily call someone in here and have it moved," Cole said.

Gabriel sighed. "Aye, that she could."

She looked from one warrior to another. "I wouldn't. I swear."

"What you don't understand," Hugh said, "is that magic is being used. It wouldn't matter if we tied you up, gagged you and locked the chamber door. If it is you, magic can undo all of that."

"Then what do you suggest?" she asked.

"Bring her along," Cole said.

Her eyes brightened. It was just what she wanted.

"She's still injured," Gabriel pointed out.

"If I can walk to the hearth and back without falling can I go?"

Hugh leaned his head back. "I'm going to regret this." He turned his gaze to her. "If you can walk to the hearth and back, without stumbling, you may go."

After Gabriel removed the platter, and Cole had moved the drawings, she shoved the covers off her legs and swung them over the side of the bed.

Hugh was within reaching distance, and it took every ounce of Mina's willpower not to reach out and touch him. She managed to get to her feet without weaving, but now Hugh was so close she could feel his heat.

It brought back powerful memories of their night together, and she felt moisture between her legs. He had done that to her. She glanced his way and found him watching her intently.

She raised her chin and lifted her left foot to begin walking. Her right leg trembled and almost buckled, but she refused to give in to the weakness that consumed her. She would make it to the hearth and back. She wouldn't stumble. She would go with them this night.

There wasn't any other choice. She couldn't be left behind.

One step at a time, she walked steadily to the hearth. When she reached it, she was out of breath and sweat covered her body. All she wanted to do was steady herself, but she wasn't about to do anything that would show them she hurt.

She took a deep breath and slowly turned to face them. She focused her gaze on Hugh, and began the trek back to her bed that seemed as long as the road to London. In order to keep the pain and weakness from taking over, she kept her eyes locked with Hugh's. She became lost in his dark gaze, recalling how they deepened and blazed when passion consumed him.

The next thing she knew, she was standing in front of him as he looked up at her. He reached up and touched a strand of her hair that had fallen over her shoulder. Slowly, he stood until it was she looking up at him.

Their bodies were just a breath away from touching. His heat surrounded her, and her loins ached to feel him touch her again. His gaze darkened as his eyes fell to her lips. Her breasts swelled, and her nipples hardened.

Her lips parted as she waited to taste him again, to be pulled out of her world into a world where only she and Hugh existed.

"You did it," he said softly.

"I did."

Still they stood together not moving. Out of the corner of her eye, she saw his hands rise toward her. He was going to touch her, kiss her. The wonderful pleasure would once again sing through her veins.

But Cole cleared his throat before Hugh could touch her. "Sorry to interrupt, but we don't have a lot of time."

Hugh stepped back and lowered his arms. "Do you need help dressing?"

She almost asked if he would be the one to aid her if she said aye. Instead, she shook her head and reached for the poster of the bed to keep her standing. When the door shut behind the men, she collapsed on the bed and shut her eyes.

She had almost made a fool of herself. Again. Then her eyes opened. She had seen the desire in Hugh's dark eyes, she had seen his breathing quicken.

He had wanted her.

A smile pulled at her lips. Maybe he did care for her a little. With that thought, she rose and began to dress. It proved difficult, especially since she had used almost all of her energy just to walk to the hearth and back. But her life hung in the balance, as well as proving her innocence. She could rest tomorrow. Tonight they would find that cursed blue stone.

Holding on to anything she could grab, she hastily

pulled off her nightgown and reached for a gown. Thankfully, the first one she came to could be fastened in the front. She sat on her trunk and pulled on her shoes. When she was finished, she shook so roughly from her effort she could barely stand.

But stand she would.

She slowly walked to the door and opened it to find all three men waiting for her. "I'm ready," she said, as she tried to tie her annoying hair back out of her face with a navy ribbon that didn't come close to matching her worn, faded navy gown.

"Let me," Hugh said and took the ribbon from her. When he was done, his hands fell to her shoulders, and she had the urge to lean back against his chest.

"Ready?" he asked, and held out his arm for her.

She ignored it and walked past him. "I think we should start in the upper levels first where we are less likely to run into anyone."

"And by the time we reach the lower levels everyone will be asleep," Gabriel finished.

"Exactly." Mina stopped as a thought took root. "What if Bernard comes to check on me?"

"He won't," Cole said.

Mina turned to him. "How do you know?"

Cole looked uncomfortable in the torches lighting the hallway. "He...ah, he has company tonight."

"Company?" she repeated. "We have no guests this night." She looked to Hugh. "Did guests arrive today?"

"Cole is speaking of a woman to warm your brother's bed."

"I see. Shall we continue on?"

"By all means," Hugh said, his eyes twinkling.

She made it to the end of the hallway without collapsing, but her steps had slowed. She waited for Hugh to comment on it, but he continued to keep his silence. When she came to the stairway that would lead them up to the top levels and the two towers, she leaned against the wall to catch her breath.

Hugh had seen enough. He knew it had been a mistake to allow Mina to come, but he had to give her credit. She had courage. Loads of it.

He motioned Cole and Gabriel ahead of him. Once they had started up the stairs, he reached down and picked Mina up in his arms.

"What are you doing?" she asked.

"You wouldn't make it up the stairs, and we both know it."

"Fine," she said. "Once we reach the top, set me down. I'll walk from there."

He didn't answer her. He knew what strength she had was about gone, and they hadn't even begun to search the castle. They would be lucky to finish the search of the upper levels by the time dawn arrived.

Try as he might, he couldn't ignore the soft curves of the warm woman in his arms. He was already hard and wanting from nearly kissing her in her chamber. How she had this effect on him, he would like to know, but he knew he wouldn't get an answer even if there was one.

At the top of the stairs, he found Cole and Gabriel waiting for him. He looked around. To the left was another hallway, shorter than the one below them that led to a few chambers. To the right was the stairway that led to a tower.

"Is there anyone in these chambers?" he asked Mina.

"With the villagers here, I would assume so."

Cole stepped toward the hallway. "Then I suggest we search them before they make their way up here."

Hugh nodded. "How many chambers, Mina?"

"Four."

"Let's hurry then."

He didn't set her down as she had requested, but he noticed she didn't ask him to either. Not that he minded. Actually, he liked having her in his arms. She fit comfortably there, and with her arm wound around his neck and her fingers playing with his hair, it seemed right.

They came to the first chamber. He stood with Mina still in his arms against the wall as Cole knocked on the door. There wasn't an answer. Cole tested the latch and found it open. They left Gabriel to stand watch as they hurried inside.

"I've searched these chambers many times as a child. There are no hidden rooms or moving stones. If the stone is here, it will be easy to find," Mina said.

Hugh sat her on the bed as he and Cole quickly, and effectively, searched the chamber.

"Nothing," Cole said.

Hugh whistled to Gabriel who went to the next chamber while he gathered Mina in his arms. Again, they got lucky and found the chamber empty.

"I wonder where everyone is?" Mina said. "Usually they have retired for the night by now."

"Listen," Gabriel said from the doorway.

They stilled, and heard the beating of the creature's wings as he circled the castle.

"Why isn't he calling out?" she asked.

"The same reason there isn't anyone in the bailey to eat," Cole said.

Hugh sighed. "If we don't come up with a plan, I can almost guarantee the creature will find a way into this castle tomorrow night."

They searched the chamber, but again found nothing. The other two chambers also came up empty. Hugh tried to pick Mina up, but she was already walking down the hallway. He stopped beside her as she stared at the darkened stairway that led to the top of the tower.

"What's up there?" Cole asked.

"An unused chamber. One of my ancestors locked his wife up there when he found her in the arms of one of his knights. She mysteriously died, and no one has been up there since then."

"How long ago was that?"

"About a hundred years. They say the chamber is haunted by her ghost."

Hugh took the torch from Gabriel and elbowed Cole out of the way. "I've seen more than my share of monsters. There isn't anything up there that will scare me."

He started up the stairs and took them two at a time until he came to a closed door. He didn't know why he knocked, but he did.

Just as he expected, there wasn't an answer. He tried the handle, but it was either stuck or locked. Since there were no chains barring the way inside, he figured it was stuck. He put his shoulder against the door and pushed, but it didn't budge.

"You can't get in, can you?"

He looked down to find Mina, Cole and Gabriel behind him. "Nay."

"No one has, not since she died."

"It would seem the perfect place to hide something."

"If one could get in it," she pointed out.

Cold air swiftly surrounded him. Despair, grief and the sudden need to harm someone engulfed him.

"Hugh?" Cole called out.

He heard them, but he couldn't answer. The cold had taken over, and the feelings surrounding him were like a whirlwind of emotions that drained him.

"Get him down," he heard Mina say.

A slap on his face made him jerk his eyes open. He looked at the three in front of him. "What happened?"

"You met the ghost," Mina said. "Trust me, there is nothing up there except her. She allows no one past her door."

"It was worth a try," he said and tried to smile.

"Let's move on," Gabriel said as he helped Hugh to his feet.

It was just fine with him if he never saw that tower again. He brought up the rear as they walked down the hallway to where the other tower was. A shiver ran down his spine, and he turned to see something out of the corner of his eye. But when he tried to focus, there was nothing.

It was time to leave. He could deal with any type of monster, but dealing with ghosts was another matter all together.

He quickened his steps, and easily caught up with Mina. She raised her eyebrow at him as she looked over her shoulder.

"I thought I saw something."

"I'm sure you did," she retorted. "The ghost."

"How come I never heard you mention her before now?"

Mina laughed. "I think I had a few other things on my mind."

He had to give her that one. "Are there other ghosts here that we should know about?"

"Nay. Just the one."

"That's comforting," Cole said.

Hugh had to agree. One was quite enough. They had only gotten halfway down the hallway when Mina began to slow her steps and hang onto the wall. Without a word, Hugh picked her up again.

"I can walk," she said.

"I know."

"Then set me down."

He didn't respond as he caught up with Gabriel and Cole who had walked ahead of them.

She leaned close and whispered. "I don't want them to think I'm weak."

"They don't."

She lowered her eyes. "They will."

He noticed she winced slightly. "Are you in pain?"

"Nay," she answered a little too quickly.

He whistled to his men to slow them down and asked Mina, "How much farther to the other tower?"

"Within another twenty or thirty steps we will come to it."

Gabriel held the torch near her. "I knew it was a bad idea to bring her. If she doesn't rest she'll get a fever."

"I'm fine," she argued.

But Hugh only listened to Gabriel. He looked out the window above them just as the creature flew at it. They all jumped back. Hugh immediately turned to protect Mina as they creature screamed in fury at not being able to reach them. It flew away, and they hurriedly walked away from the window.

"We have to kill that damn beast," Cole thundered.

Gabriel snorted. "Without the blue stone it's pointless."

"Why?" Mina asked

"Because whoever has control of the blue stone can call another one," Hugh answered.

She sighed and laid her head on his shoulder. "All my life I wanted adventure, and now I just want to be able to walk outside at night without dodging this thing."

Hugh stood against the wall and thought for a moment. "Gabriel, you and Cole continue to scour around up here. You have the map of the castle that Mina described for us."

"What are you going to do?" Cole asked.

"I'm going to take Mina back to her chamber so she can rest."

The men nodded and hurried off.

"I'll be fine," Mina said.

"I know you will because you'll be in your bed."

Mina knew quarreling with him was futile. Not only did she know he would win, but she didn't have the strength to keep up the argument.

When he entered her chamber, he quickly put her in her bed and gave her more of the herbal mixture Gabriel made her drink several times a day. She drank it all and leaned back on her pillows.

"How do you feel?"

"Better," she said, hating that he was right. "I wanted to help find the stone."

"You will," he said as he paced the chamber. "I have a feeling the stone isn't in the castle."

She raised her head and watched him. "Then why are we looking here?"

"Just in case."

She watched as his forehead furrowed. "It would be easier to kill the creature and find the stone with Val and Roderick here, wouldn't it?"

"Much. But, Aimery had need of them."

"And you don't?"

He stopped his pacing and looked at her. "I learned long ago that it is pointless to try and change a Fae's mind. They know what they are doing."

"You trust them that much?"

"I have to. I owe them my life."

She let that bit of information sink in. "How are you going to kill the creature?"

"I think it's time that we tried the trap you were using

the night we came."

She bit her lip. "You think it might actually work?"

"It's worth a try. Now," he said as he took the chair beside her bed, "I need you to tell me exactly how you had it planned. Down to every detail."

CHAPTER SEVENTEEN

Mina rubbed her tired, itchy eyes. She had gotten little sleep between planning the creature's trap, and the creature itself continuing to fly around the castle screaming its rage and banging against the castle.

At first, she'd been afraid that it might actually try and come into the castle, but when it did nothing more than bang against the castle doors, she knew how silly her thoughts had been.

"You're going to need to rest today," Hugh said.

She turned her head to find him stretching. His long, brown hair was messy, and dark whiskers littered his cheeks and neck. She yearned to run her hands over his face and feel the stubble. "So do you."

"I'm used to getting little sleep, but this is the second night in a row you haven't slept."

She looked around her small chamber. "I thought Cole and Gabriel had returned?"

"They did. They have other duties."

She knew he was keeping something from her. She opened her mouth to question him, but Bernard chose that moment to walk into her chamber.

"You're looking better," he said and leaned down to kiss her forehead.

She smiled. How long had she wanted to be a part of the family, and she was finally getting one of her greatest desires. "I feel better."

"You had us all worried." He nodded to Hugh, then turned back to her. "Do you remember anything of your attacker?"

She shook her head. "The only person that attacked me is Theresa, and everyone saw that."

"She didn't have a weapon, or we'd have seen that as well," Bernard said as he leaned his shoulder against the bedpost.

"I'll leave you two alone," Hugh said and moved to exit the chamber.

She didn't want him to leave, but there was no reason for him to stay. She watched him walk from her chamber, then turned toward her brother.

"You like him," Bernard said.

She laughed. "He is the first man to really look at me."

"I doubt that."

"My own betrothed wanted Theresa instead of me. She put aside her betrothed for mine."

"Your betrothed was stupid."

She laughed. "I wish we had talked like this years ago. It would have been nice to have a friend and be a part of the family."

"Let's not dwell on the past," he said and gave her a smile meant to charm. "We have each other now, and if Theresa doesn't come around, we'll just ignore her."

~ ~ ~

Hugh yawned and scratched his neck as he rose from

his bed. He'd tried to rest, but there was too much going on for him to get any sleep. He hadn't been able to eat any of his morning meal with Theresa's incessant prattle. She was either yelling about Mina or trying to seduce him. Frankly, he'd had enough. He wanted to order her to her chamber, but it wasn't his castle. He was merely a guest, and while there, he had to keep a smile on his face and be amiable.

But, damn, it was becoming impossible to do.

He had no idea how Mina had managed to survive her entire life under the same roof as Theresa. He knew he would have throttled Theresa years ago. The fact that he was beginning to relate to Mina showed him that he had grown too close to her, and he pushed his growing irritation at how Bernard constantly touched and kissed her aside. He was her brother after all.

There had been many times while he led his men that he had found himself attracted to women. It had only taken that one time of finding himself involved with a lady who had been controlling the creatures to make him see he needed to keep his distance. That act had nearly cost him and his men their lives. He refused to allow that to happen again. Too much was at stake, especially if the Fae queen was right.

He put his head in his hands, and the image of Mina as he brought her to orgasm flashed in his mind. He squeezed his eyes shut, and tried to think of something else, but all he saw was her eyes glazed with desire and her mouth open on a groan.

A bath. He would take a bath and let the warm, soothing water wash away his troubles, if only for a short time. But no sooner had he grabbed fresh clothes, than he remembered when Mina had come into the bathing chamber.

His cock pulsed with need. By the saints, he needed

some relief.

He focused on their upcoming plan to kill the creature, and headed to the bathing chamber. When he reached it, he saw the door opening, and for a moment, he thought it might be Mina. But it turned out to only be a servant. He recalled seeing her around the castle. She was tall with kind gray eyes.

"Is the chamber empty?" he asked.

She opened her mouth, then stopped and looked at the door. "Aye, my lord, it's empty," she said with a smile and hurried away.

"Peculiar," he mumbled, and opened the door only to stop in his tracks.

In the giant wooden tub with her back to him sat Mina. Her strawberry-blonde hair was piled atop her head, and her bandaged arm rested on the side of the tub. She hummed softly to herself as she squeezed a sponge of water on her neck.

His already aching groin grew heavy and tight as he caught glimpses of her breasts as she raised her arm. Control was something that had always come easy to him, but now he was finding that it had abandoned him. He fought to keep his feet right where they were instead of walking to the tub and dragging her out of it to mold her soft, wet body to his.

His mouth became dry as he imagined kissing her heated skin to skim down to her full breasts. She would lean her head back and moan softly as he took a taunt nipple in his mouth.

He closed his eyes and begged for the power to walk away. But his feet didn't budge. The clothes he had gripped tightly in his hand dropped to the floor as he stepped toward her.

~ ~ ~

Mina swirled the water around with her finger as she summoned the memory of Hugh at his bath. He was the type of man that made a woman want to rely on him, but she knew there was only one person she could truly rely on...herself. Life had shown her that the hard way, and she wasn't about to forget the lessons she had learned.

It had been easy to stay away from men such as Hugh, but then he had arrived and claimed all her thoughts while she was awake, and even some as she slept. He wanted her trust, and to her surprise, she had easily given it. It didn't help that he had shown her pleasures that would haunt her for the rest of her days.

She continued to hum as it had always soothed her. She heard movement behind her, and thought it was a servant. She didn't wish her thoughts to be disturbed, so she didn't speak or turn around.

With her head leaned back against the tub, she closed her eyes and let herself daydream. It was a beautiful daydream of she and Hugh married and starting a family. She would be happy, cherished, and loved.

In what realm are you living in?

She laughed at her own imaginings, and sat up to begin her bath. That was the way it was with her, she always dreamed too big. She knew by now that things like that didn't happen to people like her. This was her lot in life, and she had survived this long, she would survive once Hugh was gone.

She would have to.

The water stilled, and it was then that she saw Hugh's reflection in the water as he stood behind her. Her stomach clenched tightly as excitement unfurled within her.

She watched as his hand reached up and loosened her hair. It fell around her and into the water. His image distorted for a moment, and when the water stilled again he was gone. She closed her eyes and fought the cruelty of it all. But when she opened her eyes he was once again behind her.

"I shouldn't be here," he said, his voice low and husky.

"Nay," she whispered.

"I should leave."

"Nay."

His hands came to rest on her shoulders as he slowly turned her to him. His dark eyes sizzled with desire, and the ache between her legs began. Her lips parted as she dropped her eyes to his mouth.

"You're going to be the death of me," he murmured as he lowered his head to her.

"It's such a sweet death."

He smiled. "You only know a part of it."

"Then show me the rest."

"Ah, but you tempt me."

She gathered her courage and stood. She watched as his eyes moved down her as the water dripped from her body.

"By the saints, woman, you are magnificent."

"As long as you think so."

His eye jerked to her face. "I cannot be here."

"But you are."

He touched her cheek, then moved his hand to the back of her neck. His touch was soft, but firm as it scorched her skin.

She licked her lips and heard him groan. The boldness that had never resided in her suddenly sprang to life. She lifted a hand and trailed it from his throat down his chest to the waist of his trousers. How she wished he were as naked as she. She wanted to see every inch of his skin.

That thought was thrown aside as he drew her closer and closer until their bodies touched and he molded her to the hard planes of his body.

His mouth descended on hers, and his tongue delved deep and rapid as he kissed her as if he hadn't kissed a woman in a hundred years. She tasted his hunger that only fanned the flames of her own desire. When his hand trailed down her back to cup her buttocks, she moaned and moved closer to him.

She couldn't stand much more of this. She needed him. Desperately. "Hugh," she whispered as she moved her mouth to his neck.

"St. Christopher," he moaned and leaned her back so he could suck on her breasts.

Mina raked her fingers across his broad shoulders as his tongue scraped across her nipples. He straightened her and took her mouth again. This time, she wound her arms tightly around his neck, and let the fire of their passion consume her.

His rod pressed against her stomach, and she had the sudden urge to feel him. The fact that she had almost died made her realize that she couldn't stand in the background anymore, she needed to take what she wanted.

Before she changed her mind, she unwound her fingers from his hair and trailed a hand across his broad shoulders, and down his thick chest and chiseled abdomen until her hand rested at his waist. She took a deep breath, and moved her hand until his thick, hard arousal rested against her hand.

He gasped and ended the kiss. She looked up to find his jaw clenched and his eyes tightly shut.

"Mina," he whispered as though he was in great pain.

She immediately let go.

"Nay," he groaned. He opened his eyes, and she saw his yearning flare. "Touch me again. Know me as I have known you."

It was all the encouragement she needed. Her hand

once again found him, and she was amazed at the length of him, hot and hard, even through his trousers.

His mouth blazed a trail of tingling kisses along her neck as she continued to move her hand over him, but it wasn't enough. She wanted to see him, and touch him, without clothes between them.

"I want to see you," she whispered as she closed her hand around his manhood.

He moaned and pressed against her.

"I hope I'm not interrupting anything...pressing."

Hugh felt Mina tense in his arms as he ended the kiss. He leaned his forehead against her. "It's not meant to be, love."

He turned and shielded her from Aimery's eyes. "What do you want?"

"We need to talk."

Hugh nodded, and in a blink, Aimery disappeared. He turned back to Mina to find her sitting in the water. He shook from his desire, and the flush on her cheeks and her swollen lips didn't help him find the calm he needed. "I cannot keep away from you."

"Is that a bad thing?" she asked, as she nonchalantly rinsed her arm.

"For me it is. For you as well. I'll be leaving soon. You deserve more than that."

"You mean if I'm innocent."

He shut his eyes for a moment. "It isn't my intention to hurt you. I usually have complete control over myself."

She nodded and turned away from him, but not before he saw the tears in her eyes. He hated when women cried. Damn. He really hadn't planned to hurt her, but it seemed that was what he was forever doing.

He sighed, wanting nothing more than to sink into her tight sheath and lose himself in her heat, but he knew that

Aimery would only come if it was important. Hugh hurried from the chamber, his clothes and the bath forgotten, as he went in search of the Fae commander.

CHAPTER EIGHTEEN

Hugh stalked to his chamber where he was sure he would find Aimery. He wasn't wrong.

"Sorry for interrupting," the Fae said as Hugh shut the door.

"Nay. I'm glad you did. I had no business kissing her."

Aimery laughed. "You are a strong man I'll give you that, Hugh. But I know something you don't."

"What is that?," Hugh murmured and leaned against the door.

"You can fight the demons inside you, and you can fight the creatures that roam this world, but you cannot fight lust...or love."

Hugh fought the urge to roll his eyes. "Over the years you have trained us, guided us and even helped us. Never, in all that time, have you given us guidance when it came to our own lives. Not even when that bitch I was sharing my bed with controlled the creatures. Why now?"

The Fae shrugged and ran his hand down the burgundy material that hung around Hugh's bed. "Would you have listened to me had I warned you about that woman?"

Hugh started to say he would, but then stopped.

"I knew even then you wouldn't listen," Aimery said. "Now is not any different, but I thought I would try."

Hugh raked his hand through his hair. "Just tell me if she is innocent. Tell me if she was with you."

"I cannot."

"Cannot or will not?"

Aimery lifted a shoulder. "Take your pick."

Rage simmered just below the surface. Hugh fisted his hands and itched to wrap them around the Fae's neck. "I don't know why I bother."

"None of that matters now. Have you found a way to kill the creature?"

"Mina designed a trap that I think will work."

"Then I pray it does," he said and disappeared.

Hugh blew a breath out of his mouth. He had a feeling Aimery had intentionally interrupted him and Mina, and frankly he owed the Fae a debt of thanks for that. He needed to focus his mind on the creature and the blue stone. Everything else needed to be set aside.

~ ~ ~

Mina bit her lip and looked into the mirror. Her hair was loose around her shoulders and fell nearly to her waist. She rarely let it down because it got in the way, but she liked the way Hugh played with it.

The pink gown she wore was a couple of years out of fashion, but she loved the way the soft material clung to her body and molded her breasts. She wrapped her newer braided leather belt around her waist and hips, and let the ends fall down the front to her knees.

She raised her gaze and looked at herself. The pink brought out more of the red in her hair. She had never liked her hair much, but over the past couple of days she had paid more attention to it. When she was with Hugh, she felt pretty.

"Ah," she said and pushed away from the mirror.

Hugh had said it best. He would leave once the creature was dead, and she would fall into her silent world once again. She needed to put some distance between them, and most of all, she needed to keep from being alone with him. The temptation to taste his lips was too great.

She had always known she was weak, she just didn't realize how much until he had come along. All those years of telling herself she didn't need anyone was a lie. Hugh had proven that. In the end, it would just be her, and she knew she could survive. Gertie, her mother's nurse, had taught her all she needed to know. It was time she remembered Gertie's words.

With her resolve in place, she walked from her chamber and slowly made her way into the great hall. She ran her gaze around the hall and noticed that not many were about. It was midmorning, and the people had returned to their homes.

She expected to find Hugh sitting at the dais, but he wasn't there. Her stomach growled, reminding her why she had ventured from her chamber. She made her way to the kitchen and grabbed some bread and cheese. She didn't think her stomach could handle anything heavier.

The weakness from the night before still assaulted her, but she was determined to get past it. By the time she sat down at one of the tables, she was shaking from the exertion.

"You should be abed," Gabriel said as he sat across from her.

"There is too much to do for me to stay there."

The corners of his mouth titled up in a smile. "Where is Hugh?"

"I thought he was with you. Aimery came to see him this morning."

"He must be with him then."

Gabriel raised his hand, and she looked over her shoulder to find Cole walking toward them.

"Are you feeling better?" Cole asked as he sat beside her.

"Some."

Gabriel snorted. "She's going to make it worse if she doesn't take it easy."

"It won't matter if we don't kill the creature," she pointed out. "I take it you didn't find anything last night?"

"Nothing," Cole said. "Hugh showed us the design for the trap. I think it might work."

She beamed at his compliment. "Thank you."

He smiled in return.

"So," she said, "which one of you is to watch over me while Hugh is occupied."

Both men refused to meet her gaze. "Surely not the both of you?"

"Nay," Cole finally spoke. "I have other orders."

She turned her gaze to Gabriel. "You're the one stuck with me."

"I don't find it hard to be around you, my lady."

She chuckled. "No one has called me that since my betrothed."

"It's what you are, and they should treat you with that respect."

She cocked her head to the side and studied him. His silver eyes intrigued her. She had never seen the like before. "I'm glad you all came here."

Cole excused himself just moments before Theresa entered the hall. She took one look at Mina and made straight for her. Mina sighed and waited for the verbal onslaught. But it never came.

She looked up to find Cole escorting Theresa to the kitchens. With food in her stomach, Mina felt her strength return, and rose to walk outside.

"I'm not sure that's wise," Gabriel said as he placed a hand on her elbow and walked from the castle by her side.

"It's a good thing you'll be there to catch me if I faint then," she said with a smile.

"Don't even tease about that. Hugh would have my head if he caught you in my arms."

She laughed, thinking him jesting her, but one look at his stern features told her it was the truth. Never would she understand men. Her feet took her leisurely around the bailey. Where once it was filled with laughter and children playing, there was subdued silence and the threat of death on the air.

It pained her to see her home turned into this. "Why are the creatures being released?"

"That is something I cannot tell you."

She had expected Gabriel to answer in such a way. "It must be a lonely way of life."

"We don't have time to become lonely."

She snorted very unladylike. "Pigs wallop."

He laughed.

She stopped in her tracks and stared at him. "That's the first time I've heard you laugh."

"In our line of work, there isn't much to laugh about."

She nodded and started to turn away when something on one of the castle towers caught her eye.

"What is it?" Gabriel asked and turned to see what had drawn her gaze. "It is only a gargoyle. They are meant to keep away evil spirits."

"I know," she said slowly. "They scare me."

"Then it's doing its job."

She turned her gaze to him. "Hugh said the same thing."

~ ~ ~

The day passed entirely too slowly for Mina. She caught glimpses of Hugh as he took Bernard and some of their knights to the forest to set the trap. She and Gabriel searched more of the castle, but discovered nothing, much to her frustration.

She found herself gazing out the windows to try and catch sight of Hugh when he returned. Both she and Gabriel became worried as the sun began its descent and Hugh had yet to return.

"Hugh will make you stay," Gabriel stated as she braided her hair.

"Then he will be the one, not you."

For the past hour, she had listened to Gabriel ramble about how she was still too weak to venture out, and a woman should know her place. She was becoming so annoyed she could pinch his head off, or at the very least, throw a loaf of bread at him.

"I'll make sure of it."

She rolled her eyes and slid her feet into her boots. Once again she had dragged out her man's attire. Her gowns and skirts would be too cumbersome with what she needed to do tonight.

A knock sounded on her chamber door. Gabriel opened it just as she straightened from adjusting her boot.

"Tell me you weren't in here while she dressed," Hugh said dangerously as he glared at Gabriel.

Mina closed her eyes and prayed for patience. "Of course he wasn't."

Hugh looked at her then. His dark eyes raked over her,

and her body instantly reacted.

"My day was boring," she said and walked to him as she noted the padded jerkin over his sky blue tunic. "Thank you for asking."

One side of his wide mouth lifted in a grin. "I see you're in a fit mood."

"With my bodyguard always near to catch me if I fall," she said and smiled sweetly. "I've had a wonderful day."

Hugh's eyes snapped to Gabriel. "What did you do?"

"You must be jesting?" Gabriel said to the ceiling. He turned to Mina. "See what you've done? Fix it. Now."

"Do not threaten her," Hugh warned and took a step toward him.

Gabriel threw up his hands and turned away.

Mina watched Hugh closely. Why was he so protective of her? Could it be he lied, and that he did care for her a little?

"I was teasing," she said. "Gabriel was a perfect gentleman."

Hugh stared at her a moment, then turned to Gabriel. He held out his arm. "Once again, I must apologize."

Gabriel clasped his arm. "Don't think twice about it."

"Did you find anything?" Hugh asked.

She and Gabriel shook their heads. "Nothing," she said. "Did you finish the trap?"

"Aye. It's ready and waiting for the creature."

She smiled. "Good. Shouldn't we head out?"

For a moment, she thought Hugh would also tell her she had to stay behind. She refused to allow that to happen.

"You have limited men," she reminded him. "The knights need to be here as well to watch over the people. You cannot afford to leave me behind. Besides, I've kept myself alive before you arrived. I know how to take care of myself."

He moved to stand beside her. "You aren't well enough yet."

"I have drunk Gabriel's herbal four times today. I even took a nap this afternoon so that I would be rested for tonight. I walked the bailey this morning, and this entire castle after the noon meal in search of that stone."

Still he stared at her.

"Don't leave me behind," she begged. "I need to go."

"If anything happens to you..."

"It won't. I swear."

He nodded, and it was all she could do not to throw herself into his arms.

~ ~ ~

Hugh sat atop his horse in the clearing as he waited for any sound of the creature. He had stationed Mina beside Gabriel and Bernard. He didn't want to take any chances with her life.

His horse's ears pricked forward, and he tossed his great head. It was the signal Hugh needed to let him know the creature was coming. It was a testament to what his mount had seen that kept the horse calm as they waited for the evil.

Total silence surrounded them except for the occasional snort from one of the horses. The creature was near. Very near. Hugh began to turn to check on Mina, when a shadow out of the corner of his eye made him turn forward.

His mount reared just as the beast lunged at him. Hugh fell to the ground, and immediately rolled to his feet with his sword in one hand and his crossbow in the other. But the creature was gone.

He stood still and listened, but there was no flap of

wings or the eerie scream. He looked at his feet to see his faithful mount.

"Nay," he said and fell to his knees beside his mount. He gently patted his horse's neck. The animal had saved his life by rearing up, but in doing so, had given his. The horse was the only constant in his life, the only thing he had allowed himself to become attached to.

"I'm going to miss you," he said.

He grabbed his sword and crossbow. The creature would pay for this. His horse had been a good, faithful friend to the very end.

"Enough of this," Hugh roared to the trees. "I know you can understand me. Let's finish this, you and me!"

Before he had finished his sentence, the beast landed in front of him, a smirk on his evil, pointed face. "I thought that might get your attention, Demon Seeker," the creature said in a hissing voice.

"Who controls you?"

The creature laughed evilly. "Do you think I am that dim-witted? The ones before me might not have been able to speak, but we have always been able to understand your words."

Hugh digested the new information and prayed Aimery could hear it. "How much do you know?"

"Everything."

"Why didn't you kill me before?"

"I was told to leave you be. You are wanted by someone."

"Me?" Hugh repeated. Who, or what, could want him?

"And her," the creature said as he looked over Hugh's shoulder.

Hugh breathed in deeply to calm his racing heart. "So your master wants both of us. Why?"

"That is not meant for you to know."

"At least tell me why your master wants Mina," he said.

"I've had enough talk. You wanted a fight, and I am more than ready to give you what you want."

Hugh barely had a chance to duck and roll before the creature lunged at him.

"I suppose I should tell you that your weapons won't kill me," the creature said as he spiraled toward the heavens then stopped and stared down at him.

Hugh looked at the trees where he needed to lead the creature, and then to his dead horse. He doubted he could make it there on foot, but he had to try. He began to run toward the trees and didn't look back.

He heard the flap of wings behind him an instant before he was thrown forward. He lost his hold on his crossbow when he landed on his shoulder. He got to his feet and continued to run, but the creature once again knocked him forward.

His entire body ached, as did the new cuts on his back and arms. He rolled to his side and tried to get to his feet when the creature landed beside him and put a foot on him.

"You are finished," the beast hissed.

"I thought you were supposed to leave me be?" Hugh asked.

"That is what one master wants."

Hugh stared at the forked tongue and red eyes and knew it was over. He had failed.

"I think you would rather have me," he heard Mina yell.

Both he and the creature looked to where Mina stood near the trees. Hugh held onto the hope that she had enough strength to make it.

The creature immediately flew at her, its scream echoing through the forest. Hugh rose up on his elbow as he reached for his sword, and saw Mina take off toward the trees. He got to his feet just as she shouted to Cole and

Gabriel. They released the log they had sharpened to a deadly point and hidden in the branches of the tree.

"Duck," he called out to Mina as the log flew out of the trees toward the beast.

He watched as Mina rolled out of the way before the log impaled itself through the creature. It fell to the ground withering and crying out in pain.

Hugh waited for it to explode as the others had done when they died, but this one continued to scream and claw at the log. It wasn't going to die.

He ran to Mina. "Where is your horse?"

"There," she pointed to the left.

"Get on it," he said and pushed her toward it. "Ride!" he called to his men.

He started to run through the forest when Mina rode up beside him.

"Get on," she said.

Hastily, he mounted behind her and nudged the horse into a run. They started yelling before they left the forest for the gate to be opened. He looked over his shoulder and found all the men on their horses following close.

Then, he saw the creature fly above the trees. They would be lucky to reach the bailey before it struck. The horse's hooves banged loudly as they crossed under the gatehouse and ran the horses into the stable.

"This won't hold it," Mina said as she dismounted.

"Spread out," Hugh called. "Make your way to the castle as quickly as you can."

He pushed Mina into an empty stall as the creature flew above the stable. After he had run to both ends of the stable and bolted the doors, he waited for the attack. He and Gabriel had spent the past two days fortifying the stable in case something like this should happen.

Never before had he been so happy to be prepared. He

walked to Mina and looked down into her frightened face. His bloodlust begin to take over as it always did in battle.

"Find Gabriel. He'll take you to the castle."

She stared at him, her face showing her confusion and determination. "I'm not leaving your side."

"Mina," he warned and looked away from her. "You don't understand."

She pulled his head toward her. "I'm not leaving you."

CHAPTER NINETEEN

Hugh had to make her understand. He closed his eyes and fought the growing need for physical release that battle always brought. He opened his eyes and took her by the shoulders. "Leave now, because if you don't, I can't promise I'll keep my hands off you."

"I'm not leaving," she repeated, never looking away from his gaze.

He shoved her too roughly against the wall and gazed into her blue-green gaze. There was no fear now, only...desire.

And God help him, it sent him over the edge. He took her mouth and thrust his tongue inside to duel with hers. She wound her arms around his neck and plunged her hands into his hair. He growled and pushed his body hard against hers.

Mina eagerly gave herself to Hugh. The strange light in his eyes should have frightened her, but it didn't, it only added to her growing passion. The ache between her legs had only intensified since that morning, bringing a burning need she could neither deny nor ignore. She needed him as she needed air.

His body pressed her against the wall, pinning her to his solid form. She couldn't feel much of him through his padded jerkin, but she wasn't about to break the kiss to remove his clothes.

Yet.

She groaned when he moved away from her and ended the kiss. Her eyes opened to see his hand braced on the wall above her head, his breathing harsh and ragged. She saw how he held himself in check. Barely.

"Last chance, Mina."

In answer, she untied her tunic and pulled it over her head. He growled and dragged her roughly against him. The padded jerkin was warm against her bare skin. Horses snorted and moved around the stables as the creature continued to fly overhead, screaming in anger.

But all of that faded as she succumbed to Hugh's luscious mouth. She moved her hands from his shoulders to her trousers where she quickly unlaced them.

Her breath locked in her lungs as he bent down and trailed kisses from her mouth to her neck to her breasts. He fell to his knees, and teased her nipples with his fingers and tongue. She took hold of his head to keep him just as he was, but he had other plans. He kissed down her stomach to tickle her navel with his hot tongue.

She grabbed hold of the stable wall for support when his hands began to move her trousers down her legs. He quickly removed her boots, and the trousers soon followed until she stood naked before him.

No man had ever seen her thus, and she knew no man would again. Whatever might happen tomorrow, tonight she was Hugh's.

And he was hers.

She let his eyes roam freely over her. His hot, passionate gaze made her shaky with longing. She felt the moisture between her legs, the hunger for more of him fanning the flames of her desire. She couldn't stand not touching him a moment longer. She moved to him, and together they quickly shed his clothes.

When he stood before her without a shred of clothing to hide him from her view, she stepped back and finally got to feast her eyes on him. He was magnificent. Tall, muscled, and every bit the warrior. His legs bulged with sinew, and the hard ridges of his stomach contracted when she touched him.

She traced a scar on his shoulder, and walked behind him letting her hand trail after her. She caressed his sculpted back, making sure not to touch his new wounds, and down to his firm buttocks.

He spun around so fast she barely had time to catch her breath.

"I cannot take much more," he said before he yanked her to him and captured her mouth.

Hugh had waited as long as he could for Mina to look at him, but the feel of her soft hands against him was his undoing. His blood swelled with need, and the very woman who had driven him mad with desire was naked before him.

He could wait no longer.

He told himself to be gentle, but his bloodlust was too far gone. He picked her up, and she wrapped her lean legs around his waist as he pushed her against the wall. She moaned and whispered his name between their frantic, fiery kisses.

His cock could feel her hot, sleek moisture. He tried to tell himself to go slow, that she was an innocent, but his hunger for her drove him ever onward.

The blunt head of his arousal slid into her hot, wet core. He wanted to plunge inside her, to seat himself fully. But somehow he pulled out, and slid back inside her. Again and again he rocked his hips back and forth, gaining entrance farther each time until her maidenhead stopped him.

Hugh held her hips tightly as he pulled out of her. He hated to hurt her, but the quicker he broke through her maidenhead, the better. In one hard thrust, he filled her.

Mina's scream of pain locked in her throat as her body stretched to accommodate Hugh's long, hard length. The pain had diminished her desire, and just when she thought it was finished, he moved within her.

Her nails sank into his back, the passion rushing through her instantly. Her world was spinning, and Hugh was at its center, urging her body to answer his primal call. She was powerless to deny him. Her body was his to do as he wished, his to take.

His to claim.

With each thrust of his arousal inside her, she felt her body tightening, reaching for that place of bliss he had taken her just a few nights earlier. She wanted to move against him, but his powerful hands kept her in place.

Mina squeezed her legs to grip him tighter. His low groan made her blood burn hotter in her veins, made her body quake, as he drove deeper, faster, harder inside her.

Sweat glistened on his skin, his breathing harsh to her ears. A moan escaped her lips as he whispered her name like a caress upon her skin. Her body grew taut, each fiber within her stretched thin as if her skin could barely hold her together.

She could feel herself drawing closer and closer to that wonderful decadence, and Mina reached for it. Until she came apart, lights flashing behind her lids as pure pleasure rippled through her.

Hugh felt Mina's sex clench around him, heard her soft cry as she peaked. And that's all it took for his climax to claim him. He gave one last thrust, burying deep within her, as his seed spilled from his body into hers.

He held tight until the last tremor had left her body.

With her head on his shoulder, he pulled out of her and lowered them to the hay. He kissed her forehead as she snuggled against him. In moments, her breathing evened into sleep, and he wasn't long in following, his body sated as never before.

~ ~ ~

Mina awoke with a smile on her face. Something tickled her nose, and it wasn't until she opened her eyes that she found herself lying on Hugh's chest. Images of the night before flashed in her mind.

Her smiled deepened. She finally found out what it was to be a woman, and by the most handsome man she had ever known.

She looked down to find their fingers entwined, and for some reason, that gave her pause. Slowly, she sat up and disengaged their hands. She missed his warmth already, but the sounds of the bailey had begun to reach her, and she needed to get inside the castle.

When she turned around, she found a pail of water and a rag. She knew John had left it. She would have to thank the lad later. After she had taken the pail and her clothes to another stall so as not to wake Hugh, she hurriedly washed off. The sight of her virgin's blood did not bother her, and in fact, proved that she hadn't dreamed last eve.

Once her clothes were on, she cast one last look at Hugh. Even in sleep, he was gorgeous. She itched to run her hands along his warm bronzed skin and see his rod harden by her caress.

Before she did just that, she turned and walked from

the stable.

~ ~ ~

Hugh came awake with a start, but didn't open his eyes. He felt the rough hay beneath him, but knew something was wrong. He opened his eye a slit and looked around. The stable.

It was then he recalled what had happened. Or at least he thought he did, until he sat up and saw his nakedness.

"Mina," he whispered as he looked down at the hay stained with her blood and his semen. "Mina," he called out, hoping she was still in the stable.

But it wasn't Mina that ran into the stall. It was John.

"Has Lady Mina left?"

The lad nodded and pointed to the other side of the stall. Hugh got to his feet to see what John pointed to. That is where he saw the water and rag.

He sighed and patted John's head. "Thank you," he said as he made use of the water.

Once dressed, he hurried from the stable in search of Mina. He had to talk to her. He could only recall fragments of their night together, but if he had done what he thought he did, he should take a lash to himself. No woman deserved her first time that way, but especially not Mina.

His steps faltered and stopped before he reached the castle doors. Would she hate him? Scream at him? Probably, and he deserved much more than that. He had never treated a woman like that. Usually he stayed far away from anyone, especially women, when the bloodlust came upon him.

"There you are," Gabriel said as he walked from the castle. "I've been looking for you."

"Why?" His face must have mirrored his misgivings,

because Gabriel narrowed his eyes at him.

"I wanted to make sure you were still alive after last night. Is there something you need to tell me?"

Hugh ran his hand down his face. "Have you seen Mina?"

"I thought she was with you last night in the stable. That's what I told Bernard," Gabriel said his arms now crossed over his chest. "The baron wasn't happy to learn that tidbit."

"She was. Now answer me."

"Aye," he said. "I saw her come into the castle and head for her chamber. Did you hurt her last night?"

"I pray I didn't," he said and moved past him.

Gabriel caught up with him. "What happened?"

Hugh refused to answer, but it didn't take Gabriel long to figure it out. He cursed and put his hand out to stop him.

"Hugh," he started.

"Don't," Hugh stopped him. "I'll deal with it."

"Not right now you won't," said a voice Hugh could have gone all day without hearing.

He turned and faced Aimery. "What now?"

"You've been called to court."

"What? Why?" The only time he had been into the Fae realm was when he had first taken on the assignment of becoming a Shield.

"You can ask the queen when we get there," Aimery said before he disappeared and took Hugh with him.

~ ~ ~

Hugh stared at the blue and white checkered floor. It was the same bright blue as the stone they hunted, he realized. The last time he'd been in the Fae realm, he had begged to stay and look more at the beautiful wonders that made up their world, but there hadn't been time.

Now was no different.

He and Aimery appeared inside the palace to stand in front of the throne of the king of the Fae. Hugh glanced at Aimery, but the Fae patiently waited for the king and queen to appear.

Hugh looked around the giant room. The ceiling was so high that it looked as though it were open to the sky with its painting of blue with white clouds. The walls of the palace were painted with pictures of the Faerie history, some terrible battles, peaceful gatherings, and the crowning of kings.

The sound of heels hitting the unusual floor drew his attention. He turned to find the royal couple making their way toward him.

"It is good to see you again," the king said cordially as he stopped in front of Hugh.

Hugh went down on one knee and bowed his head. "Sire."

"Come, Hugh, we have much to discuss," the king said and pulled him to his feet.

Hugh stood to find Rufina before him. "My queen," he said and raised her hand to his lips.

"Ever the charmer," she said and followed Theron.

Aimery slapped Hugh on the back. "I don't know why, but they both like you."

"As the queen said, I'm a charmer."

Hugh's smiled died when he saw they were headed into the chamber behind their thrones. That meant whatever they wished to discuss was extremely important.

~ ~ ~

Mina found Gabriel in the bailey looking around as if he'd lost something. "Take me to the monastery."

"Now?"

"Now," she said and walked to the stable.

"I don't think that wise."

She stopped and looked at him. "Why? The creature isn't about during the day."

"It isn't that," he edged and reached for her arm. "Let me take a look at this."

"Then what is it?" When he wouldn't answer, she moved so that he had to look at her while he unwrapped her bandage. "What aren't you telling me? Has Hugh told you to keep me here?"

Gabriel shook his head and looked closely at her arm. "Actually, I'm waiting on Hugh. It's looking much better," he said of her arm. "The green tint is completely gone."

"Good, then he can go with us," she said as Gabriel rewrapped the bandage on her arm. "Where is he?"

"I still don't want you overexerting yourself. The dark magic used on you isn't something I've dealt with before."

"Gabriel," she said slowly so that he would know she was at the end of her patience. "Where is Hugh?"

"Ah...not here."

She raised her eyebrow at his words. Something was going on, of that she was sure. "I know he's not here with us. Is he in the castle?"

"Not exactly."

She took a deep breath and tried again. "Is he still in the stable?"

"Nay," he said and looked down at his shoes.

"Is Hugh even in this realm?" she asked in exasperation.

CHAPTER TWENTY

Several heartbeats went by before Gabriel answered Mina. "Nay. He's with the Fae."

Mina licked her lips and faced the stable. "I'm going to the monastery, and I'd like you to come with me."

"I'm going to regret this," he said as they walked to the horses. "What do you hope to find?"

"I'm not sure. I just have a feeling we need to look around there."

Once their horses were saddled, they rode from the bailey, through the gates, and to the forest.

"Is Hugh coming back?" she finally asked when she could hold it in no longer.

Gabriel glanced at her. "I honestly don't know."

She could tell by the way Gabriel answered that he was as worried as she was. Out of the corner of her eye, she saw him watching her. "What is it?"

"How do you feel?"

She looked at him, wondering if he knew of her night with Hugh.

"Your arm," he said when she didn't answer.

"It's fine. Did you get a chance to look at the injuries

on Hugh's back?"

Gabriel shook his head. "I barely got a chance to speak to him this morning before Aimery took him."

"He'll be back," she said, though she wasn't sure if she said it to reassure herself or him.

They rode the rest of the way in silence, her thoughts on Hugh and why the Fae would take him to their realm when it was so vital that he be here. She barely took notice of the birds and their vibrant songs that she usually enjoyed hearing.

She regretted leaving Hugh that morning. Now she wished she had stayed and watched him wake. Would they have made love again? Or would he have rolled away from her?

When she and Gabriel reached the monastery, they dismounted and tied the horses to the gate.

"Wait," Gabriel said as she started to walk through the gates. "Let me go ahead."

She let him go, and could have sworn he mumbled something about Hugh having his head if something happened to her, but she couldn't be sure.

Instead of asking, she walked behind him and let her eyes wonder as she took in the sights she hadn't bothered to notice when she and Hugh had been there. Weeds and wild plants mingled with piles of leaves and limbs littered the courtyard. She could only imagine how nice the grounds had once been before the monks had abandoned the monastery.

"What are you looking for?" he asked.

"I'm not sure." She tilted her head and looked at the outside walls of the monastery. "I just had a feeling we should come here."

Gabriel sighed. "Then, let's look. Outside or in?"

She looked at him and shrugged. "Inside."

He shook his head and led the way into the old monastery. "I wish I had an idea of what you were looking for."

"You grumble worse than a woman." She smiled, and pushed past him to step inside the door.

"I take exception to that," he protested with a grin.

She laughed and stepped over some fallen stones. Sunlight filtered through a stained glass window to shed a rainbow of color throughout the dusty room.

"I bet this place was magnificent in its day."

"Makes you wonder what happened to them," Gabriel said and drew his sword.

"You won't need that."

He turned his gaze to her and lifted a brow. "How do you know?"

She let him hold her back, and once again fell in step behind him. Movement to their left had him spinning around and holding his sword out. She spotted the cat hiding behind some stones. "It's just the cat Hugh found the last time we were here."

"What a relief," Gabriel said and rolled his eyes.

She ignored him and let her gaze wander. "What secrets are you hiding?" she whispered to the walls.

~ ~ ~

Hugh waited for Theron and Rufina to begin. He was anxious to return and speak with Mina. Not knowing if she was angry with him or not was driving him daft.

"She will still be there," Theron stated as he took a seat at the small square table. "Be seated, Hugh, there is much to be said."

Hugh glanced at Aimery to see his worried gaze on Hugh as well. "Is something wrong?" Hugh asked as he took the chair opposite the king.

"More than you know," the queen said. "We have recently come upon some interesting news that we need to share with you."

Hugh waited for the worst.

Theron leaned forward and rested his elbows on his knees, his shiny white tunic sparkling in the sunlight that trickled through the window above him. "No weapon in your possession will kill the creature while it is awake."

"You tell me something I already know," Hugh said more restless than ever to return to Stone Crest. To Mina.

"Do you think this information is something to take lightly?" Aimery thundered as he stepped forward.

Hugh rose to his feet to stare eye to eye with the Fae. "Nay, I do not, but as I already said, this information we know. You took me away from my men, away from a dangerous situation, to tell me nothing new. Why?"

Rufina, her hand on the back of her husband's chair, said, "Then you did not listen, Hugh."

Hugh looked at her while he replayed Theron's words in his head. *While it is awake.* "This creature must be asleep for it to be killed."

"Exactly," Theron said and then blew out a long breath. "But therein lies the problem."

Hugh once more took his seat. "How so?"

Theron didn't answer but looked away.

"How many times have you sent me and my men to kill these creatures?" Hugh asked. "How many times have we willingly gone into battle, no questions asked?"

"Too many," the king finally answered in a voice filled with doubt and resignation. "You and your men are all we have. The few other groups we put together are…gone. If you fail, then everything fails."

This news stunned Hugh. He didn't know if it was the

king's words or his tone, but regardless the unease was there. Firmly settled in his gut. "Why can't Aimery and his men help? They are more lethal than the Shields."

"I would go in an instant," Aimery stated, anger making his words harsh. "If I could."

Theron held up his hand to quiet his commander. "We cannot interfere, Hugh."

"Seems to me you have already interfered," Hugh said as his irritation grew. "Not only have you trained us, armed us, and informed us, but you have also moved us through realms and time."

Theron rose to his feet so quickly his chair tipped over backward. "And that is the extent that we can do!"

Hugh looked from one to the other, the chamber deathly quiet after the king's outburst, and rare show of fury. There was something else at work here, something that was holding the powerful Fae back. But what?

It came to Hugh suddenly. "Who set the boundaries on you?"

"It doesn't matter," Rufina said and pulled Theron back down beside her. She ran her hand through Theron's long, flaxen hair. "If your realm is destroyed, then so is ours."

Hugh laughed wryly, and rose to pace the room as his agitation threatened to consume him. Just when he thought things couldn't get worse, they did. He paused beside a wall and leaned a hand upon it, his chin dropped to his chest.

In his mind, he saw his men standing beside him. And then he saw Darrick's still body before they lowered him into the ground. How many more of his men would die before they won? If they won?

The Fae had given them aid, and it had helped. For a while. The more Hugh thought about it, the more he wondered if he could continue to count on the Fae.

Then he recalled the stories running rampant through

the Fae realm while he was training about Druids. Three sisters, in fact, who were all that stood between good and evil.

"Was it just a rumor I heard while training, about a trio of Druids that were all that was left to save your realm and ours from total domination?"

"It was no rumor," Aimery said. "It was a prophecy that was fulfilled."

"So they saved you?"

"In a manner."

"For a race that is all knowing and all powerful, you rely heavily on my people and my realm to keep yours alive."

Hugh must have hit a nerve for all three Fae refused to meet his eyes. "First the Druids, now me and my men. What happens if we fail?"

"Our realm and yours will cease to exist," Theron answered softly.

"Cole," Hugh murmured suddenly thinking of his friend. "His realm was destroyed. Was it by the same people?"

Theron rose and went to a table next to the door. He uncorked a long slender white bottle that was rounded at the bottom, and poured the liquid into four small goblets. He gave one to Rufina and one to Aimery, then turned and offered Hugh a goblet. "In truth, we cannot be sure, but we have our suspicions."

Hugh eagerly accepted the small silver goblet. He didn't know what it contained, but he needed something strong to cope with this new knowledge. He lifted the goblet to his lips and inhaled a sweet, heady fragrance before it touched his lips. It tasted of honey and liquid fire as it slid easily to his stomach.

Immediately, he felt the effects of the liquor as it eased some of his fears. He wondered if he could bring a bottle when he returned to Stone Crest.

"Can you give me any clues as to where to find the creature?" he asked Theron.

"Find the one that controls it, and you will find the creature," Rufina answered. "Time is running out. For all of us."

Hugh sat the goblet down, and turned to leave the chamber, when Theron's voice halted him.

Don't do anything stupid regarding Mina."

Hugh didn't respond, and he could tell Theron wished to say more, but Rufina's hand on the king's arm stopped him. Hugh nodded and followed Aimery from the chamber, his mind heavy with unwanted information.

~ ~ ~

Mina wanted to curse. Loud and long. But she was a lady, and ladies didn't do such things. Fortunately for her, she was with a man that didn't hold those convictions. She leaned against the monastery wall and listened as Gabriel used several curse words she knew – and many she didn't.

"I was sure we would find something," she said when Gabriel finished venting.

Gabriel kicked at a small stone. "To be honest, you had pretty much convinced me as well."

She looked at the sun. It was high in the sky. "We've missed the noon meal. I suppose we should return to the castle."

"Is there nowhere in your history that tells why the monks left?" Gabriel asked as he went down on his haunches and examined the earth

"None that I know of."

"And the Druids?" he asked as he stood.

"Again, nothing." She watched as Gabriel looked

around thoughtfully. "If there is a history of it, it has been kept quiet, for I asked many people."

"The ruins from the Druid temple aren't far from here?"

"Not at all." She pointed into the trees behind their horses. "Take the trail we used from the castle and venture to the left. It will take you to the Druids. Why?"

"I don't know," he said pensively. "Something doesn't fit. Christians all but killed off the Druids. Doesn't it seem odd they would be so close to one another here?"

"I suspect the Druids were here long before the monks."

Gabriel nodded. "Exactly. So, why would the monks build a holy place so close to the Druids before they had them eradicated?"

"How do you know the Druids were here when the monks came?"

"Because he's smarter than he looks."

Mina spun around at hearing that deep, melodic voice. Her heart pounded loudly as her gaze soaked up the sight of Hugh. He seemed somewhat different, as though he had a great weight to bear and struggled with it.

"Hello," he said softly, his brown eyes staring at her.

She grinned, unsure of how to react to the elation that welled within her at seeing him again. "Hello."

He nodded to Gabriel, and walked closer to them. "What brings you here?"

Gabriel jutted his chin in her direction. "She had a feeling we might find something."

"There is nothing but stone, dust, and a cat," Hugh said.

It was then she noticed something vastly different about High. It was almost like a light had dimmed within him, and she had a notion the Fae had told him something that wasn't good. "Did everything go all right with the Fae?"

She wanted to roll her eyes when Hugh glared at Gabriel. "He didn't tell me," she said. "I figured it out. I'm smarter than I look as well."

Hugh turned to Gabriel. He had no wish to delve into his conversation with the Fae just yet, not until he had a better grasp on it. Not to mention, he had many things he wished to speak with Mina about, the first of which was her virginity or lack thereof.

"Go on about the Druids and monks. How do you know the Druids were still here when the monks came?" he asked Gabriel.

Gabriel shrugged. "I just know. Look around the growth of both places. If the Druids had departed this place before the monks, wouldn't the weeds and such encompass more? If you take a close look, you'll see the growth is the same both here, and at the ruins."

"So why did they both leave at the same time?" Mina asked absently.

"More importantly, how long did they coexist with the other?" Hugh asked.

Gabriel shook his head. "That, my friends, I cannot answer. Not to mention, I have doubts that it has anything to do with the creature or the blue stone."

"This trip was a waste of time," Mina said and walked past Hugh toward the horses.

"Nay," he said and reached out a hand to stop her. "I had a sense the stone wasn't within the walls of the castle. It was a good idea to look here."

"But it isn't here either," she said.

He smiled and stared into her blue-green gaze that was filled with frustration. "There are other places to look."

She looked around them. "Really? Where? It sure isn't

in the Druid ruins. And do you have any idea the size of the forest? We'd be searching for years. I have an inkling that the creature won't give us that long."

His smile widened as his eyes crinkled at the corners. "Have you lost hope?"

"I don't think that is something you should ask while smiling." She turned to Gabriel. "Does he always act so strange after speaking with the Fae?"

Gabriel nodded. "Always. He even starts talking in circles like they do."

"Great," she said and slapped her hands on her legs. "Everyone is daft but me."

"Maybe you should join in," Gabriel taunted with a grin as he walked to his horse.

Hugh waited for her to face him. He'd worried about her reaction to him, and now that he'd faced that, he wasn't ready to be surrounded by others. Or let her go. She slowly turned to him, and he had no choice but to drop his hand.

She stared at him with her blue-green eyes as if trying to peer into his soul. For just an instant, Hugh almost let her. "Did you really think to find the stone here?"

"I don't know what I thought I would find," she admitted, her lips turned down in a frown.

"It must have been something, or you wouldn't have followed your instinct to come."

She shrugged her dainty shoulders. "It was like something told me to look here. I just *knew* I would find something. Instead, all we discovered was lots of dust and the cat again."

Hugh crossed his arms over his chest. "You took a huge chance coming back here if it was this place that caused you to become sick and nearly die."

She shrugged. "I guess we will know in a little while if it happens again."

He dropped his hands and took the two steps that put him face to face with her. "That isn't something to joke about."

"Why do you care? You think I'm controlling the creature."

CHAPTER TWENTY-ONE

As soon as the words left Mina's mouth, she wanted them back. Hugh hadn't mentioned her involvement since the night she agreed to help him, and now she was throwing it in his face. She waited for him to answer, hoping against hope that he would say the words she longed to hear. But the moments ticked by with nothing.

Just as she was about to turn and go to her horse, his hand reached out and stopped her.

He moved closer, their bodies brushing. "I asked you to prove me wrong."

"And so I shall," Mina said breathlessly. Hugh was too close, too overwhelming to her senses. She couldn't think straight when all she wanted was his arms around her, his mouth on hers. Somehow she pulled her gaze from his, and made the mistake of looking at his wide, sensual lips. "We should return to the castle."

For long moments he didn't answer, and she silently prayed he'd kiss her. Just a brush of his lips, anything to help the yearning inside her.

"Aye," he murmured.

His head lowered toward her, and her breath locked in

her throat as she waited for his kiss. He blew against her shoulder, sending dust billowing around them. Their gazes locked, held for a brief instant, before Hugh started toward the door.

It wasn't until Mina was on her horse that something continued to nag at her memory. She turned and looked at the monastery.

"What is it?" Hugh asked as he and Gabriel waited.

"Just a feeling that we've overlooked something important."

She shook herself mentally, and turned her horse back toward the castle. She couldn't help but wonder if Hugh would mention their night together. When she had first seen him, he'd a particular sparkle in his eye. Had she been the cause if it?

Their return ride to the castle was spent listening to Gabriel and Hugh plot ways in which to keep the villagers safe for the coming night.

"The creature has had enough," Gabriel said as they crossed under the gatehouse. "You realize he'll come at the castle tonight."

"Aye," Hugh agreed and looked at Mina once they had stopped near the stables in the bailey.

"There is nowhere else for the villagers to go," she said.

As they dismounted, Bernard met them and kissed Mina on the cheek. "I wondered where you went off to."

She smiled at him, comforted at his ease around her. "I thought you weren't supposed to do that."

"Bah," he said with a roll of his eyes. "Theresa knows we've reconciled. She has vowed to see you dead, by the way."

Mina sighed. "Nothing new."

When she looked at Hugh, she found him watching her and Bernard with a funny look in his face. "What is it?"

"Nothing," he said tersely. "Baron, is there some place your people can go until this creature is dead?"

"You know there isn't," Bernard said as the smile on his face died. "This home is all they know. Why can't they continue to sleep in the castle?"

"We have a feeling the creature will attack the castle tonight," Hugh answered.

Mina wanted to reach out to her brother as he ran his hand through his short blonde hair, his face darkened in thought. "The only place I can think of is the dungeons, but I wouldn't want to subject them to that if I didn't have to."

"I don't think you have a choice," Hugh said. "I'd rather see them face another day than die tonight."

"Then I'll see it done," he said and walked off barking orders to his men.

"He's a good man," she said to no one in particular.

"Few men could lead with such a clear head when faced with such evil," Gabriel agreed.

Mina turned and found Hugh staring at her again.

"We need to talk," he said softly.

She followed him as he walked toward the castle, both unsure and thrilled to be alone with him again. He held the door for her, and she strode past him only to hear him whisper, "Why did you leave this morning?"

His question caught her off guard and caused her to trip. He easily righted her, and she glanced at him as he guided her into the castle. "I didn't wish for Bernard to barge in to the stable and find us. I wasn't sure how my brother would react. I thought it best he find me in the castle."

"You could have woken me," Hugh said as they entered the great hall.

She grinned at the memory of him sleeping so soundly.

"I didn't wish to rouse you when you looked so peaceful. How is your back, by the way?"

"Don't change the subject," he warned with a sharp glance in her direction.

It didn't wipe the grin from her face as she recalled the feel of his hard body beneath her hand. She walked into the solar and turned to face him. By the stern look on his face, she knew she wasn't going to like what he had to say. The smile slipped, and she squared her shoulders. "I'm simply concerned about your back. Am I not supposed to ask?"

He shut the door and leaned against it. "What happened last night —"

"Was wonderful," she said before he could continue and say something she'd never forgive him for. "Don't say that you regret it," she cautioned. "Don't you dare."

He briefly closed his eyes, and when they opened, his golden brown orbs held guilt and regret. "You deserved better than to be taken standing up in a stable."

"Why?" she asked. "Because I'm a lady?"

"Aye."

She snorted. "All my life I've lived alone, wondering if I would ever experience any adventure. Or find a man who would really look at me the way you do. I rely on no one but myself, or at least I used to. All that has changed. Because of you."

He shook his head. "Don't paint me into a pretty picture, Mina. You won't like the outcome. I tried to warn you last night I'd be leaving."

"I know. I'm not asking you to stay."

"You don't want me to stay?"

The distress in his dark eyes shattered her heart, but what she did, she did for the both of them. "You and your men have a mission ahead of you. Your men need you to lead the Shields. I knew going into last night that I would get no more from you than that."

He pushed off from the door and glared at her. "You used me?"

"No more than you used me."

She dug her nails into her hand to keep her from running to him and throwing her arms around his neck. He glowering at her, but she stood her ground no matter that it was the hardest thing she'd ever done.

Because he meant that much to her. She'd suffer the same agony every day. For him.

"You should've run from me," he finally said.

"I'll tell you again that I don't regret it. It was everything I could have hoped for and more."

"You're ruined for a husband now."

She waved away his words. "You and I both know I'll never marry. Theresa will see to that. As it is, I am past the marrying age."

"Men will look past that once they see your beauty."

His words caused her stomach to flip. She smiled, because only Hugh could make her smile through tears. "Put your fears to rest, Hugh. I'll not trap you into marriage."

He nodded at that and left the solar. It was strange that she should feel so alone now after she'd been that way all her life. Yet, after sharing such an incredible night with Hugh, everything had changed.

The world was a vastly different place. It was still as scary, but Mina's soul wasn't the shriveled thing it had once been. She knew her fate now, and she would take whatever it was that life gave her.

Hugh didn't know how he managed to walk from Mina with his emotions in such turmoil. He had half expected Mina to beg him to marry her, or at least to make him feel as though he should ask her. But she'd done neither.

He mentally shook himself. There were other, more important, things to concentrate on. He motioned to Gabriel who sat at a table in the great hall, and caught Cole's eye as he stood guard behind Theresa.

They followed him into his chamber, and each took a chair. He stared at them a moment, briefly wondering who would take over as leader of the Shields if something happened to him.

Gabriel was the first to ask, "What did Aimery want?"

"What?" Cole asked as he looked from Gabriel to Hugh. "Aimery came to speak with you?"

Hugh shook his head. "Actually, I was taken to court."

Cole whistled. "The king and queen called for you?"

"They wanted to let me know a few things."

Gabriel sat forward. "Like how to kill the creature, perhaps?"

"If only," Hugh said and raked his hand down his face as he sat on his bed. "I do know that no weapon we have will kill the creature while it is awake."

Cole and Gabriel exchanged glances.

"We're to kill it while it sleeps?" Cole asked.

"That is the only way to kill it."

Gabriel said, "How are we supposed to do that when we have no idea where it goes during the day?"

"We'll have to follow it," Hugh said.

"What else did the king and queen tell you?" Cole asked.

Hugh looked into the eyes of his men. "That, if we fail, it won't be just our world that is destroyed, but also the Fae's."

"How is that possible?" Gabriel asked.

Cole stood and turned to look out the window. "It is easier than you think," he said. "I watched my world destroyed. I've no wish to see any others come to the same fate."

"I think it has something to do with the fact that the Fae once roamed this realm. They are connected to us in a way that no human can fully understand," Hugh explained.

Gabriel stood and clapped a hand on Cole's shoulder. "Then I suppose we had better find the blue stone and the creature."

"Bernard is seeing to readying the dungeons so the villagers can stay in there tonight," Hugh said. He raised his eyes to find both men staring at him. "What?"

"Did you speak to Mina?" Gabriel asked.

Hugh lowered his gaze. "Aye."

"Well?" Cole prompted. "What happened?"

"You know our way of life," Hugh said. "We live solitary existences with only each other for company."

Gabriel crossed his arms over his chest. "No one blames you for what happened with that woman. It was many years ago."

"Besides," Cole said. "We all deserve some happiness when we can get it."

"I don't see either of you with any women here," Hugh pointed out.

Cole shrugged. "None have gained my interest."

"Mine either," Gabriel said.

"It doesn't matter," Hugh said. "Mina isn't interested in more than what we shared last night, and that's just the way I want it."

"Right," Cole said his voice dripping with sarcasm. "I must get back to watching Theresa."

Hugh watched him leave before he turned to Gabriel. "You don't believe me either?"

"I don't know," Gabriel answered thoughtfully as he stood in the doorway. "But I do know that if you continue with that line of shite you just gave us, you'll be lying to yourself."

Hugh couldn't stand to be by himself once Gabriel left. Being alone made him think of things he had no business thinking, like a future with Mina in it.

"Who am I kidding?" he asked the empty chamber. "I'll be lucky if I leave here alive, much less with my heart intact."

CHAPTER TWENTY-TWO

Hugh got no farther than his door, when he found Gabriel standing there. "I thought you left."

"I need to look at your back," Gabriel said.

Hugh stood aside and took off his shirt. He straddled the chair backwards, but his mind wasn't on his wounds. Try as he might, memories of the night before filled his head. Mina's cries of pleasure, her body opening for him, accepting him.

The desire and unimaginable pleasure.

In all the years he'd been alive, not once had he ever experienced anything that could compare. No matter what he wanted, he had no choice but to let Mina go.

Gabriel whistled when he glimpsed Hugh's back. "That creature likes leaving you with scars."

"This set deeper than the last?"

"Aye, but they healed well. I wish I'd have gotten to take care of them earlier," he said as he cleaned off the caked blood. "But it looks like that journey to the Fae realm did something to help."

Hugh gritted his teeth as Gabriel poked around the fresh wounds. They had bothered him since he woke. He hissed when Gabriel smeared some foul-smelling cream on the wounds.

"I'm amazed you were in any condition to make love last night," Gabriel murmured.

"It was the bloodlust."

Gabriel straightened, and slowly came to stand in front of Hugh. His jaw was clenched, his gaze blazing with anger and disappointment. "You didn't."

Hugh looked away from the scorn in his friend's eyes. "I tried to get her to leave, but she wouldn't. I couldn't keep away from her. She's too much of a temptation for me."

He sighed. "I would ask if she was a virgin, but I know she was."

"She was," Hugh agreed.

Gabriel returned to Hugh's back. "If I hadn't seen her smile at you this afternoon, I'd tell you to be prepared for Bernard's attack. But she *was* glad to see you."

Hugh recalled her welcoming smile, the way her eyes had warmed when she caught sight of him. "She said she enjoyed it."

"Well," Gabriel said with a chuckle, "that's a good thing, my friend."

"I could have hurt her."

"But you didn't."

Hugh laid his head on his arms. "I've got to stay away from her."

This time Gabriel laughed loudly. "I wish you luck, because frankly, I think you're fighting a losing battle."

~ ~ ~

Mina pushed up her sleeves and wiped the sweat from her face. The dungeons had never been a place she wanted to be, even when others surrounded her as she was now, cleaning in preparation for the coming night. The dungeons hadn't been used in more than a score of years, and the musty, damp walls were no place for the elderly, or the young.

But they had need of it for the night to come, and who knew after that.

She pushed a lock of hair from her face with the back of her hand, and bent down to pick up more of the old rushes that lined the floor. Women were going behind her sweeping and mopping the floors before placing new rushes down.

They had much to do before nightfall, and she doubted if all of it would be accomplished. The kitchen was alive with women cooking while men gathered what they could and began stacking it in the hall to be moved down once the dungeons were clean.

She had no idea how long she had been hunched over cleaning when someone came to offer her water. But when she tried to rise to get the water, she cried out from the pain in her back.

Immediately strong hands came around her. She turned her head to find Hugh holding her.

"Drink," he ordered.

When she had drunk her fill and replaced the ladle, Hugh straightened her into a standing position.

"You should take more breaks."

"There isn't time," she said.

He stared at her a moment. "Take more breaks," he repeated and walked off.

She watched as he went to stand with some other men who were carrying up the bundles of old rushes. A movement out of the corner of her eye caught her attention. She turned to find Theresa at the top of the dungeon stairs looking down at everyone. Mina wasn't surprised to find her sister as far away from work as possible.

She bent down to pick up more rushes, and glanced around for Bernard. Sure enough, he stood with other men cleaning. Her brother had made a drastic turn- around. Too bad Theresa couldn't do the same.

Sweat poured down Mina's face, and her hair clung to her face and neck and rolled between her breasts making it itch. She promised herself a nice long bath once the dungeons were clean. That bath might not be until tomorrow, but she would have one.

"Hello, milady," an older woman said as she came to work beside Mina.

"Hello," Mina said and offered her a smile.

The woman smiled in return. "It's good to see you smiling. For many years, we all despaired of ever seeing the light in your beautiful eyes again."

Mina sat in stunned silence as the woman continued to work. Had it also been a lie when she had been told that no one in the castle wanted to have anything to do with her? That no one would be her lady's maid? Since it had been Theresa that had told her, Mina seriously doubted if any of it had been true.

Anger began to well inside her, because she would never know the answers. She had always thought her parents good, kind people, but now she didn't know anymore. Suddenly, the dungeon walls began to close in on her. She could barely catch a breath as her world began to spin.

From a distance, she heard someone call her name, but all she could think of were the lies she had believed. She grabbed hold of the wall, and not even the sticky damp stone could snap her out of her anger.

She ran for the stairs and fell as she started up them.

Theresa's mocking laughter only spurred her anger more. She slowly rose to her feet and faced her sister.

"What's the matter," Theresa taunted. "No one to help you? It's no wonder looking the way you do."

Mina pushed past her and ran for the castle doors. She needed some air. Once she was in the bailey, all she could think about was the ruins. She needed their warmth and compassion, but someone blocked her way.

She glared at Gabriel and said, "Move."

"Nay."

Tears welled up in her eyes, but she refused to allow them. "I need to go to the ruins."

"It isn't safe, Mina, and you know it."

"Mina," Bernard called as he reached her. "Are you all right?"

She turned away from her brother so he wouldn't see her distress. "I'm fine." When she raised her face it was to find Hugh staring at her.

"What happened?" Hugh asked.

"Nothing," she lied. "I'm just tired, and I needed some air. The dungeon is very hot."

Before they could question her more, she turned and retraced her steps back to the dungeon. She would cry later, but her village needed her, and she would finish what she started.

Hugh watched Mina's departing back. "What did she want?" he asked Gabriel.

"She wanted to go to the ruins."

Bernard sighed. "She only wants to go there when she is upset."

Hugh waited for Cole to join them before he asked. "What happened between Theresa and Mina?"

"The usual," Cole said. "Theresa goaded her, and Mina ignored her. Nothing different."

"Something else happened," Hugh said. "She looked ready to faint one moment, then the next she was racing up the stairs."

"Was it something you said?" Bernard asked Hugh. "I saw you talking to her while she took a drink of water."

Hugh shook his head. "I only told her to take more breaks."

Bernard shrugged. "I'll keep an eye on her while we are down there."

Hugh nodded and followed him back to the dungeon. He wanted to know what had happened, but if he pressed any harder Bernard would begin to wonder why he was interested.

Why are you interested?

Because I can't stand to see anyone upset.

If that's not a lie, I'm a donkey's hairy arse.

It had been a long time since Hugh hadn't been truthful with himself. So, why was he so concerned?

I made love to her.

He groaned silently. God help him, but he was in way over his head.

~ ~ ~

Finally, it was done. Mina helped place the last bag of belongings in the dungeon as families gathered into the open cells. She stretched her back and walked up the stairs. One look out the window showed her she had time for a bath before she would need to return to the dungeon for the night.

She retrieved a clean gown and hurried to the bathing chamber. Fortunately, it was empty. She stripped and climbed into the hot water.

A sigh escaped her as she lowered herself into the water

and submerged. She rose and wiped the water from her face, feeling better already. Without pause, she picked up the soap and began to scrub the grime and sweat from her body. She washed her body twice, and her hair thrice.

She was just about to leave the tub when Hugh walked into the chamber. He stopped in mid-step, water dripping from his hair and down his shirtless chest. He must have gone for a swim in the stream.

"Hello," she said.

"I didn't realize you were here," he said.

"I was just about to leave." Although she knew he didn't want to have anything more to do with her, she couldn't stop the desire from throbbing in her body.

His voice was low, silky smooth as he said, "It must be Fate that we continue to meet here. I should go," he said a heartbeat later.

"Stay." And then with a deep breath, she stood.

Hugh knew he was a fool. But knowing it didn't make it easier to bear. He dropped his boots and shirt, and in two steps reached the tub. He grabbed hold of Mina and lifted her from the water.

Her legs wrapped around him as he sat her on a table beneath the window. He leaned back to look into her blue-green eyes. "No matter how hard I try, I cannot stay away from you."

His body hungered for her gentle touch and her sweet mouth. He jerked her against his chest before he devoured her mouth in a kiss he'd been thinking of all day. He swept his tongue inside and explored every nuance of her mouth.

A surge of pure desire rushed through him as she sighed into his mouth. His hands moved toward her buttocks and squeezed. She moaned and broke the kiss.

"Hugh," she said as she kissed his neck.

Ripples of pleasure raced across his skin. It had been so

long since he had allowed himself to bed a woman. But it wasn't just any woman in his arms. This woman gentled him in his most volatile moments, and she didn't even know it.

He leaned his head back and closed his eyes as her hands roamed over his bare chest, touching, stroking. Caressing.

His stomach quivered in anticipation when her fingers slid into the waist of his trousers. But it was her hot mouth on his chest that was nearly his undoing.

With a flick of his wrist, he unlaced his trousers and quickly shed them. Her welcoming smile only intensified his desire. He moved between her legs and felt the wetness against his cock. She was ready for him.

He cupped her face in his hands and stared into her amazing eyes. There was no guile, no evil, only beauty and innocence. He kissed her slow and gentle, but her hands reached down and wrapped around his aching rod. He groaned and whispered her name as she guided him into her.

A hunger like he had never known consumed him. Took him.

Seized him.

He wrapped his arms around her and thrust into her tight, hot sheath.

"I need you," she whispered into his ear.

Hugh looked into her eyes. "You have me."

Her smile was bittersweet, but he didn't allow that for long. He held onto her with one arm while his other cupped her breast.

Mina held onto him as if her life depended on it. The need, the hunger, began to throb and grow with each of Hugh's thrusts. He plunged long and slow, then quick and short, but with every movement her body climbed higher and higher. She squeezed her legs tight around his waist to bring him closer.

His fingers skimmed over her nipples, wringing a cry of pleasure from her. Her breasts were full and heavy as they eagerly awaited more of his touch. Each roll of her nipples between his fingers ignited her already heated sex until she was mindless with need.

But when he raised his hand to his mouth and licked his finger before moving between their bodies to touch her clitoris, she nearly climaxed right then. He must have sensed it, because he stilled and held her tightly. After a few moments, his thumb found her swollen clitoris and moved back and forth across it as he thrust inside her hard, fast.

Her hands gripped his shoulders, ready to reach the pinnacle, when he removed his hand and pulled her tight against him. His thrusts became slower, longer, as his hands roamed over her back to her hips and across her buttocks. Mina's mouth had found Hugh's neck and placed kisses on his flesh as his hands roamed over her bottom.

His hips jerked as he began to pound into her, going deeper than ever before. She wanted to hold off her climax, but he was having none of it. Her head fell back as the release came hard and intense.

She didn't complain when his lips silenced her moans as he thrust into her one last time as his orgasm engulfed him. She buried her head in his neck, and let the pleasure sweep them, take them.

Swallow them.

"Hugh," Cole said as he walked around the corner into the bathing chamber.

She instinctively hid her head, but she knew Cole could see her legs.

"What?" Hugh snapped.

"Ah," Cole stammered. "Nothing. It can wait."

When they were alone once more, she smiled up at Hugh.

He returned her grin and said, "You really need to put a lock on that door."

She laughed and kissed his chin. "I'll speak to Bernard about it."

The smile left his face as he pulled out of her body. She longed to call him back, but she knew he had distanced himself from her.

For the moment.

She watched as he gripped the wooden tub and wondered what thoughts were in his mind. But she was likely to never know. She moved to get off the table, and in an instant, he was there to help her.

His closeness was her undoing. She reached up and touched his sculpted chest, his heat scalding her. Her gaze rose until she stared into his dark brown eyes. "Don't tell me you regret this."

"That's the problem." Sadness radiated from him. "I enjoy it too much."

She smoothed the frown from his forehead. "If this is your expression for enjoyment I would hate to see the one where you are sad."

He grabbed her hands and stepped back from her. "I don't want to hurt you."

"Then don't push me away."

"We have so little time."

"Exactly," she said and stepped toward him. "Don't throw away what little time we have together."

When his hand came up to cup her cheek, she laid her head against his palm and closed her eyes. It was then she realized what could help ease his mind. She had to prove she was innocent by finding the blue stone and giving it to him. And she had an idea of just where to look.

CHAPTER TWENTY-THREE

Hugh's thoughts were constantly of Mina. Even now as they were about to lock everyone in the dungeon, all he could think of was their time together in the bathing chamber.

Dusk had fallen rapidly, and the hall was filled with the sounds of cries from the children and the worried voices of their parents. Hugh hoped and prayed the dungeon would keep the villagers safe.

He and his men, along with a few of Bernard's knights, were stationed in the castle to make sure the creature didn't find the villagers.

"Everyone is inside," Bernard said as he walked up. "I've checked the castle twice."

Hugh nodded. "Good. We'll see you in the morn then."

"I'd rather be out here," Bernard argued.

"The people need their baron. Keep your family and your villagers safe."

Bernard stood for a moment before he turned and walked into the dungeon. Hugh nodded for Gabriel to lock the doors. It was a chance they were taking, but Hugh didn't want to risk anyone trying to leave the dungeon.

He walked to Cole and Gabriel. "Is she inside?"

"Aye," Cole said. "I watched her enter myself."

Hugh sighed. At least Mina was safe for the night. The scream of the beast let them know the long night had begun.

"Take your places," Hugh bellowed as he ran to his spot behind the tapestry beyond the dais. It gave him the perfect view of the front of the castle and the stairway to the dungeon.

"Here it comes," someone yelled from above.

Hugh braced himself for what was to come. He readied his crossbow and fingered the dagger at his waist. He might not be able to kill the creature with his weapons, but he could slow it down.

The flap of the giant wings could be heard as thunder rumbled in the distance. Lightening flashed, enough that he was able to glimpse the creature flying toward the front of the castle. His heart raced with anticipation as his eyes focused on the door. He could just make out sounds above the thunder, but surely it couldn't be the beast.

The castle doors slowly opened, and to their surprise, the creature stepped into the hall. Hugh blinked to make sure he was seeing correctly, but he and his men stayed hidden, watching. The fiend's red eyes looked around slowly. Its hands clenched briefly before stretching its long talons.

It walked toward the stairway that led to the dungeon. Hugh's gut tightened in fear. But just as he was about to stand and get the creature's attention, it turned and walked away from the stairway.

"What the Hell just happened?" Cole whispered

Hugh glared at Cole. "What are you doing out of your spot?"

"I was on my way to distract the creature when it

stopped. What made it turn away?"

"I'm not sure," Hugh said. "I think it doesn't want to chance harming whoever is controlling it."

Cole snorted. "That's the whole damn village."

Hugh held up his hand to quiet Cole as the creature turned toward them. Its long tail swished behind him and its claws clicked on the stone floor as it made its way to them. Then, just as suddenly as it had flown in, the beast screamed and flew out of the castle. Hugh and Cole walked from behind the tapestry.

"That was close," Cole said.

"Very," Hugh agreed.

They raced up the stairs toward Gabriel. "It's flying away," he said as they neared.

"Where?" Hugh asked.

"Northwest."

"The forest," all three said in unison.

"We'll head out tomorrow," Hugh said as they walked back to the hall. "Unlock the dungeon, but we need to keep watch to make sure it doesn't return."

The quiet hall vanished as the sounds of the villagers once again filled it. Hugh stood back and watched Mina and Bernard as they helped their people. Theresa sat on the dais with her arms crossed over her chest glaring at Mina.

It had been a long day and exhaustion had its hold on Hugh. He nodded to Cole and made his way to his chamber. A few hours to rest was all he needed.

~ ~ ~

"Maybe we should tell him," Aimery said as he paced the throne room.

"Nay," Rufina said.

Theron looked at Aimery. "If we do, then he won't

learn that there is more to life than instincts."

"He asks so little of us," Aimery argued. "I've never before had him ask me such a simple question."

Theron shook his head. "We cannot meddle with their lives."

"We do it every day."

Rufina rose from her chair and walked to Aimery. "Many times it would have been so easy to just tell a human what they wanted, but their lives are based on learning."

"And it's high time Hugh learned to trust with his heart," Theron said.

Aimery turned toward his king and queen. "And if Mina is the one controlling the creature? Do you know what that will do to Hugh?"

"It'll destroy him," Rufina answered solemnly. "I hate that she is unreadable to us."

"We must find a way to see who has the blue stone."

Theron shook his head. "If only it were that easy, Aimery, we would never have needed men like Hugh."

"You know what is blocking our vision don't you?"

Aimery waited for them to answer, and instead they turned away. Which was all the answer he needed.

~ ~ ~

Mina waited until the last villager was settled before she made her way toward the stairs. She smiled at Cole and Gabriel, and wondered where Hugh had disappeared to. Her feet were quick as she walked to her chamber. Maybe Hugh was there waiting for her.

But when she opened the door all she found was a dark chamber. She lit the candles and then sat to unbraid her hair. It was still damp from her bath and hasty dressing. She looked to the bed, but found she wasn't sleepy.

She briefly thought about trying to find Hugh, but realized that was foolish. Instead, she sat in her chair and stared into the empty hearth. The candles were almost gone when a knock sounded on her door. She jerked in surprise, and was about to rise when the door opened and in walked Hugh.

"I saw the light under your door, and wanted to check that you were all right," he said.

She nodded. "I'm fine."

"And your arm?"

"Just about healed. Gabriel's medicines are wonderful."

He glanced at the bed. "Why aren't you asleep?"

She shrugged and rose from her chair. "I couldn't sleep. Why aren't you abed?"

"Same reason."

She stood in the center of her chamber and waited. Silence reined as they stared at each other. She was about to give up when he dropped his chin to his chest.

"I knew I shouldn't have come," he said. Then he raised his head and stepped inside. He shut the door behind him, but he didn't move from it.

"Why did you?"

"I had to see you."

A glimmer of hope burst from those five words. "And now that you are here? Do you wish to leave?"

He pushed away from the door and walked to her. "I don't think I could leave if you asked me to."

"I'm not asking you to."

"The more we are together, the harder it'll be when I leave."

She gave him a small smile. "Don't think about that. Think about us. Right here, right now. We'll deal with the tomorrows when they happen."

He reached up and smoothed her hair out of her face.

"So wise for one so young."

She stepped into his arms and lifted her face for the kiss she knew would come. He didn't disappoint. His mouth moved slowly, seductively over hers, leaving her flushed and wanting more.

"You're teasing me."

"Nay," he said and kissed her eyelids. "I'm going to show you how you should have been made love to."

Her heart fell to her feet when he bent and picked her up to carry her to the bed. He stood her beside it, and turned her around to unlace her gown. With each string he unlaced, he placed a kiss where it had been.

Chills raced down her spine at his feather light kisses. When he pushed her gown over her shoulder, he twirled his tongue on her neck. Then, he turned her to face him, and knelt to pull the gown from her arms.

She had dressed so hurriedly that she hadn't bothered with any underclothes. As the gown came off her shoulders, it bared her chest to him. His eyes heated at the sight of her breasts. Her sex clenched and her heart raced at the look on his face. He wanted her, and if that was all she remembered of their time together, it was enough.

Slowly, he lowered her gown over her hips until it pooled at her feet. She was about to take her shoes off, but he stopped her and did it himself. When she was naked, he kissed her ankles and ran his hands up her legs and over her hips to circle her waist. He kissed and teased her stomach and hips with his lips and tongue. Her hands plunged into his hair and held onto him.

In the next heartbeat, he picked her up and laid her on the bed. She watched as he pulled off his tunic, his muscles flexing with each movement. He sat on the bed and took off his boots, then stood and faced her. His fingers slowly unlaced his trousers.

She bit her lip, as inch by inch, his skin was exposed. When his thick arousal stood straight and tall, all she could think about was holding his velvety, hot rod in her hands. When he had shed his trousers and laid beside her, her hands instantly went to his body.

"You are so hard and solid," she said as she caressed down his bulging arm to his hip.

He nuzzled her neck. "And you are all softness and curves."

When she reached between their bodies for him, he stopped her and pulled her arms over her head.

"Tonight, my lady, I am going to make love to you."

"You've already made love to me. Twice."

He shook his head. "That wasn't making love. At least not how it is supposed to be."

She gave up trying to argue when his lips claimed hers in a kiss that made her toes curl. He stroked her tongue and plundered her mouth fiercely, but lovingly. His hand moved over her arms, down her side to her hip.

But he didn't release her arms.

He held them firmly as his kiss moved from her mouth to her neck and down to her breasts. He took a nipple into his mouth and swirled his tongue around it, bringing it to a hard bud.

Mina cried out and rocked her hips against him. Her breasts swelled until they ached for more of his touch. He cupped her other breast and fondled her nipple while his tongue continued to tease the other one.

The pleasure was so intense she didn't know how she was going to survive it. She moved her hips against his abdomen, and felt a spurt of desire at the contact.

"I have to touch you," she said.

He let go of her hands immediately, and she gripped his wide shoulders. His hard, hot body pressed against hers as she felt every move he made. He slid his hands across her skin, awakening her body.

She closed her eyes and lost herself in the power of his touch. While in his arms she felt beautiful, as though nothing could stand in her way. In his arms, she had the missing part of her world.

He rolled over, and she found herself straddling his hips. She smiled down at him as she ran her hands up his abdomen so her fingers could curl in the black hair that littered his chest. He grinned and cupped her breasts. Mina let out a groan and let her head fall back from the pleasure of his touch.

Her hips began to rock back and forth, and Hugh instantly stilled her. She looked down at him, a silent question directed at him.

"I want you too desperately, Mina," he whispered.

Her heart ached for him. How lonely he must be, maybe as lonely as she was. She leaned down until her nipples brushed his chest. He gasped and stiffened. She bit her lip to keep from smiling as she realized the control she had.

She moved from side to side rubbing her breasts against him. He tried to stop her, but she shoved his hands aside and wielded what little power she had. He didn't allow her much time before he rolled over and pinned her with his body. His weight on her was exquisite, and she relished the feel of him.

His cock pressed into her stomach, and she knew by his darkened eyes that he needed her, yearned for her. Her stomach felt as though it had butterflies flying around inside.

She opened her legs for him, inviting him. His lips touched her as he rested the blunt head of his arousal against her sensitive sex. She wrapped her legs around his waist and tugged him against her. Slowly he filled her. Fully. Totally.

Completely.

Mina gasped at his fullness, her body recognizing his in a heartbeat.

Hugh thought he would spill his seed right then. He had wanted to make slow, sweet love to Mina, but she brought out the passion in him like no other woman ever had. He lost control so easily while in her arms.

He looked into her blue-green eyes filled with desire, and felt himself swell even harder. He pulled out of her until only the tip of his rod remained, then he sank into her and heard her sigh with pleasure. He knew if he continued on this course he would climax in a matter of moments, and he wanted this time to last longer for her.

With a groan he withdrew, and turned her onto her stomach. He placed kisses from her shoulders to her delectable behind. He urged her onto her hands and knees, and reached around to fondle her clitoris. Moisture coated his fingers as he sunk them into her heat and smeared her juices around her sex, teasing her until she shook with the desire flooding her.

She moaned and moved her hips back against him, seeking more. He grasped his cock and moved it to her sex. He pushed into her as he griped her hips. She tried to rock back, but he held her in place. Inch by inch he filled her, the angle sinking him deeper into her slick heat.

He clenched his jaw as he struggled to keep his climax away. Hugh focused on Mina, on giving her as much pleasure as he could. She cried out his name as he plunged in and out of her, her moans music to his ears.

And then she peaked, the walls of her sex clenching around him until he was lost in the desire. No longer could he hold off his climax, and he stopped trying. Hugh threw back his head and pumped furiously into her until he roared his release, finding a peace he had never imagined.

They fell together on the bed, his heart hammering rapidly while the euphoria of their lovemaking enveloped him. He pulled out of her, and she turned to nuzzle his neck and kiss his face while her hands roamed over his back. His last thought was that he wanted to make love to her when he woke.

CHAPTER TWENTY-FOUR

Hugh woke and reached for Mina, but all he found was an empty bed. He opened his eyes and looked around the chamber to find it vacant as well. He ground his teeth and made a mental note to talk to her about leaving him in the mornings.

He wasn't happy that he had slept soundly either. He looked out the window and saw the sun already up. A knock sounded on the door, and it only took a heartbeat to realize Mina wouldn't knock on her own door. He quickly rolled off the bed to land on the far side.

"Mina," Theresa called.

From under the bed, he could see Theresa's feet walk into the chamber. As quietly as he could, he moved under the bed. Just in time too, as Theresa walked to the bed. He heard what sounded like her moving her hands over the linens.

"What are you doing?" Mina asked as she walked into her chamber.

"Who slept in your bed?"

"I did," she answered.

Hugh held his breath.

"I don't believe you," Theresa said.

"Get out of my chamber."

He longed to see Mina's face. He could well imagine her eyes were shooting fire, and her face was flushed with anger. She had changed quite a bit since his arrival.

His thoughts came to a stop when he heard the door slam. He peered out, and found he was once again alone. With a sigh, he rolled from under the bed and hurriedly slipped into his clothes that he had taken with him under the bed.

When he was dressed, he walked to the door, but stopped short of opening it. He could only hope there was no one in the hallway. He took a deep breath and opened the door a crack. After a careful look, he found the hallway empty.

As quickly as he could, he slipped from Mina's chamber and hurried to his own to change clothes. When he opened his chamber door, he found Gabriel and Cole waiting for him.

"Where have you been?" Gabriel asked crossly.

Cole laughed. "If I had to hazard a guess, I'd say with a woman."

Hugh turned and went to the chest that held his clothes. He pulled out a black tunic and a pair of fawn colored trousers.

"Well?" Gabriel prompted. "Is Cole right? Have you been with a woman?"

Hugh didn't want to answer them, but he knew better than anyone that they wouldn't let up unless he gave them what they wanted. "Aye," he whispered.

Cole clapped him on the back. "About time."

Hugh rolled his eyes as he changed clothes and ran his fingers through his unruly hair. He splashed water on his face, and had a thought that he might visit the bathing chamber later.

"By the heavens, he's smiling," Gabriel said.

Hugh looked in the mirror and found himself doing just that. He wiped the smile from his face. "Come, men. We need to see if we can track the creature."

When they walked into the great hall it was overcrowded with the villagers. The atmosphere was one of a party. Something was definitely wrong.

His eyes roamed the hall until he spotted Mina. She sat surrounded by villagers laughing and smiling. He watched her, noting how well she belonged here despite what she thought.

He moved his eyes down the table and found Bernard's stare fixated on Mina. There was something odd in his gaze that made Hugh take notice. He couldn't put his finger on it, but he found himself wanting to rip Bernard's head off.

He is her brother.

But that didn't stop the anger rolling within him. His gaze traveled back to Mina, and he found her eyes on him. His anger dissipated in an instant with the smile that she gave him. He nodded and returned her smile before turning to his men.

"What is it?" Gabriel asked.

Hugh shook his head. "I don't know. Go see what you can find. Cole," he called.

"I'm off to find the shrew," he said of Theresa.

Hugh turned and made his way toward Mina only to be stopped by Theresa.

"Come sit," she beckoned. "I have saved a place just for you."

Not to take her invitation would be an insult, and one he couldn't afford. He sat beside her, and glanced at Mina to see a frown marring her beautiful face. He would make it up to her later, he told himself.

Instead of a cheerful morning conversation with Mina, he had to listen to Theresa complain about everything from the food to the villagers crowding the castle. He was about to put a gag in her mouth when Bernard spoke.

"Enough," the baron said. "Hugh's eyes are glazed over from your ranting."

Out of the corner of his eye, Hugh saw Theresa's face flush with anger.

"You are insulting me now?" she hissed furiously.

Bernard shook his head. "I'm taking pity on our guest."

"Bah," Theresa said and rose to her feet. "You are treading on dangerous ground, brother. I would remember that the next time you think to go against me," she said before she stormed out of the hall.

Hugh looked after her and just spotted Cole trail after her. When Hugh turned back, he found Bernard staring at Mina again.

"Something wrong?" Hugh asked as nonchalantly as he could.

Bernard sighed and leaned back in his chair. "Mina has changed."

"And that's bad?"

"Not at all. I just worry about her. Theresa sees what everyone does. You should have seen the smile on Mina's face when she came down this morning. She lit up the entire hall."

Hugh smiled inwardly. He had done that to her. "And you think Theresa will react to it."

"I don't think," Bernard said. "I know it as surely as I breathe. We'll have to watch Mina."

"I had planned for us to find the creature today."

"During the daylight? Do you think we can?" Bernard asked, hope shining in his blue eyes.

"It's possible. Gabriel saw the creature fly to the

northwest."

"The forest," Bernard said.

"Exactly."

The baron stood. "Then Mina must come with us. I dare not leave her here alone with Theresa."

Hugh wasn't about to tell Bernard nay. In fact, he wanted Mina with him just so he could have her by his side. "As you wish, my lord."

He watched as Bernard walked to Mina and told her the news. Her gaze jerked to him and they shared a secret smile.

"The villagers think the creature is gone," Gabriel said as he sat beside him.

Hugh couldn't believe his ears. "Are you sure?"

"That's what they're celebrating."

"Didn't anyone tell them that as long as the creature lives it will terrorize them?"

Gabriel nodded. "I tried. They think because it left last night that it's gone for good."

Hugh wiped his hand down his face. "They'll be massacred tonight."

"Not if we find the creature today."

Hugh looked into Gabriel's silver eyes. "Find Cole. We'll need him."

~ ~ ~

Mina decided against her male attire. She wanted to be the lady that Hugh thought she was. She patted her two braids that hung across her shoulders, and found herself giddy at the day ahead of her.

She opened the door to find Theresa waiting for her. "Do you need something?" she asked.

Theresa eyed her. "Who was in your bed?"

"I already told you. Me."

"Who else?"

Mina laughed. "You actually think a man would look at me?"

"You're right, of course," Theresa said and threw her long blonde braid over her shoulder narrowly missing Mina's face. "No man would have you."

Even though Mina knew that there was a man who wanted her, Theresa's words still cut deep.

"Ready?" Cole asked as he walked toward her.

She waited until Theresa turned the corner before she faced him. "Hugh let you off of guard duty?" she teased as she walked from her chamber.

Cole laughed. "For the day. It could all end today if we get lucky."

She stumbled at his words, and his hands reached out to steady her. "Are you all right?"

"Aye," she managed to say around the lump in her throat. She was so distraught at the thought of Hugh leaving that she didn't see Cole watching her.

She still hadn't recovered when they reached the bailey, but she put a smile on her face for Hugh, and to her surprise, Bernard helped her mount her mare.

Hugh fisted his hands and silently cursed. He hadn't thought of helping Mina mount, she had always done it herself. But a gentleman would help her.

He turned to find Gabriel and Cole staring at him. "What?"

"Nothing," Cole said and turned away.

But Hugh wasn't fooled. He looked at Gabriel. "What is going on with you two?"

"We've never seen you like this."

Hugh swung up in the saddle. "Like what?"

"You're happy."

Hugh started to snort until he realized Gabriel was right. "What makes you think I'm happy?"

"The way you look at Mina. That's who you were with last night, wasn't it?"

Hugh leaned down. "I don't ask who shared your bed, Gabriel. Don't ask who shared mine."

"Even if that woman got nervous when I said we might kill the creature today?" Cole asked.

Hugh straightened and sighed. It wouldn't leave him. The evidence that said Mina controlled the creature. "Are you sure?"

"Unfortunately."

"Damn," he said and nudged his horse forward needing to think through his thoughts.

He led the small band of men, which included Bernard, Cole, Gabriel and two of Bernard's knights as well as Mina, into the forest.

Many times he felt Mina's eyes on him, but he couldn't allow himself to look at her, not yet. But when they stopped just inside the forest, his gaze went to her on their own accord. Her expression was one of uncertainty, and it tore at his gut.

Could she be so great an actress that she had fooled even him?

"Hugh?"

Her soft voice called to him. She had whispered his name, but to his ears it was a shout. He gave her a brief smile before he turned to the men.

"This is a large forest. We have no idea where the creature is, so it would be best if we split up," he said.

"Good idea," Bernard said. "Mina, you come with me."

Hugh fought his anger and jealousy as Bernard helped her dismount. "Cole, you go north. Gabriel, south. I'll head farther west."

Bernard nodded and turned to his men to give them direction. "Mina and I will head northwest."

"If you find anything give a shout," Hugh said

"What happens if we discover it?" Mina asked.

"I'll tell you when we find it."

Mina saw the suspicion in Hugh's eyes, and she couldn't blame him. She had no idea what had happened. One minute he was smiling, and the next he could barely stand to look at her. She needed to speak with him.

She had awoken and went down to get some food for them, but Bernard had stopped her. When she returned to her chamber it was to find Theresa inside and Hugh gone. Since then, she had not a moment alone with him.

"Come," Bernard said and took her hand.

She stared down at their hands as he pulled her after him. She looked over her shoulder and saw Hugh watching them. Bernard set out on a fast pace, and she could barely keep up with her skirts getting tangled in the underbrush.

"Slow down," she called.

He immediately let go of her hand, and she took that time to sit and rest for a moment. "Why are you in such a hurry?

"I want to find that creature first."

"You don't even know what to do with it if we do find it."

He shrugged and looked around the forest. "Hugh said it flew this way last night."

"That's why you chose this direction?"

He nodded and reached for her hand. "You've rested enough. I want to keep moving."

She jumped up to keep from falling on her face as he pulled her. Bernard was acting so strangely, yet she couldn't figure out why.

They walked for hours looking in caves and through

underbrush for any signs of the creature, but there was none.

"It's like it only exists at night," she said.

"It has to live somewhere."

She smiled at her brother. "That's true. But where?"

"Maybe the monastery? It's just up ahead."

Something told her not to tell him she had already looked there with Gabriel and Hugh. He started walking without her, and she hurried to catch up. Many times she had to yank her skirts free from the underbrush.

"It's much easier with pants on," she mumbled when her shirts wouldn't come free.

She gave a jerk and found herself flat on her back staring at the tops of the trees as they swayed in the breeze.

"You should have told me you had fallen," Bernard said as he leaned over her. "Here, take my hand."

She smiled and accepted his hand as he pulled her to her feet. "I think I might have ripped my gown."

"I'll buy you another."

She raised her gaze to him, not sure she had heard him. Never before had he offered to buy her anything, not even when she needed it. She had always had to take discarded gowns from Theresa or sew her own.

He reached up and touched her face. "You have a smudge of dirt on you," he said. Then his hand began to caress her face. "You are so beautiful."

CHAPTER TWENTY-FIVE

Hugh had seen enough. His rage broke the surface as he walked from behind the tree.

"Hugh," Mina said and tried to back away from Bernard.

Bernard turned to him, and for a moment, Hugh thought the baron was going to keep his hold on Mina, but he eventually let her go.

"Did you find something?" Bernard asked.

Hugh looked from Mina to Bernard. Mina wouldn't meet his gaze, which bothered him immensely. "I heard something," he lied.

"It was only Mina," Bernard explained. "Her skirts became twisted in the underbrush and she fell."

There was no reason for Hugh to stay, but he couldn't make himself leave, either. He turned to Mina. "Are you all right?"

"Just fine," she mumbled, but still wouldn't raise her eyes to him.

He found it difficult to breathe. Why was she afraid of him? Had he stumbled upon something he wasn't meant to see? She had been an innocent when he took her, so he knew there wasn't another man.

Or was there?

It was time he left. He nodded and turned away from them when Mina stopped him.

"Wait."

He slowly turned to her, hoping she would say something. "Aye?"

"I suppose your hunting brought you here. Why don't you search with us?"

Before he could answer, Bernard stepped between them. "This is a large forest, Mina, and we don't have much time to look before nightfall. I think it would be better if we had as many men as we could searching."

Hugh watched as Bernard reached for Mina and turned her away. His instincts told him to follow them, but he needed to find the creature. It was more important than his jealousy.

When they were out of his sight, he swiveled on the heel of his foot and resumed his search. Yet, the image of Bernard caressing Mina's face wouldn't go away.

He's her brother. And, he did say she had fallen. He was just checking to make sure she wasn't injured.

Then why wouldn't she meet his eyes?

Because she can tell I still don't trust her. I made no attempt to hide that while still at the castle.

None of it made him feel better. In fact, it made him feel worse.

~ ~ ~

Mina looked back through the trees hoping Hugh followed them. She wanted to talk to him, to find out why he still distrusted her.

"Keep up," Bernard called harshly over his shoulder.

She jerked her head around and hurried to reach him. In moments, the ruins of the monastery appeared through the trees. Apprehension snaked down her spine. She had no desire to return to the monastery. Ever.

Her hands became clammy the closer they walked to the holy place. And she tried to tell herself it was just that. A holy place, but her heart wouldn't listen. It pounded so loudly in her chest, she feared Bernard would hear it.

When they came to the gate, she stopped and watched Bernard walk though it. It didn't take him long to realize he was alone.

He turned and quirked an eyebrow at her. "Aren't you coming?"

She swallowed and shook her head. She took a step away from the gate. "I'm tired," she said. "Running through the forest with the weight of these skirts has worn me out. I thought I would wait here for you."

"All right." He smiled and waved. "I won't be long. Don't move," he said over his shoulder.

She shuddered and sat on a fallen tree as she watched him disappear inside the monastery. It wasn't long before she realized that the normal sounds of the forest were no longer around her. Silence as still as death encircled her. The longer she sat there, the more she was sure someone or something watched her, yet she could find no one.

So she sat with her arms wrapped around her, her eyes constantly looking around her as apprehension and fear began to control her thoughts. A twig snapped behind her, and she jumped up and twirled around. But only forest surrounded her. She was starting to regret staying by herself.

She screamed when something touched her shoulder, and turned around to find Bernard standing behind her.

"Mina? What is it?" he asked.

She shook so badly she couldn't speak, and she didn't try to jerk away when he pulled her into his arms.

"Shh. It'll be all right," he said as he rubbed his hands up and down her back.

There was a loud crash in the underbrush. She pulled out of Bernard's arms and saw Hugh and Cole running toward them. So Hugh couldn't see how frightened she was, she turned away.

"What happened?" Cole asked. "We heard a scream."

She saw Bernard shrug out of the corner of her eye. "I'm not sure," he said.

"Mina."

Hugh's deep voice beckoned her. She turned and faced all three men.

"I frightened myself," she admitted.

Hugh's brow furrowed as he looked beyond her to the ruins. "Something in the monastery?"

"Nay," Bernard said and wrapped an arm around her. "It was the strangest thing. She didn't wish to go inside."

She kept her gaze on Hugh as he stared intently at her. There were many questions he wanted to ask her, she could tell, but they would have to wait.

"I thought I heard something behind me," she said. She pulled away from Bernard and went to look where she had heard the twig snap. "There," she pointed.

She watched as Hugh and Cole searched around the tree and shrubs.

"Nothing," Cole said.

Hugh walked to her. "What did you hear?"

"A twig snap. It could have been anything," she said and shrugged. "Sitting out here by oneself can get an imagination turning."

"I'm sure that's all it was," Bernard said with a small laugh.

Hugh's dark eyes went to Bernard. "Did you find anything in the monastery?"

"Nothing," Bernard said. "And I was hoping I would find the blasted creature. Did either of you locate anything?"

"Not a thing," Cole said.

A loud whistle sounded around them.

"Gabriel," Cole and Hugh said in unison before they took off through the forest.

Mina barely had time to gather her skirts before Bernard grabbed her hand and raced after them. It was a good thing the men were in front of her, because she had to hike up her skirts above her knees to be able to keep up with them.

With one arm holding her skirts and the other being pulled along by Bernard, she wasn't able to keep the branches out of her face or her hair. She gritted her teeth as a branch tangled in her hair and nearly yanked her bald-headed.

Her lungs burned, and an ache in her side started, when they finally came to a halt. She dropped her skirts and braced her hands on her knees to catch her breath.

It took her a moment to realize that there was total silence around her.

She began to straighten when Hugh took her arm and turned her away.

"Don't look," he said.

There was something painful in his eyes that made her hesitate. "Why?" she asked.

He didn't get to answer her. From behind her, she heard Bernard and someone else moving something heavy around.

"Has the creature been found?" she asked.

Hugh shook his head solemnly.

"Then what? Is Gabriel injured?"

"I'm here," Gabriel said as he came into her line of vision.

"What is going on?" she demanded. She looked from Gabriel to Hugh. It was Gabriel who finally answered her.

"One of the knights has been killed."

Hugh watched the surprise register on her face as she covered her mouth with her hand. She shook her head and took a step away from them.

"Why?" she croaked.

"I want the murderer found," Bernard raged from behind her. "Who would kill a knight like this?"

Hugh reached to keep her from looking, but he wasn't fast enough. He held her as she took in the site of the decapitated knight. She jerked out of his arms and ran to a tree where she emptied her stomach.

He strode to her and patiently waited. When she straightened and wiped her mouth with her sleeve, he opened his arms and she walked into them. He held her for a moment before he backed away.

"This is no place for you. You should be at the castle."

"No one is safe while the beast is loose."

"This wasn't the creature," Gabriel said to everyone. "It's daylight. The creature only comes at night."

"Then who?" Bernard asked. "And why?"

"Questions I would like answered myself," Hugh said. "I think it's time we returned to the castle."

They waited as the horses were retrieved, and the body of the knight wrapped and slung across his horse. Hugh lifted Mina onto her mare and kept his hand a moment too long on her leg. When he turned around it was to find Bernard studying him.

"Baron."

Bernard smiled tightly. "Hugh."

The return ride to the castle was done in silence. Hugh wanted the body of the knight kept secret to keep the panic at a minimum, so Bernard and his other man carried the knight through the postern door.

Hugh was surprised to see the bailey alive with activity as though there wasn't a being terrorizing them.

"What are they doing?" Mina asked as her gaze swept the bailey.

Cole nudged his horse close to them. "Celebrating."

She looked at him as if he had suddenly sprouted wings. "Celebrating what?"

"They think the creature is gone," Hugh explained.

She shook her head as they stopped in front of the castle. Hugh dismounted and reached for her. She slid into his arms and gave him a weak smile. He reluctantly sat her on her feet.

"I think I'll go to my chamber," she said before she walked into the castle.

He watched her until someone cleared their throat. He turned to find Gabriel and Cole behind him. "She didn't kill the knight."

"I know," Cole said. "There was no way she could have done it and returned to the monastery in time."

"Not to mention she had no blood on her," Gabriel pointed out.

"And," Hugh said, "she did not look as though she had just run a race when we found her at the monastery."

"So who does that leave?" Cole asked?

Hugh sighed and looked around him. "Everyone at the castle."

"What about Bernard?" Gabriel asked.

"Definitely not," Cole said. "Not only was he with Mina at the monastery, but I just don't think he would have it in him. Did you see the way he reacted to the knight's death?"

"I agree with Cole," Hugh said. "Bernard isn't our man. But who is, and why kill the knight?"

Hugh looked around and found people beginning to stare. "I think it's time to take this conversation elsewhere."

He walked into the castle and to his chamber. He waited for Cole to shut the door and take a seat. "Did you see anything?" he asked Gabriel.

"Nothing out of the ordinary. I hadn't found anything when I went south, so I headed southwest when I stumbled upon him."

"No one had shouted out?"

Gabriel shook his head. "If he did, I didn't hear it."

"Could it be the other knight?" Cole asked.

"Could be," Hugh said as he leaned against the door. "There wasn't any blood on his clothes though, and whoever severed the head would have blood all over them."

"There was enough blood on the trees and ground to justify that," Gabriel said.

"The knight had to have found something for someone to kill him."

Cole's brows shot up. "The blue stone perhaps?"

"Perhaps."

"Or perhaps not," Aimery said as he appeared next to Hugh.

"By the gods," Gabriel said and jumped back.

Aimery merely smiled.

"You enjoy doing that?" Hugh asked him.

"It's one of the little pleasures I have," the Fae answered.

"How much do you know?"

"It only takes me a moment to gather the information," Aimery said as his smile dropped. "I know of the knight's death."

"And you don't think he found the stone?" Cole asked.

Aimery shrugged. "Would someone leave a blue stone in the middle of a green forest to be easily found?"

"Just once, couldn't something be simple," Hugh said. He pushed off the door and moved to sit on the bed.

"If it was easy you wouldn't want to have anything to do with it. You thrive on this," Aimery said.

Maybe he was right, Hugh thought.

"So," Cole said as he rubbed his hands together. "We don't know where the creature lives, we still don't have the stone or who controls the creature, and now we have an unknown murderer."

Gabriel sighed. "Just another day for us."

Hugh turned to Aimery. "Tell me you've come to give us some good news."

Before Aimery could respond, a soft knock sounded on the door.

"Mina," Aimery said.

Hugh walked to the door and opened it. "Hello," he said and couldn't help but smile at her.

"Hello." She looked past him. "Am I interrupting?"

"Nay," Aimery said and came to stand beside Hugh. "Actually, I think it would be wise for you to hear this."

Hugh shut the door behind Mina as she smiled at Gabriel who offered her his chair. Hugh sat on the bed and made himself look away from her.

The Fae looked at each of them, then stopped at Hugh. "Information has recently come to us that might be of help. Not too long ago, a realm had the same troubles plaguing this one."

"The same creatures?" Cole asked.

"Always different creatures, but wreaking the same destruction."

Hugh leaned forward to brace his elbows on his knees. "To annihilate the realm."

"Exactly," Aimery said.

"What happened to them?" Mina asked.

Aimery looked down and sighed. "They didn't survive."

"How did you discover this?" Hugh asked.

"We have our ways," Aimery said with one side of his mouth raised in a rueful smile. "However, not all died. Twelve infants were sent from that realm. Six boys and six girls."

Hugh rose to his feet at the information. "Where were they sent?"

"Here."

CHAPTER TWENTY-SIX

Hugh was sure his ears had heard wrong. "Here?"

"Here," Aimery repeated. "But to different times."

"What has that to do with us?" Gabriel asked.

Aimery walked to the window. "It has everything to do with you."

"I think you had better explain," Hugh said. "Nothing you've told me lately has made sense."

"When does it ever," Cole muttered under his breath, but loud enough that everyone still heard.

Hugh narrowed his eyes at him and turned back to the Fae. "Aimery?"

The Fae issued a long, deep sigh. "We don't know where all the children went. In fact, we don't know where any of them are, but we think maybe they could tell us something that could stop the destruction of this realm."

"Maybe? You want to search out these children on a maybe?" Hugh asked.

"It is all we have to go on."

"And how are we to know that they would give us any information?" Gabriel questioned. "They were infants when they came to his realm. How would they know anything?"

Aimery arched his brows as he gazed at Gabriel. "I would not have brought you this information if they weren't able to give us something to aid us in stopping this realm from being annihilated." He turned his attention to the others in the chamber. "Those children weren't brought to this realm by mere chance. They were sent here for a reason."

Cole drummed his fingers on the back of the chair. "I agree that they may give us some information, but there aren't enough of us to look for the children as well as what we're doing."

"This I know," Aimery said. "But, you won't be looking for children. By our calculations, they are all grown now."

"Well, that makes it easier," Gabriel grumbled. "I suppose we could stop every man and woman we come across and ask if they were born of this realm or were sent here."

Hugh noticed that Aimery didn't comment. "What are you keeping from us?"

"I don't know if all of our information is true or not," Aimery hedged.

"Just tell us."

"The men are dead," he said after a moment. "It is how we know the children were distributed throughout the times."

Gabriel shook his head in irritation. "All six of them?"

"Unfortunately. None of them knew what they were, and we had no idea they were even here, so they didn't think twice about volunteering for wars."

Cole began to laugh. "Are you telling me all six of them died in wars throughout history? That not one of them is in the future?"

"All but one died in war."

"And the other?" Hugh asked.

"He died in a duel over a woman."

Mina sat and listened with interest. She had no idea why Aimery wanted her to hear this, but she found it fascinating. "You travel through time don't you? Can't you just go back and save these men from their deaths?"

"It doesn't work that way," Hugh said sadly.

Aimery smiled at her. "We cannot alter the past, present or future."

She looked at the men. "Isn't that what you're doing now?"

Gabriel laughed. "She does break it down rather simply."

"We wouldn't be here if the creature wasn't here," Hugh said. "It's a matter of righting what is being altered."

"Oh," she said.

"It was a good question, though," Hugh said.

She bit her lip and hastily looked down, but not before she noticed Aimery watching her.

"What about the women?" Cole asked. "How are we supposed to find them?"

Aimery once again looked out the window. "Our information says that they have a mark that will distinguish them."

"What kind of mark?" she asked.

"It's a symbol of their realm, though we don't know much about it, we do know that it has three sides and is ringed."

"And if we find one of these women, what are we supposed to do with her?" Gabriel asked.

"Call to me," Aimery said. "It's very important that we find them. I must go."

"Wait," Hugh said, but the Fae had already departed.

Mina knew the three men were irritated at what little

information they had gotten. "At least he told you something that could help."

"Always just bits and pieces. Just once I'd like to be told everything," Gabriel said.

Cole stood and put the chair against the wall. "Think of it as a puzzle. I like puzzles."

"Good. Then you can figure this one out. Oh, and remember we don't have a lot of time," Gabriel said, annoyance clear in his deep voice.

"Enough," Hugh said. He turned to Mina. "Tell me what happened at the monastery. Why did you go back?"

"Bernard wanted to look inside. I'm not sure what stopped me from telling him it had already been searched by you and Gabriel."

Gabriel stood close to her. "It could be because you're still becoming used to having a brother acknowledge you. It will take awhile to trust him."

"I hadn't thought of that." She raised her gaze to Hugh. "Do you think that's why I did it?"

Hugh shrugged. "I don't know. It's a plausible reason."

She tamped down her feeling of disappointment and continued. "When we came to the monastery I didn't want to...nay, that isn't right. I couldn't, go in. I have never felt so cold and scared and helpless in my life."

"Evil," Cole said. "That's what you felt. Evil in its purest form."

She shivered just thinking about it. "Regardless, I never want to feel it again. Bernard didn't seem affected. He walked through the gates and into the ruins while I waited in the forest."

"And that's when you heard something?" Hugh asked.

She stood because she couldn't stand to sit and be stared at a moment longer. She walked to the window and leaned back against it so she could see all three men.

"I had this strange feeling someone watched me, but when I turned around there was nothing. I began to imagine all sorts of things," she admitted.

Gabriel nodded. "That happens to all of us."

"When I heard the twig snap, I jumped up to see what caused it. That must have been when Bernard walked from the ruins. I never heard him, and when he touched my arm, I screamed."

"And then we came," Cole said.

"Aye," she said. "It was nothing."

"Oh, it was something, all right," Hugh said. "No one feels evil for nothing, Mina. Remember that for future use. There was something, or someone, there."

A chill ran down her spine at his words. "You're scaring me."

"You need to be scared. Evil is a dangerous minion. Do you have any idea how many of the Shields there once were? Several hundred of us. Now it is down to just us five."

She saw the pain in Hugh's dark depths, and wanted to wrap her arms around him. "I didn't know."

"You couldn't have," he said and took a deep breath. "We'll have to return to the monastery."

"I felt nothing when I took Mina," Gabriel said. "Even you were there, Hugh. Did you feel the evil?"

"Nay, but that doesn't mean there isn't something there now."

Mina had a sick feeling in her stomach. "You aren't going are you?" She cast a glance out the window. "It's getting late."

"She's right," Cole agreed. "The villagers need to be told to stop celebrating and get ready for the night."

Mina watched as Hugh's eyes came to rest on her. His gaze was unreadable, and she had the impression he had closed himself off.

"I'll go," he said. "You and Gabriel take care of the villagers."

"Nay," she, Gabriel and Cole said.

She walked to Hugh. "You shouldn't go out there alone. You need someone to watch your back."

"Are you worried about me?" he asked softly.

"You know I am. Too many people have died needlessly. As you told me just recently, your men need you."

Cole came to stand beside her. "As long as I've known you, Hugh, you've never done anything rash. Don't start now."

"It's going to take all three of us to get the villagers inside," Gabriel said. "Besides, I want my shot at this creature for taking Darrick."

Mina waited one heartbeat, two, and then three, before Hugh finally nodded. She sighed in relief and silently thanked God.

"I'll wait," Hugh said. "Until first light. Then I ride out."

~ ~ ~

"They won't listen," Mina said to Cole. "I've tried everything, but they truly think the creature is gone."

"Bernard is the only one who could make them get into the castle," Hugh said as he joined them.

"Then where is he?" Gabriel asked.

"Mourning. He agrees with the villagers."

Mina couldn't believe her ears. "Surely you jest. Regardless if he agrees or not, he should get them inside before nightfall just in case."

"I concur," Hugh said, "but your brother does not."

"Then I'll talk to him." She turned to go find him when Hugh's hand snaked out to halt her.

"He won't see you. The knight's death has upset him greatly. He almost wouldn't see me."

She sighed and looked at the castle to see Theresa standing in her window looking down at them. Her sister wore an evil sneer. "Did anyone search her chamber for the stone?"

Hugh stood beside her and raised his gaze. "The entire castle has been searched. Including Theresa's chamber. Why?"

"I think she has something to do with it."

"But she was attacked," Cole pointed out.

"True," Mina agreed as she turned to them. "But she could have staged it."

Gabriel shook his head. "If it had been a man, aye, I would agree with you, but I cannot see a woman doing it."

"Why?" Hugh asked. "Do you forget so easily how I was deceived before by a woman?"

Mina's stomach rolled at his words. He had been duped by a woman. "D...did this woman control the creature?"

His eyes came to light on her. "Aye."

She put her hand on her stomach as it became queasy. So much made sense now. Why he couldn't take her word of innocence, and why he trusted his instincts.

Her lungs refused to give her air. He would never believe her, she realized suddenly. She had foolishly thought he would come to understand that she couldn't possibly control the creature because she didn't have the stone.

Yet, they hadn't found the stone to prove her innocent.

"Mina?"

She raised her eyes to him. "You still think I'm guilty. All this time, I thought you believed I was innocent, regardless of what the evidence proved. I foolishly assumed you were allowing me to look for the stone with you so I could prove my innocence."

Her feet took a step away from him as the truth dawned on her.

"You kept me with you to keep an eye on me. Thought that if I was with you, I couldn't control the creature." The tears came quickly, and she didn't bother wiping them away as they coursed down her face. "You used me."

Hugh stood silent as Mina pieced everything together. He yearned to tell her she was wrong, but in truth she was very much correct.

He didn't stop her when she turned and ran into the castle. Part of him wanted to run after her and comfort her, but the logical part of him knew it was for the best. He needed to distance himself from her, and it was the perfect time to begin.

"Did I ever tell you what a fool you are?" Cole asked furiously.

He looked at his friend. "Every instinct I have says it's her. Should I ignore that?"

Cole walked stiffly away. Hugh turned his gaze to Gabriel.

"You didn't have to use her," Gabriel said.

"I didn't," Hugh said softly as Gabriel too walked from him.

CHAPTER TWENTY-SEVEN

It was useless, Hugh realized several hours later. The sun had begun to set, and the villagers had not heeded their words. No matter how hard he, Gabriel, and Cole coaxed, begged or ordered, the people continued to celebrate and drink to the now dead creature.

"They'll be slaughtered," Cole said tersely.

"There's nothing we can do other than help them into the castle once the creature comes," Gabriel said.

Hugh grunted. "If they're not too drunk to run."

"Good point," Gabriel said.

Cole looked at them. "Now what?"

"We make sure the castle is ready. We have only an hour at the most."

But no one in the castle would listen without Bernard there to give the order. The food, wine and ale flowed freely, and it hadn't taken anyone long to become drunk.

"By the gods," Gabriel hissed.

Hugh sighed and sat at one of the empty tables. "It was all in vain then. We've done nothing to prevent them from dying."

"There's nothing we can do," Cole said as he sat. "Not

unless we pick them up and bring them inside, but they do outnumber us, and I don't think they would stay here unless we chained them."

Hugh put his head in his hands. "What did we fail to notice? There must have been something we missed today. We could have killed it."

"If we had found it," Gabriel said. "It isn't your fault the creature wasn't discovered. We didn't have much to go on."

"For all we know, it could have flown past the forest," Cole said. "We've had tough assignments before, Hugh."

"True," he agreed. "But not one such as this. Those creatures were able to be killed."

His men were silent after his words.

"I sure wish Val and Roderick were here with us," Cole murmured.

And Hugh couldn't agree more. "We could use the extra hands."

His eyes went to the stairs hoping to find Mina, but he hadn't seen her since she had run from him in the bailey. Maybe he should go and check on her.

"There you are," Theresa said as she slid into the seat next to him. "I've been looking for you everywhere."

He stifled a groan. "What can I do for you, my lady?"

Her blue eyes, identical to Bernard's, twinkled. "I was hoping you would ask that," she said and ran her hand up his arm.

He had once loved blue eyes, but now he yearned for blue-green ones. Out of the corner of his eye, he saw Cole and Gabriel watching them. He moved his arm so she was no longer touching him, and turned to face her.

"Lady Theresa, the night is coming, and that means the creature as well. Shouldn't you be gathering your people into the castle?"

She laughed and ran a long fingernail across his cheek, down his neck and chest, and stopped at his waist. "I do not worry about the creature."

It was the confidence in her voice that pricked his ears. "And why do you say that?"

"You saw what it did last night. It left without killing us. It's done with us."

"I'm afraid you're wrong."

She smiled seductively. "We can debate this more in my chamber.

"As appealing as that offer might sound, I must decline." He hoped she got the point so he wouldn't have to be rude, but he had a feeling he was expecting too much.

She lowered her blue eyes for a moment, but not before he saw the spark of anger flash in them. When her gaze returned to his, she was smiling. "Not many men turn me away."

"I'm sure they do not. You are a beautiful woman." Though not as stunning as Mina, he thought to himself.

"Are you sure there isn't a way to change your mind?"

He rose to his feet. "I'm afraid not. Now, if you will excuse me, there is much I need to do."

It was amazing. He had gotten away without her detaining him any longer. He smiled inwardly, and waited for Gabriel and Cole to catch up with him.

"I cannot believe she gave up so easily," Cole said. "You should see her. Once she sets her eyes on someone she doesn't let anything stand in her way."

Gabriel snorted. "It's good you got away in time. Now, let us hope you didn't anger her."

"Me, too," Hugh agreed.

The words had just left his mouth when he was swung around. Before he could utter a word, Theresa stood on her tiptoes and planted her lips on his. He was too stunned to do anything other than stand there.

She pulled back and laid her head on his chest. "I've wanted to do that for a long time."

He kept from spitting at the cold taste of her kiss, but just barely. It wasn't until she ran her hands down his chest and looked over her shoulder that apprehension snaked through his belly.

His gaze scanned the hall until they landed on Mina at the base of the stairs. His gut twisted at the pain flooding her eyes. He tried to go to her, but Theresa held him.

"Get away, wench, you've done enough," he said. When he shoved her away from him, he looked up to find Mina gone.

"That should do it," Theresa said and moved to walk away, but Hugh grabbed hold of her arm.

"Why?" he demanded.

"Because I'm prettier than she is, and I shouldn't be jealous of her."

He shook from his anger and the realization of what Theresa had done.

"Hugh," Cole said next to him. "She's not worth it."

He turned his head toward Cole to find Gabriel there as well. With a snarl, he released Theresa and stormed from the castle, only stopping when he reached the gatehouse. He turned and looked at the bailey and the castle.

"Are you all right?" Gabriel asked as he and Cole strode toward him.

Hugh shook his head. "Do you realize what Theresa has done?"

"Aye," Cole said sadly. "She has put Mina out of your reach now."

Hugh nodded and looked at the sky. "Maybe it's for the best. I've become too attached to her."

"Looks like you got the distance you wanted," Gabriel

said. "Between using Mina and having Theresa in your arms, you've lost her for good."

Hugh found his mouth dry. His gaze went to Mina's window, but she did not stand there looking down at him.

"Dusk is coming," Cole said.

"Take your places," Hugh told them as he shoved aside thoughts of Mina. "We'll do what we can."

He was grateful to have his mind taken off of Mina and the pain on her face that broke his heart. His hand flexed and reached for his crossbow. It had been made by the Fae, and was near indestructible.

His hand fit perfectly in the groove as though it was a part of him, and in truth it was. He breathed in deeply and closed his eyes as he smelled the sweet fragrance of summer. He opened his eyes and gazed at the dark clouds rolling toward them, and heard the distant rumble of thunder.

"Perfect hunting weather," he murmured as he strode to the stable.

~ ~ ~

Mina sat on her bed and tried to breathe. The last thing she had expected to see was Theresa in Hugh's arms, though it shouldn't have been a surprise. Hugh was a gorgeous man, and Theresa a beautiful woman. It was only right that the two of them be together.

At least that is what she kept telling herself.

The tears she had shed all day continued to come. Would her pain never cease? To find out he had used her, and then to find Theresa in his arms, drove a wedge straight into what was left of her heart. Although it would have still been painful, she would have much rather seen him in anyone else's arms except Theresa's.

She wiped her wet cheeks and took a deep breath. She had expected to be hurt, just not in the way she had. At any rate, she now knew why Hugh wanted her with him all the time. It wasn't because he yearned for her or had come to care for her.

Her heart hardened against him then. She was wiser now, and would protect her precious heart that had been shattered. But never again. She had been hurt for the last time.

Hunger roused her, but she had no desire to sit in the great hall and watch Theresa and Hugh. She would sneak down later and find some food once everyone was asleep.

It was the scream of pure terror that bolted her to her feet. She rushed to her window and looked out to find the creature flying towards the castle. A glance at the bailey showed that the villagers hadn't taken the threat seriously, as they screamed and rushed to get inside the castle.

Mina ran from her chamber to the great hall to help whoever she could. Many of the villagers had gone into the dungeons, but there were many more who had been trampled and injured. She helped get many of them to the stairs of the dungeon where others brought them below.

She looked around for Bernard, but didn't find him anywhere. And neither did she see Hugh or his men. Just where were they when they were needed so desperately?

"My boys," a woman cried as she tried to rush from the dungeon. "My babies!"

Mina spun around and raced from the castle without thought to her safety. She needed to find those boys. She stood aside as more villagers entered the castle while the creature circled the bailey.

It wasn't until she was in the bailey that she saw the carnage around her. Dead bodies littered the bailey, and blood was everywhere. She began to shake with fear until she spotted the two boys running toward the castle.

"Here," she called, and motioned for them to hurry. Her eyes scanned the skies for the creature, but it had gone out of her sight. "Hurry," she whispered.

Then, the dreadful sound of the beating of wings sounded behind her. She slowly turned, and her stomach fell to her feet when she caught sight of the creature on the steps to the castle blocking her retreat. Its beady red eyes glared at her, then slid to the boys approaching.

She turned and ran to the boys. "Stay behind me," she told them. "No matter what, stay behind me."

They nodded at her through their terror. She gave them a smile and turned to the creature.

~ ~ ~

"Ah. Hugh, do you see what I see?" Cole asked.

Hugh looked up from notching his crossbow to find Mina facing the creature. "By the saints," he hissed. "What is she doing?"

"Saving those two lads, I would think."

Hugh whistled to gain Gabriel's attention and motioned for him to distract the creature. Yet, as Gabriel fired arrow after arrow, the creature did not look away from Mina.

"It isn't working," Cole said.

"I know that," Hugh snapped. "Have you a better idea?"

"I don't think it matters now."

"Naaayyyyyyy!" Hugh bellowed as the creature clamped its claws around her and flew away.

CHAPTER TWENTY-EIGHT

Mina opened her eyes to find the ground rushing far beneath her. She tried to scream, but her chest was squeezed painfully. She looked above her to see the creature holding her as it flew high in the sky.

Terror took hold of her, turning her blood to ice, and causing her heart to pound in her chest. She had wanted adventure in her dull life, but now all Mina craved was the castle and Hugh's arms around her.

To her amazement, the beast flew straight to the monastery and landed on the roof. It released her, and a scream lodged in her throat as she began to fall. She landed with a bone-jarring thud that knocked the breath from her. Once she was able to breath again, her entire body pulsed with aches and pains. She took stock of herself and found the only thing that might be injured were her ribs from where the creature had grabbed her.

She blinked and looked around the roof, the eerie silence of the night sending chills of dread over her body. Mina turned her head and found the creature staring at her. She refused to die huddled and scared. She would meet her death standing tall.

"Why didn't you kill me at the castle," she said defiantly as she gained her feet.

The being laughed harshly. "I only do as I am commanded."

"What?" she asked, not sure she understood.

"He brought you because I told him to."

She whirled around to find Bernard behind her.

~ ~ ~

Hugh and Gabriel managed to get the villagers that were still alive inside the castle and in the dungeon. The night sky was quiet and still as Hugh searched it, straining his eyes to catch a glimpse of the creature, and maybe one of Mina.

"There isn't anything you could have done," Gabriel said and placed a comforting hand on Hugh's shoulder.

Hugh knew Gabriel was right, but it didn't make him feel any better. If only he had done something to help Mina, she might still be alive. He should have run down to her. He should have done more.

"The lads have been returned to their mother," Cole said as he joined them.

Then the oddest thing happened. Hugh felt moisture in his eyes, and he hastily blinked. "She died saving their lives."

Suddenly, it didn't matter that she wasn't innocent. All he knew was that his heart ached knowing she was gone. There was a hole in his chest where his heart had been, which made it even worse because he hadn't known it had begun to live again.

"It was a brave thing she did," Cole agreed.

Gabriel sighed. "I'm not looking forward to telling the baron."

Hugh jerked as if he had been shot and clenched his fists. "How could we have been so dense?"

"What?" Cole asked

Hugh looked at Gabriel and Cole. "Have either of you seen Bernard since we returned this afternoon?"

They shook their heads.

"He isn't in the dungeon," Gabriel said.

Cole's gaze narrowed. "Nor is he with his knights."

Hugh leaned his head back against the castle wall and laughed dryly. Then murmured, "Mina, forgive me."

"Hugh," Gabriel growled. "God's blood, tell us what is going on.

Hugh stared at the inky sky as the stars blinked above him. Finally, he looked at his men. "Did either of you search Bernard's chamber?"

Gabriel and Cole looked at each other before they shook their heads again.

"It's as I thought." Hugh sighed. "I've been wrong, so damn wrong. I was deceived again, but it wasn't by a woman this time."

"The baron?" Cole asked in surprise.

All three raced to Bernard's chamber, but no matter how hard they searched they didn't find the blue stone.

"Nothing," Gabriel hissed and kicked the trunk he'd been rifling through.

"He's smart," Hugh said. "He knew we would search the castle."

Cole slapped his hands on his thighs in exasperation. "If not the castle then where?"

Gabriel crossed his arms over his chest. "That I'm not sure. I do have a feeling we'll see him by dawn."

"We'll question him then," Cole stated.

"Nay," Hugh said louder than he intended. He motioned them out of the chamber and didn't speak again until they were in the bailey. "We follow him."

"We cannot all follow him," Gabriel said.

"That's right," Hugh said and narrowed his gaze as his mind began to form a plan. "Cole, you're as quiet as a shadow. Trail the baron and find anything we can use against him."

Cole gave a brief nod and was out the door.

Hugh turned to Gabriel. "You and I need to set up a diversion to make Bernard think he's safe so he'll go for the stone."

"I've got just the thing," Gabriel said with a sly grin before he turned on his heel and left.

It wasn't until Hugh was alone that his thoughts turned back to Mina. He couldn't believe she was dead. It just didn't seem possible. How he regretted the words they had last spoken.

He walked to the window and watched the knights as they gathered the dead. The beast had killed more this night than it had since before he and the Shields arrived. The creature was so hungry for blood that it couldn't wait to sink its talons into anyone that got near it.

Hugh's gut contorted painfully. He squeezed his eyes shut as realization dawned on him. It had been in front of him the entire time.

Mina wasn't dead. If the creature had wanted to kill her, it would have done so in the bailey the first time. The creature had taken her because she was working with Bernard to control it.

Relief surged through him to recognize that she was indeed living, and though it hurt him to know she was part of the evil, it didn't stop him from wanting to shout to the heavens at having her alive.

His heart squeezed agonizingly as comprehension filled him. It wasn't just joy he felt, but love.

Pure, beautiful, love.

"Nay," he whispered. "It couldn't have happened after all these years. Not like this."

But it had.

His heart had been given to a woman who controlled evil.

"I love her."

The words spoken aloud only confirmed it. And he would do everything in his power to get her away from the evil, even if it cost him his life.

~ ~ ~

Mina shook from her panic, and wrapped her arms around herself. She wasn't sure where she was exactly since Bernard had blindfolded her. All she knew was that she was somewhere deep in the bowels of the monastery, somewhere she, Gabriel, and Hugh had not found.

Her instincts had been right to have her look at the monastery. It was too bad she hadn't found the evidence she had needed before.

Bernard.

Anger surged through her like lightning. Her *brother*. How could he? She had thought for sure that it was Theresa controlling the creature. How could she have been so wrong about it?

And how could Hugh have missed it?

If he had never been wrong, then he had truly been duped, but that didn't make her feel any better. She desperately wanted to speak to Hugh, to feel his strong arms around her keeping her safe. Did he think she was dead? If he did, then he wouldn't come looking for her, which was exactly what Bernard wanted, she realized.

Her brother hadn't said anything as he brought her into

her cage, no matter how much she begged and pleaded. But what had disturbed her the most was the kiss – on the lips – he had given her.

It had shaken her to her very core, for it hadn't been a brotherly kiss. It had been one of a lover.

She had screamed for him to let her out, but he had quickly bolted and locked the door, leaving her in complete darkness. She wished for a window or something so she could have some light. Her eyes had adjusted to the darkness, but it didn't keep her fear at bay.

It made it worse, since she knew the creature guarded her.

CHAPTER TWENTY-NINE

"She what?"

Hugh watched Bernard carefully as they sat in the great hall while sunlight began to spill into the castle. "I'm sorry, baron. She died saving the lives of two lads."

Bernard shook his head and gazed at the table. "I don't believe it. Not Mina. She was just beginning to live again."

Hugh felt Cole kick him under the table.

"Where is her body?" Bernard asked as he lifted his gaze to Hugh. "Is it with the others?"

"Actually," Gabriel said. "The creature carried her off."

To give Bernard credit, he acted the grieving brother well as he buried his head in his hands.

"We must find the stone," Bernard said as he raised his head. "I want this beast dead."

"Don't worry. We'll kill it," Hugh said.

There was much weeping in the castle as family members mourned the loss of one of their own, as well as the loss of Mina. But there was one person who didn't mourn.

In fact, Theresa looked anything but sad. The satisfied expression only confirmed how deep her hatred for Mina went. But why? They were sisters, and Mina had been nothing but civil to Theresa. It must be something much deeper.

And there was only one way to find out.

Hugh waited until Theresa left the hall before he looked pointedly at Gabriel and Cole. He wasn't worried about them. They each knew what they had to do.

He stood outside Theresa's chamber and prepared himself mentally. So much was at stake, and he couldn't make a misstep. He raised his hand and knocked before he changed his mind. The door swung open almost immediately, as if she had been expecting someone.

"Hugh," she said breathlessly as she stood gawking at him.

"Lady Theresa. I hope I'm not interrupting."

She gave him a dazzling smile and motioned him inside. "Not at all. Please, come in."

He walked through the doorway and schooled his expression. "You do not mourn your sister?"

"Pah," she scorned and shut the door. "I would be lying if I said I did. She never belonged here."

"Just where did she belong?"

She seemed to realize she had said more than she should, and shrugged. "Anywhere but here."

Hugh knew she lied, but he had more pressing things to see to. The time was at hand. He took a step toward her and twirled a lock of her blonde hair around his finger. "You needn't have hated her. Everyone knows you are the prettiest women in the shire."

She smiled and cocked her head to the side. "It was just last night that you pushed me away."

"I'm not a man who shares. I wanted to be sure you were mine alone."

She sighed and moved closer to him. "Oh, I am

definitely all yours."

"Just what I wanted to hear," he said and nuzzled her neck. He slowly ran his finger up her arm. "Is it ordinary for the creature to carry its prey off?"

She pulled away from him. "What?"

"Didn't you know? The creature didn't kill Mina in the bailey. It carried her off."

She turned away from him, but he saw the anger spark in her blue eyes. "Normally the beast kills here, but it has taken others off."

It was a lie.

He smiled as she fell neatly into his plan. He touched her shoulders, but she deftly stepped away from him.

"We shouldn't be up here," she said as she turned to face him. "There is much I need to help my brother with."

Hugh nodded slightly and walked from the chamber. It wouldn't be long now.

When he reached the hall, he found Gabriel leaned back in his chair as if he didn't have a care in the world.

"The wheels are turning," Hugh said as he sat across from Gabriel.

"Cole is tracking the quarry through the castle."

"Good," Hugh said and drank deeply from his goblet. If everything went according to plan, they would find the stone, capture the ones who controlled the creature, and kill the beast all before nightfall.

He sat where he could see every aspect of the hall without fully turning his head. He and Gabriel made it seem as though they were in deep conversation, but in reality they did nothing more than speak of their horses.

Hugh was about to give up when he saw Theresa walk from the shadows by the stairs toward the kitchens that would take her out of the castle.

"The bait has left," he whispered.

Gabriel snorted. "About time. I was about to start speaking of my horse's tail."

Hugh smiled despite himself. His eyes rose to the top of the stairs where he saw Cole. Cole nodded before slipping back into the shadows.

"Are you ready?" Hugh asked.

"I'm always ready," Gabriel said. "Has our quarry taken the bait?"

"He should. Any moment now."

~ ~ ~

Bernard downed his ale in one gulp, and looked around his large chamber. He poured himself another goblet and drank deeply. He smiled to himself as the ale filled his stomach.

Everything had worked out just as he had planned. For a while, he feared Hugh would figure out Mina's secret, but the dolt had been too blind. But Bernard planned to make him pay for touching Mina.

Too long he had acted the drunken lord to be overlooked. Despite the arrival of Hugh and the Shields, Bernard had been able to carry out his plans. And after tonight, nothing would matter any more. Not even Theresa could spoil this.

He walked toward his bed and glanced out his window. That's when he saw her.

"Theresa," he hissed.

She was headed to the forest. Surely she hadn't figured it out. But he would have to make sure she left well enough alone.

~ ~ ~

Mina's stomach growled loudly with hunger, but her fear took precedence. She kept telling herself to get up and walk around, but her legs wouldn't obey her. So, she sat huddled in the same corner she had fallen into when Bernard pushed her into the little chamber.

Her thoughts drifted to Hugh. She had only to close her eyes to envision his dark gaze tilted upward with his smile. She grinned at the memory. He was such a handsome man. She missed him terribly.

Despite knowing he preferred Theresa, she still longed to have him know she wasn't involved with the creature or the stone. She had her memories of their time together and they would have to last a lifetime, because she knew there would be no other man for her.

Only him.

Even now her body yearned for him to fulfill an ache only he knew how to quench.

A sound above her startled her. She held her breath as she heard the telltale sound of footsteps coming toward her. Would it be Bernard...or something else?

~ ~ ~

"Let's go," Hugh whispered to Gabriel when Cole motioned to him.

He and Gabriel slipped out of the castle without anyone seeing. Cole waited beside the postern door with their weapons.

"What happened?" he asked Cole.

"I'm not sure. I heard Bernard curse loudly before he threw open his door and came here."

Hugh smiled. "Good. He'll think nothing of anyone following him because he'll be focused on Theresa."

"How did you know she was in on it?" Cole asked.

"A hunch. I knew how much she hated Mina, and it seemed as though Mina's death wasn't a surprise."

Gabriel moved past them. "Enough talk. Our quarry is getting away."

Hugh picked up his crossbow and slung it over his shoulder while his left hand held the hilt of his sword in its scabbard. He waited for Cole to take the lead before he moved. Gabriel would follow behind and make sure no one pursued them.

They made it to the forest without any mishap.

"Bernard hasn't even looked behind him," Cole said.

"He's too confident," Hugh said. "I was expecting that."

They moved onward keeping hidden behind trees and brush.

"Where is he headed?" Gabriel asked as they hunched down behind a fallen tree.

Hugh had an idea. "There are only two places in this forest that he would think of hiding the stone."

He didn't say more because Bernard chose that time to turn and stare directly at them. Thankfully, they had hidden well. Bernard continued to glance around the forest, as if he expected someone to come running at him.

Cole sighed and slid down next to them. "He would have turned around when I was standing next to the tree. He's moved on."

Hugh made to move when Gabriel's hand landed on his arm. "You're sure Mina is part of this?"

"Aye," Hugh answered. "As much as I hate to admit it."

"Usually, it's only one person who controls the creature," Cole said. "You think all three of them are in on it?"

Hugh blew out a breath. "I wasn't sure about Theresa

until today. She had me fooled. Hell, Bernard had me completely mislead until last night."

"What are you going to do about Mina?"

Gabriel asked the question Hugh hadn't allowed himself to think about. He turned to his friends. "I'm not going to lie. I love her."

Cole whistled softly. "We knew you had feelings, but we had no idea they went that deep."

"Congratulations," Gabriel said.

Hugh shook his head. "I might love her, but that doesn't change the fact that she's involved with evil."

"What's your plan?"

"I'm going to convince her to let go of the evil."

Cole rose up and looked over the tree before he glanced back at Hugh. "I wish you the best of luck, old friend. We'll be there if you need us."

~ ~ ~

The door opened slowly flooding light into the little chamber and blinding Mina. She covered her eyes with her arm and waited.

"I'm going to kill him."

Mina's heart jumped into her throat at those words. She lowered her arm and looked into the hate-filled eyes of her sister. "Theresa?"

"I should have known he wouldn't follow the plan," she spat.

Mina rose to her feet with the aid of the stone wall she had been leaning against. "Let me go."

"So you can run and spill our little secret to Hugh? I think not. I have waited too many years to see you dead. Nothing is going to stop me now."

CHAPTER THIRTY

Their steps were light as Hugh and his men followed Bernard. Trepidation twisted through Hugh. His worst fears were taking shape in front of him.

But it wasn't until Bernard had taken the left path in the fork in the road that Hugh knew a moment of pure dread. Everything he imagined had indeed been true.

Even where the creature lived.

"I should've known," Hugh muttered as they stood outside the monastery's gates.

"Mina knew something was here," Gabriel said.

"Of course she did. She was part of it. Bloody hell, she led us right to it, and we were too dim-witted to see it."

Cole looked around them. "I think you're wrong. The last time Mina was here she wouldn't go in."

"It could have been a trick," Hugh said.

"Or not," Gabriel pointed out. "Don't condemn her just yet."

"After all, you were wrong about Theresa and Bernard," Cole said.

"We'll see about all of it," Hugh said as he walked through the gates.

He didn't need to turn around to see if his men where with him, he knew they were. When he reached the doorway into the monastery, he paused a moment and said a quick prayer that he was wrong about Mina.

"We could use Aimery's help with this," Cole said from behind him.

Hugh looked at his black-haired friend and smiled. "I've never asked Aimery for help before. I'm not about to start now."

Gabriel chuckled. "Let's get going then. I'm tired of waiting."

~ ~ ~

Mina didn't fight Theresa as her sister dragged her to the top of the monastery. She looked at Theresa's triumphant expression.

"Why have you always hated me?"

Theresa laughed. "You mean you still don't know? I'm surprised Bernard hasn't spilled that secret."

"It was a secret I planned on telling her this night."

Mina jerked around to find Bernard walking toward them. She looked about expecting to find Hugh, but there was no one but her brother. She watched Bernard and Theresa glare at each other.

"What secret?" she asked when neither spoke.

"Do you really want to know why you were never part of our family?" Theresa screamed shrilly, venting her rage as she glared daggers at Mina. "Why our parents all but ignored you?"

The verbal barb cut deep. "I want to know."

"Mina," Bernard said softly and came toward her. "It's nothing to be upset about. To be honest, I'm glad the truth will finally come out."

"What truth?" Mina asked. She was tired of hidden meanings and hints. She needed answers.

"You aren't our sister," Theresa smirked, and crossed her arms over her chest.

Mina couldn't have been more shocked if Theresa had told her the sky was purple. "What?"

Bernard turned around and slapped Theresa hard enough to send her to her knees. "Enough." He then turned and grabbed Mina's shoulders. "Mina, it's the truth. I've wanted to tell you many times, but my parents made me swear I wouldn't."

Mina tried to step away from him, but he held her tightly. "Who are my parents?"

"I don't know."

Her head began to ache with everything filling it. "I don't understand. You've been just as cruel to me as Theresa."

"Only because I was trying to hide how I truly felt. Have you never wondered why I haven't married?"

She shook her head. "You're still young."

"How about why I never made you find a husband?"

"Because of the way I look," she said.

"Neither answer is right. I didn't make you find a husband because I couldn't bear to see you with another man. The only reason Theresa was able to take your betrothed was because I bribed him."

Mina's head jerked up. Nothing made sense anymore, the more they talked, the more confused she became. "Stop," she said and tried to turn away.

"You need to hear this," Bernard said urgently and dragged her against him. "It's for the best."

"Nay," she screamed and wrenched out of his arms only to collide with a wall of solid muscle.

Just when she was about to fall she was caught by

strong arms she knew all too well. She raised her gaze and looked into the hard eyes of Hugh.

He didn't speak to her, just set her behind him where Gabriel and Cole stood on either side of her. She watched as Bernard drew his sword.

"I wondered if you would follow me," Bernard said.

Hugh shrugged. "Put that away. You're no match for me."

"You won't stand in my way of getting what I want. Not after all these years."

"Just what do you want?"

Bernard laughed. "You still don't know?"

"Would I ask if I did?"

She knew that although Hugh's tone was light, he was furious. All one had to do was look at the tick in his neck to know.

"I want Mina," Bernard said. "And no one," he said with a pointed glance at Theresa, "will stand in my way."

Cole cursed. "You want your own sister?"

"I don't think she's his sister," Hugh said.

Bernard clapped his hand against his sword. "Very good. When did you figure that out?"

"Just now."

"What a pity. I had thought you were smarter than that," Bernard taunted.

Hugh shrugged. "Power makes everyone think they are shrewder than the rest. Tell me, Bernard, why kill your parents?"

"Why not?" Bernard asked. "Power is a most heady feeling. You should try it sometime."

"What power you think you have is misleading. The evil that holds the blue stones is the one with the true power."

"We'll see about that," Bernard said.

Mina knew this was the time for answers and truths.

She took a little step forward. "Who drugged your ale?" she asked Bernard.

He laughed, but kept his gaze on Hugh. "I did."

"Why?" Mina asked.

"It had to look convincing."

"And Theresa's attacker?"

Bernard looked over his shoulder at Theresa. "Ask her."

Mina turned her gaze to Theresa. "Well?"

"It was me. It's amazing how much power the stone holds," she purred. "It helped me to nearly kill you by infecting your wounds."

Mina had never felt so angry and hurt in her life. "Bernard's knight?"

"All me," Theresa said and looked down at the large emerald ring on her finger.

"Dammit, Theresa," Bernard bellowed. "I knew it was you. You lied to me."

"No more than you lied to me," Theresa retorted. "You would have killed me along with our parents had I not found the stone."

Bernard turned and roared before he raised his sword and thrust it at Hugh.

Mina turned to Gabriel. "Do something," she begged.

"I am," he said solemnly. "I'm keeping you safe."

She groaned and looked to Cole, who quickly threw up his hands and shook his head.

"Don't turn those blue-green eyes at me, my lady. I was given orders, and I'll be doing just that."

She had the urge to stamp her foot she was so angry. It was then that she spotted Theresa slowly working her way toward Hugh and Bernard. Something flashed in the sunlight, and Mina caught sight of the dagger.

Without thought to her own safety, she slipped past

Gabriel and Cole and ran at Theresa. She tackled Theresa to the ground just as she was about to plunge the dagger into Hugh's back. Mina raised her head to make sure Hugh was unhurt.

Swords clanged as he and Bernard continued to fight. Her eyes were glued to the smooth, graceful movements of Hugh. Bernard was smaller, and moved a little quicker, but he was no match for Hugh's strength and ability.

Her breath caught when Bernard's sword swung at Hugh's midsection, but Hugh deftly blocked the swing. Theresa forgotten, Mina got to her feet to watch the two men when the world tilted and she was thrown to her back. She tried to grab hold of the roof when she realized that she was on the edge and about to fall off.

"Die!" Theresa screamed.

Before Mina could call for help, Bernard had turned and pulled her safely away from the edge. He cupped her cheek and smiled.

"I'll keep you safe," he said.

Her eyes moved past Bernard to find Theresa's gaze burning with hatred. The dagger was once again in Theresa's hand, and despite the fear Mina felt with Bernard, she couldn't allow him to die.

At the same time, she yelled for Bernard to look behind him, Hugh also tried to stop Theresa. But Theresa used the dagger to slash at Hugh's arm. Mina watched in horror as Theresa got past Hugh and started toward Bernard.

"No more shared power," Theresa yelled. "I want it all!"

Bernard rose to his feet. He swung his arm around to stop her downward thrust of the dagger, and the force of it sent both of them over the edge of the roof.

Mina rushed to the edge. Her heart pounded fiercely as she gazed down upon the two people she had thought family. She mourned for them. After all, they were the only family she had known.

"I didn't expect that," Cole said from beside her.

"None of us did," Hugh said from her other side.

She sighed and turned away from the gruesome sight. "Now what?"

"Where is the stone?" Hugh asked.

Her eyes closed briefly. "You still think I'm a part of this?"

His dark gaze held hers. "It doesn't matter any more. Help us find the stone so we can destroy it and the creature."

"I would if I knew where it was," she cried. She'd had enough. Hadn't he heard anything that Bernard and Theresa had said?

"All right," Hugh said.

That made her pause. "You believe me?"

"I don't have any other choice."

She turned away before she gave into the urge to wrap her hands around his thick neck and squeeze.

"What happened before we arrived?" Gabriel asked.

She opened her mouth to tell them when Hugh cut her off.

"We don't have time," he said. "We must find the stone and the creature before nightfall since we won't get any answers from Bernard or Theresa now."

"Why?" she asked. "With Bernard and Theresa dead they can no longer control the beast."

"That's just it. Without someone to control it, the creature will destroy everything in one night."

She nodded and looked around. "Right then. Where should we begin looking?"

"My guess is here," Hugh said. "You wouldn't have been brought here otherwise. Both the creature and the stone are somewhere very close."

"Cole and I will take the lower levels," Gabriel said as he and Cole walked away.

Mina wrung her hands together and looked anywhere but Hugh. "I'll look around here."

Hugh watched her. There was so much he wanted to say, but he didn't know where to begin. The first thing he had wanted to do when he had seen her was take her in his arms. Instead, he had pushed that emotion aside.

He knew he should look at the level below them, but he didn't want to leave her. He told himself it was to make sure she didn't leave with the stone, but he knew it was because he wanted to be near her.

When he couldn't stand it another moment, he reached out and took her arm. She turned to him, her eyes full of hurt and worry. He could stand it no more, and pulled her into his arms. For a moment she stiffened, then melted against him. It was the sweetest moment of his life.

"Will you help us find the stone?"

She pulled back and looked at him. "Of course. I've already told you I would. Why are you asking me again?"

"I want you to know that it doesn't matter that you were part of it with Bernard. Help us destroy the creature, and everything else won't matter."

She stepped out of his arms. He should have known by the darkening of her eyes that anger swelled just beneath the surface.

"I was not part of anything. I am innocent."

He sighed, tired of it all. He just wanted the truth from her. "No more lies, Mina. It doesn't matter anymore."

"Aye, it does. I won't have you believing me to be guilty of something I'm not. You never once considered Bernard, yet he fooled you completely."

Hugh took her hands in his. "Mina, it doesn't matter

anymore because I love you."

Her mouth dropped open then snapped shut. "I cannot believe you," she said and walked away.

Hugh couldn't understand what had gone wrong. He knew she had feelings for him. He hadn't expected her to say that she loved him, but he had expected more than what he had gotten.

He stalked off after her. "We aren't through talking."

"Aye, we are," she said as she walked down the stairs, her steps hard and hurried.

He tried to grab her, but she yanked her arm away from him. To his dismay, she lost her balance and began to fall backwards.

CHAPTER THIRTY-ONE

Mina reached for anything that she could grab hold of. Her hand caught on a stone that stuck out from the others in the stairwell. She sighed loudly when she had once again gained her balance. And in an instant, the stone slipped out and she began to fall again.

Only, this time, Hugh grabbed her. She locked her arms around his neck. Nothing she did could stop her from shaking. Too many attempts on her life, both planned and accidental, were having an effect on her.

"Are you all right?"

She shook her head. "That's the third time I've almost fallen to my death. I think I'm beginning to fear heights."

He set her at the top of the stairs. "You'll be fine up there."

"I've got to walk down sometime. I don't like this place. I wish to leave soon. Immediately would be preferable."

She hadn't expected him to agree since they had to find the stone and the creature. It was then both of them looked at his feet to see the gray stone that she had pulled free.

"You don't think..." She couldn't even finish the

sentence.

"It would be too easy," he said.

But he took a step up and looked into the hole where the stone had been. Mina held her breath as Hugh pushed his hand into the dark gap. When he pulled his hand out, he held something. He unwrapped the soiled linen to show the smooth round blue stone that had caused so much havoc.

"I can't believe it," she whispered.

"And all because you were about to fall," Hugh said as he wrapped back up the stone.

Her heart squeezed as she recalled his words. He loved her. She longed to tell him that she loved him too. She had known for quite some time how her heart felt, but she tried to keep it from herself, and him.

"I wasn't a part of it," she said again, hoping this time he might believe her. "I swear to you."

His dark eyes raised and looked at her.

"I know you think the evidence points to me, but the fact is that it was Bernard and Theresa. I didn't realize Bernard was part of it until he had the creature bring me here last night."

Hugh looked away, and she began to lose hope.

"I stayed the night locked in a dark chamber. I'll even take you to it." She swallowed as she searched for some proof she could give him. "I also learned something today."

"What?" he asked quietly.

"They weren't my brother and sister. Bernard wanted me for his wife."

This time Hugh looked at her closely. "Aimery," he called.

In a blink, the Fae stood beside them. He looked down at Hugh's hand and smiled. "Aye, you found the blue stone. Very good." Then he looked around them. "It's old and dusty in here. Come."

They followed him back onto the roof.

Mina walked to Aimery and said, "Please, tell Hugh the truth. He won't believe me."

Aimery looked down at her, and she saw the sadness in his bright blue eyes.

"Hugh has to see it for himself."

"Nay," said Hugh. "I demand you tell me. Never once have I asked for anything since I've been a Shield. This is twice now that I have asked you about Mina. Why won't you tell me?"

"The Fae are not allowed to meddle in the affairs of humans."

Mina found herself grinning at the curses Hugh said as he paced in front of them. She stopped him and said, "I speak the truth. I am not a blood relative of Bernard and Theresa."

Hugh looked at Aimery who nodded.

Mina swallowed and licked her lips. "I did not know where the stone was."

Aimery nodded again.

"I was with Aimery the day the stone was found in my chamber."

Aimery nodded.

"I am not a part of any evil involving the creature."

Hugh wanted to believe her. He saw the question in her gaze, and knew she spoke the truth. He smiled and went to gather her in his arms, but she held him away from her.

"I'm not done," she said.

He groaned. "Then finish."

"I love you."

He pulled her against him and closed his eyes. Never once had he expected to find someone like her, much less love. When he opened his eyes it was to find Aimery grinning.

"You knew?" he asked the Fae.

Aimery nodded. "But you had to realize your love despite what your instincts said."

"Now that Hugh knows what an idiot he's been, might we look for the creature?" Gabriel asked from the stairway.

Hugh laughed and gave Mina a quick kiss. "We'll finish this later."

"Aye, we will," she promised.

~ ~ ~

They searched the entire monastery, twice, to no avail.

"I don't understand," Cole said. "I can feel that it's here."

Hugh looked at Aimery. "Can you help?"

"I also feel that it is very near, and I cannot understand why we haven't found it."

"Are you telling me the beast is cloaked from you?" Hugh asked.

Aimery nodded dejectedly.

"The sun will dip into the horizon in just a few hours," Cole called from the window.

Mina jumped up and ran out of the monastery. Hugh followed to find her outside staring at the monastery.

"What is it?"

She didn't answer as she walked around the monastery, her eyes focused toward the sky.

"Mina," he urged.

She looked at him. "I think I found it."

Hugh followed her arm that pointed to the roof and a gargoyle. "There are gargoyles across England. There are even some on your castle."

"Exactly. No one pays attention to them because they are everywhere."

"It would explain why our information said it could only be killed it while it slept," Aimery said.

Hugh ran back into the monastery, but then waited on Mina, because he didn't know which one was the creature.

"I suppose we could destroy them all," Cole said.

"I wouldn't advise it," Aimery said as he walked past him to lean against the bell tower.

Gabriel frowned. "Why?"

"You really don't want to know," Aimery said ominously.

"Which one, Mina?" Hugh asked.

Mina walked around the roof. "I'm not sure." She inspected one gargoyle and then another until all of them had been looked at.

"I was so sure that was the answer," she said.

Hugh wrapped an arm around her. "It was a good guess, love."

She smiled and leaned against one of the gargoyles.

"The sun is just about to set," Cole called.

Mina was sick to her stomach to realize they had failed. "At least we have the stone."

They all nodded. She sighed and turned to look over the beloved lands that she thought were part of her. Now she didn't know where she came from or who her parents why. Or why her parents had given her up. Her eyes lowered as she realized just how much her life had changed in a matter of days. And that was when she saw it.

"Hugh," she whispered urgently.

In an instant, he was by her side.

She pointed to the gargoyle she was leaning against. "Is that not from your crossbow?" she asked of the missing part of the gargoyle's wing.

"That it is."

She stepped back as Cole, Gabriel, and Hugh tried to

shove it off the roof, but it didn't budge. The darkness beginning to surround them made it difficult to see. But she definitely saw the small movement of the gargoyle's wing.

"It's waking up!"

"Try this," Aimery said as he handed Hugh a mace.

The first swing knocked a chunk out of the stone gargoyle's wing. The second knocked the entire wing off. The gargoyle's stone eyes glowed red, and they heard the unmistakable sound of a growl.

"Hurry," Aimery warned.

When the gargoyle's mouth opened as he bared his long teeth, Mina gasped and wished she had a weapon of her own to hack away at the creature. She said a prayer that they would succeed as Hugh hammered away at the stone creature while it continued to growl and hiss as it slowly woke.

Chunk by chunk of stone fell to the ground until there was nothing left but its legs. Hugh, Gabriel and Cole were then able to push it over the side.

She rushed to the edge of the roof to see the creature shatter into pieces before it began to sizzle and melt away.

"Just in time," Aimery said.

They saw the sun sink below the horizon. She held her breath expecting to hear the creature, but there were only the sounds of the night.

"Thank you," she said as she turned toward Aimery only to find him gone.

Cole began to laugh. "Don't worry, Mina. He does it all the time."

She looked at Hugh. "What now?"

"First, we tell the villagers they are free."

He held out his hand, and she eagerly put hers in his.

CHAPTER THIRTY-TWO

Hugh watched as the villagers crowded around Mina. He and Mina had decided to keep what Bernard and Theresa had done a secret. Their bodies had been brought in and readied for burial, but for tonight, there would be celebrating.

"What do you want?" Aimery asked as he walked to him.

Hugh looked at the Fae. "What do you mean?"

"You have found what some people search their entire lifetimes for. Love. A soul mate."

Hugh tamped down the hope that blossomed in his heart. "I am a Shield. I lead my men."

"And you've been an exceptional leader," Aimery said with a smile. "I've been sent to grant you removal from the Shields, if that is your desire."

Hugh thought it over for a moment. "The Shields have dwindled to five. If I leave, there will only be four."

"Oh, you'll still be a Shield," Aimery said. "You will just be here. Stone Crest will be a safe haven for the men, and a place where you can train new recruits, and your men can have a home."

A smile broke across Hugh's face. "Truly?"

"If Mina will have you," Aimery said.

Hugh walked to Mina and dragged her away from the villagers. "I love you," he said.

"I love you, too," she said and smiled. "What's happened?"

He answered by pulling her into his arms and slanting his mouth over hers. He plundered her mouth, every ounce of hope, every yearning he'd ever had, he put into the kiss. He didn't end it until she was limp in his arms.

"I missed that," she said.

He placed a kiss on her forehead and pulled her tightly against his chest. "Will you be my wife?"

She stiffened and pulled out of his arms to turn her back on him. "Don't. That is too cruel."

He heard the tears in her voice, and turned her back around to face him. "Just answer me, love."

"I would be honored to be your wife, if you were staying."

He took her head in his hands until she was looking at him. "But I am staying."

"What?" she asked with a sniff. "You're a Shield."

"Aye, and I'll still be one. Just here. The castle will be a safe haven for the men. If you agree."

She threw her arms around his neck. "Of course I agree, you silly man."

"Well," Cole said, "I guess we'll find a way to go on without you. It won't be too hard to take over the leadership."

"Leadership my arse," Gabriel said. "If anyone is going to be the leader it's me."

Mina sighed as contentment settled around her. "I do have one question."

"What is that?" Hugh asked as he nuzzled her neck.

"You said you owed the Fae your life. What happened?" She didn't take the question back even when he stiffened and stopped kissing her.

She looked into his brown eyes. "I want no secrets between us, Hugh. There is nothing you could say to me that would make me stop loving you."

"It's no secret that I keep," he said after a moment's hesitation. "I was a poor man's son when I joined the king's army. I was looking for adventure and anything that would keep me from becoming a farmer like my father."

"That is nothing to be ashamed of."

"I rose quickly in the ranks of the army, and it wasn't long until I earned my spurs and became a knight. It wasn't something a peasant does very often, but I was determined to see myself a knight."

She smiled, knowing it was his determination that had killed the creature. "That is something to be proud of."

"I was very proud of it. I did whatever the king asked me to do and didn't ask questions. I made a name for myself, though it wasn't a good name. I lost my family while I warred for the king. My father and brother were tortured to death, and my mother was raped and then hanged. The men had come looking for me for revenge on the battlefield, but my family refused to give them any information."

Mina closed her eyes at his words. She could only imagine how she would have felt if she had been Hugh. "Did you find them?"

"Aye." His voice had become thick. "My service to the king was finished, and I had come home to become a farmer like my father. I wanted to repent for the things I had done, and instead I nearly went insane."

"That's when Aimery found you?"

Hugh laughed. "It was Aimery that came to me. I knew

I had to leave my home and the nightmares that plagued me. He took me to the land of the Fae, and there I learned to let go of the past and forgive myself."

She ran her hand down his whiskered cheek. "I owe them much then for saving you."

A smile pulled at his lips, and she was quick to rise up and give him a kiss. His arms pulled her against him as he again began to nuzzle her neck again. His warm breath and tongue were doing delicious things to her. He hit a spot that tickled her, and she laughed as she pulled out of his embrace.

"Ah, I found a spot," he said and tried to tug her against him.

Mina did her best to try to get away, but it wasn't long before he had overpowered her and had her locked against him with her back to his chest.

"Is this the spot?" he asked as he moved her braid aside and began to nip at her neck.

She wiggled around and tried to break free. Just as she was about to get loose, she heard him inhale sharply.

"Mina, where did you get this?"

She looked at him over her shoulder. "Get what?"

"This mark on your neck?"

"I don't have a mark on my neck."

"Aye," he said as his hands came up to hold up her braid. "It's on the base of your neck."

There was no denying the anxiety in Hugh's voice, and it frightened her. "What kind of mark?"

But Hugh didn't answer her. "Aimery!"

Within a heartbeat, the Fae commander was beside them. "What?"

Hugh pulled his eyes away from the mark and turned to Aimery. "Is this what we needed to look for?"

"Indeed it is," Aimery said as he traced the mark.

"Enough." Mina spun around and glared at them. "What is on my neck?"

"A symbol from another realm," Aimery answered her. "It's a three sided interlacing knot that is ringed with a solid line."

"Another realm? What does it mean?"

Hugh smiled and pulled her closer to him. "It means you were sent here from another realm to help give us answers to save Earth."

"But I don't know anything," she said, her eyes wide.

Aimery nodded. "When the rest of you are found, then we will have the answers."

"The rest of us?" Mina repeated.

But just as Hugh had expected, Aimery left. "I'll explain it all when we're alone," he said and wrapped his arm around her shoulders. "At least you have some answers now."

"But many more questions."

He looked up to find Cole and Gabriel still arguing by the stable. "Shall we slip away while there is still a chance?" Hugh asked.

"I thought you would never ask."

EPILOGUE

"Seems strange to have a home again."

Mina smiled at her husband as they looked over their people. It had been six months since they had destroyed the creature.

"You say that every day."

"And I'll say it every day for the rest of my life," he said as placed a kiss on the symbol on her neck.

A speck on the horizon caught her attention. "I think we have company."

Hugh followed her gaze. "It's a Shield."

"I'll make a chamber ready." She stopped before descending the stairs. "I wonder if it's Cole, Gabriel, Val, or Roderick."

"We'll know soon enough, love," Hugh said without taking his eyes off the rider.

"Are you really content here instead of out fighting?" she asked.

"You know I am."

"Then I think you'll be happy to know you'll be a father."

He whirled around to stare at her. For several minutes

he simply stared at her, his chest rising and falling quickly. "Truly?"

"A woman does not jest about such things, my lord," she said with a smile.

He picked her up and kissed her. "I love you. With you in my life, I have finally found peace."

"And you, my lord, gave me love, happiness, and a family."

"Then we are whole," he said.

Hugh held Mina tightly as he fixed his gaze on the approaching rider. He had felt the Fae's call for a few days. It was time again. The Shields were needed.

"Are you ready for another adventure?" he asked.

"As long as you are by my side, I can face anything."

Hugh watched the rider ride through the gates. "It's Roderick."

"And he's not alone," Mina said and pointed to the woman behind Roderick. "I wonder..."

Hugh took her hand. "Let's find out."

Read on for an excerpt of A KIND OF MAGIC, Shields book 2...

Our Fate is in their hands...

Earth is about to be annihilated by creatures spoken of only in myths and legends. The fabled race of the Fae have gathered together a group of warriors highly skilled and trained to defeat these creatures.

These men come from different times and realms, giving their lives if necessary, to end the destruction of our world.

Present Day
Houston, Texas

"Sex. It's the answer for everyone. Most especially you."

Elle Blanchard couldn't help but choke on the peanut that had been sliding down her throat. She looked at her best friend since sixth grade to see if she was serious.

Jennifer was definitely serious.

While Elle's eyes hastily scanned the crowded, noisy bar to see if anyone had overheard Jennifer, she drank some of her *pinto grigio* to help the peanut down. She slowly placed her wine glass on the bar and stared at her friend.

"I don't need sex," she whispered.

Jennifer laughed and nodded her head as she sipped her Cosmopolitan. "Oh, but you do, sweetie. How long has it been?"

Elle hated when Jennifer turned their conversation to

her love life, or lack thereof. "Can't we talk about something else?"

"Not tonight. I've let you change the subject for the last time." Jennifer grabbed her arm and grew serious. "You need more than the ancient artifacts in the museum, hon. You need a man that will spend time with you, care for you and love you."

Elle laughed. "Look at me," she said and pointed to herself. "Men don't look at women like me. They look at women like you and them," she said and pointed to two women at the end of the bar.

She stared at the gorgeous women while three guys stood around them talking. Elle might be many things, but a fool she wasn't. She turned back to Jennifer and shrugged.

"No amount of expensive clothes, make-overs or attitude is going to change what I am. Plain. I have always faded into the background."

"Elle, hon," Jennifer said, her Texan drawl coming out. "That bastard put too much into your head. If I ever find him..."

She trailed off, but Elle knew exactly what Jennifer would do--castrate him. Literally. She loved Jennifer more for it, too. Friends like Jennifer didn't come along often.

"I'd rather not talk about him. Instead, I'm going to enjoy this expensive Sterling *pinto grigio* and then head back home."

As soon as the words left her mouth, Elle regretted them.

"There's another problem. How do you expect to find a man when you live in the Montrose area? Honey, you know I'm not homophobic, but that's gay central."

Elle chuckled and shrugged. "Exactly. I feel safe there. When I see a man, I'm not worried about them attacking me to rape me."

"No, it's the women you've got to worry about."

Leave it to Jennifer to tell it like it was.

"Excuse me," a deep voice said from behind Elle.

She turned, her heart thumping that someone might actually want to talk to her. But, when she looked at him, his eyes were on Jennifer. She wasn't surprised. Jennifer was pretty. She might be of average height, but her athletic build turned many a heads.

"May I buy you a drink?"

Jennifer looked the man up and down, her dark brown eyes critical, before she answered him. "I'm fine, but my friend needs a drink."

Elle could have cheerfully rammed her foot up Jennifer's butt. She didn't look at the guy, because she knew what was coming.

"Ah....," the guy mumbled and looked over his shoulder. "My friends are calling me. I'll be right back."

"Sure you will," Elle said after him. She looked at Jennifer. "I really wish you wouldn't do that. It's embarrassing."

"I'm so sorry," Jennifer said, her lips turned down in a frown. "I just thought-"

"I know."

Elle envied Jennifer more than she liked to admit. Jennifer always got the guys in junior high and high school that Elle had a crush on. Those guys never even looked twice at her. And now, Jennifer had a guy most women would kill for. Not only was he as wealthy as Prince Charles, he could be a pin up guy for Calvin Klein underwear, *and* Alex was a nice guy. It would only be a matter of time before he proposed to Jennifer.

And then where would that leave her? Alone. As usual.

"Have you decided what you want to do this weekend?" Jennifer asked.

Elle was grateful for the change of subject. "Nothing."

Jennifer rolled her dark brown eyes and shoved her long dark hair over her shoulder. "Puh-leeze, darlin'. I know you better than that. Birthdays mean a lot to you, and this one is going to be better than ever."

Elle couldn't help but smile at her friend. Ever since their sixth grade year when Jennifer found out Elle lived in a foster home with nearly ten other kids, Jennifer had done something special for her birthday.

This year would be no different. Elle swirled her wine around in the glass, the goldish liquid catching the dim lights of the bar.

There was only one thing she really wanted, and Jennifer couldn't get it for her.

"How about we spend part of the weekend at the beach? We haven't been to Galveston in a couple of years."

The idea had merit. "All right. That sounds good."

"We can shop, people watch and soak up some rays. And one of the guys I work with at Events just bought a beach house he's renting out. It'll be perfect."

Elle looked at her when Jennifer glanced at her watch and squealed.

"Ohmigod. I'm going to be late for my dinner with Alex," she said and slid off the stool, the pinstriped dark gray Donna Karen pantsuit fitting her frame perfectly. "I'll call you tomorrow to work out the details. Oh, and I'm paying for the beach house," she said and kissed Elle on the cheek.

Elle smiled and waved her off. Once the door clicked behind Jennifer, Elle sighed. A weekend. At the beach. She wasn't fooled. Jennifer was looking for a guy for her.

Too bad the search would be in vain.

A KIND OF MAGIC
The second book in the *Shield* series

Greetings Dear Reader,

I was born an immortal prince on the realm of Thales. I lived the life of grandeur, revered and respected, but my one true love was fighting. I was given a special gift in my battle abilities and soon became known as Thales' finest warrior. But all that changed the day my brother died and an evil descended upon my realm. With Thales on the verge of ruin, I bound myself to The Shields to protect the realms from the evil that ravages them. But I have a dark secret that I must atone for. Then and only then can I return to Thales and face my family. My special battle skills and immortality help to keep my goals in front of me. They have always been clear...

Until Elle.

Elle makes me long for things I cannot have. Her innate goodness makes me want to grasp what she offers with both hands, but I know that we can never have what she seeks. Elle bears a mark that signals her one of a chosen few who were sent to Earth as infants. She and the others who bear the mark must be found and kept hidden from the ancient evil that seeks them, for they hold the key to the evil's ruination.

The only way to keep Elle safe is to keep her by my side, but can I resist the temptation to take her love?

Roderick of Thales

A DARK SEDUCTION
The third book in the *Shield* series

Dear Friend,

Most would give all they had to be raised in the Realm of the Fae. I had no choice. I was too young to remember anything of my own realm, save for snatches of memories that could be no more than my imagination. But if it hadn't been for the Fae who found me wandering between realms after mine was destroyed, I would be dead now. It was the Fae who raised me and trained me in weaponry and battle skills until I became a warrior to be feared. When the same evil that destroyed my realm threatened Earth and the Fae, I was the first to volunteer for the Shields.

With my immortality the only link I have to my past, I take what comfort I can in the arms of women. I want nothing more than one night with them, one night to forget that I cannot remember my family, one night to take what pleasure I can. It isn't until I find Shannon that I begin to think of more than jut one night in her arms.

Shannon has been brought back in time from Chicago to 1244 England because the evil knows what she is – one of the chosen. Somehow the evil has found the Chosen before the Shields. His plan is to kill Shannon, but I won't allow that. My duty is to protect her at all costs.

I've never known fear until now – until Shannon.

Cole the Warrior

A FORBIDDEN TEMPTATION
The fourth book in the *Shield* series

Salute!

As one of the youngest men ever to have the title of general in ancient Rome's great army, fame and fortune were my bedmates. I was chosen by the Fae for my mastery of any weapon. Though the Shields like to claim they are stronger because of my skills, I know I am only alive today because the Fae found me before my demons could put an end to my life.

Adventure and danger have always ruled my life, and I thrive on the thrill of the hunt. I am loyal to the Shields, willing to give my life to follow Hugh and the others to fulfill their oaths to save the world.

Who would have known following such great men would lead me to Nicole.

She's everything I've ever wanted in a woman and more. She's innocent and pure and beautiful of face and spirit. And she deserves better than me. Yet, every time I think of her in the arms of another I find I cannot let her go.

For better or worse, Nicole has bound herself to me. I just pray that the demons loosen their hold before the past catches up with me and repeats itself.

Valentinus Romulus

A WARRIOR'S HEART
The fifth book in the *Shield* series

Regards Reader,

There are those who would love to rid themselves of painful memories, to forget nasty pasts and mistakes. They say its Hell to live with those memories. I say its Hell to live without them. I have no memories of my past, my friends, or my family.

I owe my life to the Fae who discovered me bleeding and nearly dead at their doorway. They saved me and offered me a new life, regardless of my pat. So I've served the Fae and the Shields since that day. My special knowledge of herbs and healing has been needed to save the Shields countless times. They are my brethren, my family, yet I am alone.

No matter what I search or what questions I ask, I discover nothing to open a doorway in my mind of locked memories. Until I catch a glimpse of a woman who seems as familiar to me as breathing.

Danielle.

Though she claims to not know me, our bodies know each other. I agonize over what she keeps hidden in the depths of her haunted hazel eyes. I fear the dark thoughts that lurk in my heart and wonder at any black deeds in my past. If what I dread comes to pass, death will not come swift enough.

Above all, I must keep Danielle safe. She's the only one what has quieted my soul and shown what serenity was.

Gabriel the Hollow

Thank you for reading **A Dark Guardian**. I hope you enjoyed it! If you liked this book – or any of my other releases – please consider rating the book at the online retailer of your choice. Your ratings and reviews help other readers find new favorites, and of course there is no better or more appreciated support for an author than word of mouth recommendations from happy readers. Thanks again for your interest in my books!

Donna Grant

www.DonnaGrant.com

ABOUT THE AUTHOR

New York Times and *USA Today* bestselling author Donna Grant has been praised for her "totally addictive" and "unique and sensual" stories. She's written more than thirty novels spanning multiple genres of romance including the bestselling Dark King stories, *Dark Craving, Night's Awakening,* and *Dawn's Desire* featuring immortal Highlanders who are dark, dangerous, and irresistible. She lives with her husband, two children, a dog, and four cats in Texas.

Connect online at:

www.DonnaGrant.com
www.facebook.com/AuthorDonnaGrant
www.twitter.com/donna_grant
www.goodreads.com/donna_grant/

Never miss a Donna Grant book!

Be sure to visit

www.DonnaGrant.com

and sign up for Donna's private email newsletter!